HALF IN LOVE

Justin Cartwright

Half in Love

SCEPTRE

Copyright © 2001 by Justin Cartwright

First published in 2001 by Hodder and Stoughton
A division of Hodder Headline
A Sceptre book

The right of Justin Cartwright to be identified as the Author of
the Work has been asserted by him in accordance with the
Copyright, Designs and Patents Act 1988.

Grateful acknowlededgement is made for permission to reprint excerpts
from the following copyrighted works:
'Famous Blue Raincoat' words and music by Leonard Cohen © 1971 Sony/ATV
Songs LLC All rights for the British Commonwealth, Eire, South Africa, and
Zimbabwe administered by Chrysalis Songs Ltd.

The extracts from 'The Grief of a Girl's Heart' ('O Donall Oge') translated from the
Irish by Lady Gregory are reproduced by permission of Colin Smythe Ltd on behalf
of Anne de Winton and the heirs of Catherine Kennedy.

10 9 8 7 6 5 4 3 2 1

A CIP catalogue record for this title is available
from the British Library.

Hardback ISBN 0 340 76629 8
Paperback ISBN 0 340 79505 0

Typeset by Palimpsest Book Production Limited,
Polmont, Stirlingshire
Printed and bound in Great Britain by
Clays Ltd, St Ives plc

Hodder and Stoughton
A division of Hodder Headline
338 Euston Road
London NWI 3BH

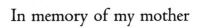
In memory of my mother

To see him [Kean] act, is like reading Shakespeare by flashes of lightning.

— Coleridge

I thought I had entered into a secret understanding with life to spare me the worst.

— *Herzog*, Saul Bellow

I was shocked by dead horses and mules; human corpses were all very well, but it seemed wrong for animals to be dragged into the war like this.

— Robert Graves

I

The sun warmed his scar and he imagined that he could feel a current in the skin itself, responding to the warmth, trickling out. As a boy he had been told that batteries placed in a fire would be encouraged to release the last electricity that they were hoarding. The scar was about three inches long and lay on his neck now, like the section of an earthworm.

The scar would fade to become nothing more than a hieroglyph, worn by weather. Your skin bears many signs. On his knee was the cartilage incision, on his calf the cut from falling off his bicycle; his nose was slightly uneven where a pony had kicked him. On his stomach there was a blurred reminder of where he had had a lump removed. Your body goes on in its own fashion, accepting with equanimity the wounds. It doesn't care. It's like a tree, impervious to cuts and slashes, but bound to succumb to an excess of injury. No principles, no ethics, are involved. The ethics lodge in the body, but are of an unconnected species. Sometimes he imagined they were like holly, living on a tree.

When King Hussein died his horse was paraded along, boots reversed in the saddle. He found that a moving image. (Although he knew of the security reports which told of little Hussein's intemperate sexual habits.) The horse was never to be ridden again, like El Cid's horse, Bavieca, which survived his master, and was buried at the gates of the monastery in Valencia, with two elm trees planted to mark the spot.

But the nobility of horses is an illusion. The illusion is in the fact that although horses have been enlisted to our purposes – war and so on – they don't give a fuck. They'll go along with it, according to their lights.

He put his fingers to his scar which was throbbing lightly and prickling in the sun. This little thing on his neck, a small pink asp, was nothing, although the knife had nicked a tendon and just missed his carotid artery. The surgeon told him, later. Surgeons abhor routine and love drama.

In a field beside the railway line – the famous railway line – three horses stood beside a pepper tree. His great-uncle, Major Dick McAllister, had written that the pepper tree was the toughest tree of all. This one provided some slight relief from the sun. On its pendulous branches you could see little berries that looked just like peppercorns, the red and pink kind that you can buy for expensive grinders, but these peppers were poisonous. Everything inviting about the tree was a sham; no part of it was of any use to man or beast, his great-uncle said. The horses were pockmarked and thin, with prominent backbones. The grey stood beween two dirty bays. All three were listless, tails swishing against the flies, feet stamping occasionally . . .

A horsefly settled on his arm and just before he could swat it, it bit deeply. There was a smear of blood on his forearm. He didn't care. He felt that the blood, his own, was connecting him to the horses, to the place and to what had happened here a hundred years ago. The horses had come from Australia, from Ireland, from Argentina, from India and from Britain to die in their hundreds of thousands. And the soldiers had died in hundreds of thousands too, not really knowing much more about what they were doing here than the horses.

The blood on his arm, just a smear, just pale Japanese calligraphy now, was already drying; soon it would be a few flakes of rust. That's how they died out in the sun, the blood quickly forming a crust on the wounds or a burnt caramel on the ground.

He would have liked to know more about death. He knew nothing about war. In a way he regretted it, because the experience of war was an eternal human experience. Sometimes people said his generation might be the first to grow up and die without any direct knowledge of war. Perhaps you could never be fully human without having seen war or without having been in mortal danger. When he was stabbed in the throat he had been in danger, but the incident was too minor, too random, too tawdry, to have any meaning.

The scar was throbbing in the sun. The horses glanced up at him as he approached. He stopped a few yards off, close enough to get the cereal smell of horses and close enough to hear the attendant flies and the click of cracked hooves on the hard ground and the small snorts and stomach rumbles. One of the bays was in foal; her belly slung beneath her bowed like a hammock in which someone is lying hidden. No, he didn't know anything about death, although here in this expanse of bare clumpy grass near a railway line, he could faintly hear the cries of the dying. He wanted to hear their cries. From the railway line came a humming, and he imagined a train was approaching, but nothing happened

3

and the noise died. The dry wind vibrated the telegraph wires along the track and riffled the horses' thin, oily manes.

The grey snapped at one of the others half-heartedly. Greys are more temperamental than other horses; perhaps, like redheads, they are more passionate. He stood in the sun, feeling the scar and watching the horses.

Horses have no sense of time passing

Stick the Eiffel Tower up your arse, we 'ate the French, we 'ate the French, stick the Eiffel Tower yup your arse. We 'ate the French. Bald cunt, goalie. Stick your garlic up your arse. We 'ate the French. Wanker cunt ref. Wanker. Bald cunt Barthez.

He turns to look at the man who is chanting. He's a boy really, a pudgy, pale boy with earrings. It's a freeezing night but he is wearing an England team shirt, three lions bowed over his nipples. His forearms are goose-bumped and his pale soft cheeks are chapped. Although he is young, rolls of fat push his shirt out. It hangs down over his jeans. He raises his right arm: *Ingerland, Ingerland. We 'ate the French. Ingerland, Ingerland.*

'Would you do me a favour?'

'You what?'

'Would you shut the fuck up for five minutes?'

The fat boy looks at him, uncomprehending. The referee blows the whistle for half time. The whole of Wembley moans. It's a sort of hungry, discontented lowing.

He walked slowly up to the horses. They were small, not much more than ponies. He reached out with his hand, gently, to the mare, but she backed away, one eye showing white and defensive.

'Good girl, good girl.'

He talked soothingly in that way you do to horses – horses apparently like a calm monotone – but she backed away and began to walk into the bright sun, and he backed off too, guiltily. The mare stopped. Her ears were lopsided, so that one was upright and the other leaned sideways at an angle. Slowly she turned and trudged back to the tree.

Now a train could be seen, a goods train, moving slowly towards them. The rails were whining in anticipation. It was a long train, at least thirty wagons, mostly open and piled with coal, and it took a few minutes to pass the horses under their lone pepper tree. They were used to trains and did not move.

The lavatories are heaving. He stands at a low wall, dividing one line of latrines from another, facing a boy in a white, soft top hat, with a red Cross of St George on it. His shoulders are draped in a flag, also emblazoned with a cross. The boy suddenly shouts *Ingerland, Ingerland* and smiles as he zips himself up, as though he has said something inexpressibly witty.

He eases himself from the lavatory, through the milling crowd. As he exits, near the fried-chicken stand underneath the cement cliffs, he hears a low, urgent voice: 'You're a posh cunt, aintcher?'

He turns and at that moment he feels an appalling pain in the side of his throat. He cannot see who was talking to him, but he finds that his legs have given way and that he has fallen onto the stained and strewn concrete and that his face is irrevocably at the same level as crushed polystyrene cups, discarded wrappers, work boots and colourful trainers. Helplessness rushes over him.

It's a sensation which is strange to him: he feels himself floating away serenely, but in his heart there is wild fear, made worse by the sense that his heart and his body are going in different directions.

He walked from the dried field along the edge of the railway line towards the cemetery. The train had entered the shunting yards and stopped. A small steam locomotive was moving out of a shed. The sky above the yards was salmon-coloured, the colour of those glasses of water at the dentist's. He wondered if it was dust or the fumes of the trains which were causing this colourful display.

The cemetery was ringed by prickly pears and watched nervously by lizards. Here a few troopers were buried. The stones were broken. By an accident of history, by virtue of the fact that it lay on a key railway line, this had become famous. There was no other reason. Mafeking was a dump.

His scar was throbbing, baking now like the lizards on the broken gravestones. The gate of the cemetery hung loose. The few square yards enclosed by the stone wall were returning to their natural state. Another century and there would be nothing here but scattered rocks. The lizards were lively, darting creatures, skins as lustrous as newly caught fish, but with the implacable eyes and mouths of snakes. His scar now prickled. It was never still.

He found a small bronze plaque screwed to a rock:

In tribute to the Cape Boys Regiment, sixteen of whom died in the heroic defence of Mafeking and are buried here.

Beyond the stone wall he could see the three horses, moving, heads held low, in the direction of a group of shacks. The shacks were positioned around an older house, built of stone and mud. A car on blocks stood at an angle to the main house. The horses were following a path. They dipped out of sight suddenly; he was anxious until they reappeared just as suddenly, smaller now. Off to the left the town looked far from heroic. It was dusty and dilapidated, an African town selling cheap goods: furniture in velour and the sort of clothes that the poor believe are modish, adorned with pictures and slogans and brand names that mean nothing.

He asks the nurses in the hospital as he comes round: 'Am I a posh cunt?'

They are used to the effect of anaesthetic, but they smile. Nurses have huge backsides, like working horses, and sturdy legs. He has an urge to ask them if they went into nursing because from behind they look so sensible, so dependable, but not the sort of women you would leave home for. It's cruel, this question of beauty. He wants to reassure them, but his tongue is thick and his mouth is very dry. He wants to give them some comfort from his position as a man who has known plenty of women, and maybe even from his position as a minister in the Government of his old chum, now Prime Minister. And then he remembers how he got here, as the narcotic tide begins to recede, and he sees that he is wearing a sort of thin shift which leaves his own backside exposed to draughts and he sees that he has a tag on his wrist.

'Did I nearly die?'

7

'You are fine, just fine, Mr McAllister,' says the sister. 'Just a little blood lost. Mr Brough stitched you up.'

She squeezes his hand. He wants to hold her to him and speak to her about Galway or wherever it is she comes from and kiss her and tell her that her great big arse and her large turned legs and her over-filled bosom, which is pushing out her apron and watch, make her the most attractive woman he has ever seen. But he can't tell her. Nor can he tell her that he himself is in love with a woman so beautiful she makes his heart lurch, because it would be unfair to mention her in this company. Now he sees in this solid Irish woman a reproach, although he is not sure why she should care, for having been stabbed. And he feels guilty himself about having been stabbed.

He's moved from the recovery room, rolled from a sheet of rubber, like one of those dolphins that beach themselves, onto a trolley.

'Am I at Wembley?'

'No sir, you were brought here to University College in an ambulance,' says the orderly who is pushing him down the corridor. He sees that a policeman in body armour is walking behind the porter.

'Nearly there, sir,' says the porter. His hair is very close cut and he has a stud in his tongue which bobs as he speaks, a fish rising.

The three horses were still there as he walked towards a fort which had once formed the forward defence of the town. He wondered if these horses could have been descendants of the remounts his great-uncle had sent over the seas. Horses grew smaller and more wiry with harsh conditions.

Half in Love

The grass underfoot was dry. Over there behind the shanty town, a fire was burning on the open plain, burning listlessly and slowly, sending an immense column of smoke into the unenthusiastic, still sky. It's things like this that make you see for the first time: the farmhouses lying on the vast plain, columns of smoke rising every ten or fifteen miles, columns of horses stumbling wearily down one ridge and up another, columns of soldiers in khaki and kilts walking through Africa. You could see now how it would have looked, a game, like a train set in an attic; from this distance you couldn't have seen death. What was death? What you saw as you came up close was not death, but the dead. Death is a personal moment, when consciousness flies, or seeps, or scuttles, away. When he fell on the Wembley concrete, he might have been dying. It wouldn't have been any different. That would have been it: he wouldn't have woken up. Could it be possible that death was nothing? Nothing at all?

Three small boys came by pushing cars made of wire along the worn paths, guiding them with long steering wheels, also of wire. Their noses were frozen fountains of mucus. The boys stopped and looked at him. He smiled at them. Their legs were dusty and their feet were bare. He reached into his pocket and gave each of them twenty rand. They stared at the money, bemused. Then they began to run, dragging the cars behind them, wondering if he was a madman.

And he had an aberrant thought: I will never know what happens to these dusty little snot-streaked boys. I'll never know them, but perhaps they will remember me for a time. It wasn't sadness he felt, but a sort of elation. He had seen something, a filament in the dark, which suggested to him that death was a communion. They would all be dead together, all differences and misunderstandings and longings gone. There was a memorial at Hyde Park Corner, to forty-nine thousand and seventy-six soldiers of the Royal Artillery who had died in the First World War. There was something heroic and defiant about publishing the exact numbers, an unimaginable number of dead, with the suggestion that they were at peace. For the first time he saw that there might be some peace in death, some redeeming sacrifice in war. And he saw what is meant by history: those not dead trying to explain how those who are dead became so.

The horses had stopped wandering. They were drinking from a galvanised-iron trough near the huts of mud and tin, out in the open without even the shade of a pepper tree.

He reached the road, passing a memorial to the Boers who had died. Their struggle was commemorated by an obelisk, on which their names were inscribed. But now the memorial was fenced against goats and vandals. He walked down the road, busy with taxis, actually small Japanese vans full of women wearing berets and blankets.

Mercifully, the town was softened by the fading light.

2

'Of course,' said the journalist to Joanna, 'acting is a strange thing
for a grown-up to do. I've interviewed lots of actors and it strikes
me they are emotionally needy.'

'That's probably true. Most people are emotionally needy. By
the way, I don't like the phrase.'

'Yes, but actors seem to require a fix. They're addicted
to praise.'

'Maybe. I just think that it's in the nature of acting that if you
offer yourself up for judgement, of your performance, your . . .'

She paused wearily.

'Your looks?'

'Yes, your looks. The public infer a lot from what they see.
They assume. Too much.'

The journalist, as he leant forward to write in his notebook,
exposed his bare skull to her. He had shaved his head so that the
sides, where there was still some hair, looked like the grindings of
a pepper-mill, while the top was smooth. In London, this shaved
head was very common now. It levelled the bald and the hairy.
But it also seemed to signal a kind of deliberate self-effacement.
Her own hair was quite short and spiky at the moment. The
journalist had asked her why she had it so short.

'Why the fuck shouldn't I? It's my hair, not public property.'

But she said it amiably, and then she qualified too: 'Anyway, they do what they want with it on the set.'

And it was true, directors — and their shadows, the producers — were obsessed with hair.

The journalist was not the usual show-business type; he was more serious, more harsh in his manners.

'How long have you been in London?'

'I have to promote the film obviously ...'

'That's in your contract?'

'Yes. Of course.'

'But you hate doing it?'

'No, I like quite a lot of it. Do I look as though I hate it?'

She gestured at the room. He paused for a moment, looking at his notebook, his bare head flat onto her, as she sat across her huge chintzy armchair.

'Can I ask you something else?'

She felt it coming now, cutting through the water, sending vibrations ahead of it.

'Go ahead,' she said.

She glanced at Sophie from the PR company, who was whispering brightly on her cell-phone near the bedroom. Sophie had a few more interviews lined up for her today.

'Is there any connection between you and Richard McAllister?'

'We're friends. We have houses in the same village.'

Now Sophie put down her phone, her plump face performed a swift rearrangement as she stood up, pulling down her short, black skirt.

'Unfortunately, Jim,' she said, 'there's no time for the kind of in-depth personal interview on our schedule. Sorry to say this, but, you know how it is, how it works, we have to remain focused.'

'So the Minister's absence from office and your moving to the Savoy are purely coincidental?'

'Miss Jermyn won't be answering that, Jim. As Duncan knows, and I told him, when he rang requesting an interview, we haven't got much time. I'm afraid there are three other journalists waiting.'

'Do you deny that you and Mr McAllister have been having an affair?'

Joanna wanted to answer. She wanted to say that the word 'affair' was demeaning, a tawdry word which implied something hasty, makeshift and unworthy.

The journalist was standing up now, and Sophie placed herself directly in front of Joanna.

'That's it, Jim. I'll speak to Duncan about the photos. And the tickets he wanted. I'm afraid we've just run out.'

The journalist was tall, so Joanna could see his gulag head over Sophie's shoulder.

'And the Minister's disappearance? Could that be to keep out of the way?'

'As far as I know,' said Joanna, 'he's in Africa looking at horses.'

'Jim, the interview's over.'

Sophie moved to try to block the journalist's view of Joanna.

'He's in Africa, and you've moved into the Savoy?'

Sophie began to push him.

'Miss Jermyn is on a major promotional tour. Would you get out now, please.'

The journalist moved steadily backwards under pressure, until he fell over a Chinese lacquered table.

'You've killed the bastard.'

He lay still for a moment: 'I'm going. If you don't mind my pointing it out, you are over-reacting,' he said, from a kneeling position. The batteries for his tape recorder were lying across the room.

'And you are well out of order,' said Sophie, standing over him.

Joanna wondered at the way she said 'well out of order'. PR women come from a pool of poorly but expensively educated young debutantes. But this Sophie had obviously lived a little.

'Weh outta oardah,' she said again. 'Right outta lahn. Now fuck off outta it.'

After he had gone, they ordered coffee and a glass of champagne.

'Well outta lahn, Soph,' said Joanna. 'But it's true of course. I love him.'

'Shall I tell the next one to go, or wait?'

'You tell him to fuck off outta here, Soph.'

'I'm from South London really.'

Her laugh was as rasping as any old dear's sitting in a corner of the snug bar.

'So we both have secrets.'

'What are we going to do?'

'You don't need to worry. Whatever he writes, it can only help get bums on seats.'

'And you?'

'I don't know. I want to speak to Richard. I miss him terribly.'

'I'll get on to the little twerp's boss, Duncan Follow, who I know well, and see if I can shut him up.'

'What's the point? It's all going to come out.'

'I can probably delay if you need to speak to . . .'

'To Richard. If I can find him. He's in the middle of nowhere. Can you order me a cab? I think I have to go home and talk to my husband.'

'Does he know anything?'

'Not really. He's a writer.'

'What about your agent?'

'He knows. I should speak to him right away. Can you ask him to come and see me?'

While Sophie made her phone-calls, Joanna looked out of the window. A sightseeing boat was passing under Hungerford Bridge. Another boat passed in the other direction, loaded with what looked from this height like sand. From here she could see both ways, up along the river, from Westminster to Canary Wharf. She hadn't realised that the river curved in this way, in huge, lazy arcs. The river itself was sand-coloured today; she had watched it from up here over the past few days; it changed with the tides and the winds, from a grey, uneasy, wintry turbulence, to a dappled sparkle. The water itself was at times full of discords and conflicts, heaving and rolling, and then it would unexpectedly become as gentle as a mill pond.

Living here at the Savoy was a strangely muted experience. The view from outside was silent. There were no familiar domestic sounds; vital parts of her normal life had been excised, so that there was no connection, for example, between eating and the raw ingredients. The strangely subdued waiters and maids were from another world too, a world which had different natural laws and different hierarchies. There was a nostalgia for the perfect guest, a rich civilised man of a type which had probably not crossed the threshold for sixty years. Actors, of course, were only acting. They could be admired – as she was – but the staff knew actors weren't the real thing. All the same, she was aware that her face, her new fame, had an electrifying effect on people she met, as though fame were really the vital spark that could ignite what was dormant in them.

And now she would have to go back and tell Jeremy the whole truth. Jeremy had said a strange thing to her when she told him she would be housed at the Savoy for the whole promotional tour. He said: when you brush your teeth in the morning these days, it's as if you were looking after an idol. What sort of idol, she asked. He meant an idol in a temple but, for a moment, she thought he meant screen idol. It was true that fame made your every action more significant. Jeremy had poured scorn on the screenplay of *Half in Love*, when it was offered to her, but she wondered if Jeremy recognised it for what it was, a story which could take her out of the world of theatrical artifice and into the landscape which only movies can create, a sort of parallel world, where feeling reigns just as it does in the dreams of ordinary people, dreams which save them from embracing the reality of their lives.

Jeremy said that it was a banal idea. From the comfort of their farmhouse, he wanted to produce abrasive work; he wanted people to understand what he understood; he wanted people to learn. But Joanna knew that people didn't want to learn or to understand, they wanted to feel. History had become feeling. Politics had become feeling. It occurred to her when Princess Diana died that millions of people – probably lonely, miserable people as Jeremy said – had wanted a communion, an opportunity to express their feelings. Nobody, of course, was interested in their daily lives, but that only gave the pent-up emotions greater intensity. Jeremy found the whole thing pathetic. He wanted people to face up to reality. His plays were all about issues, but they were issues which he manufactured in his study, an old granary next to the house. The sacks of grain had gone, replaced by sacks of unsolicited wisdom. Now she would have to go down to the farmhouse, to leave her silent sub-aqua world, and give him the real, true, facts.

A waiter arrived with a tray loaded not just with a glass or two, but an assortment of nickel-plated jugs and pots and a small vase of orchids, invitations to the health club, a plate of cookies, an elaborate wine cooler, three types of sugar, and a bowl of coffee crystals attached to lollipop sticks, which in turn had streamers on them so that you could launch them like navigational buoys into the coffee. There was also a silver dish of almonds and brazil nuts, chosen for their plump good looks. Sophie put the phone down.

'Are you all right?' she asked.

'I was dreading it, but now it's got to be faced.'

Sophie opened the champagne expertly. Joanna imagined that she applied the same dexterity in her sex life.

'Cheers.'

She didn't really want to drink champagne, but it was PR people's first aid, the PR antibiotic. She sipped it, while Sophie gulped.

'I've rung Stan and he's on his way. A car is coming. Umberto, the doorman, will keep it standing right outside, and I've told the journos you're not well. Is that all right?'

'Yes, that's fine, Sophie.'

Adversity had thrown them together.

'There are more calories in one brazil nut than in a Mars Bar,' said Sophie, eating two. Her clothes, the South Kensington rig, were straining, but Joanna guessed that there were men who found her attractive. There was more than a hint of sexual complicity about her. The women Jeremy wrote about were bitterly conscious of men's selfishness and insensitivity, but this girl belonged to that subversive legion of women who encouraged men in their folly.

'What did you tell Stan?'

'I said you needed to speak to him very urgently.'

She was Stan's biggest client by a long way now. He was out of his depth in Hollywood, but he knew people at ICM, who shared the commission with him and consulted him. In the past when she had just left Webber-Douglas, Stan had taken her out for meals and tried, rather forlornly, to seduce her. Once that phase was over, they became very close. Stan had a wry kind of Old Testament kindness, a kindness matched by a faintly exasperated wisdom, as he watched the passing show of producers, directors and television executives and listened to their plans sympathetically. He too had seen instantly that *Half in Love* could be a huge success, particularly when directed by Joel Mannix. She was nominated for an Oscar, she won a Golden Globe and a BAFTA, and went from being a respected television and theatre actor to being a star in a few heady months. Stan knew all about Richard. He was also contemptuous of Jeremy, although he tried to hide it. Once he had said: 'Look, you probably have to be Jewish to understand this, but this is a wonderful country, and I can't stand people who are always trying to suggest that there's something sinister going on. David Hare, people like that, for instance.'

People like that included Jeremy, no question of it.

Jeremy. Jeremy, sitting there writing his almost-brilliant television plays and his slightly-tedious stage plays and his run-of-the-mill serials, which were always loaded with big ideas. A critic had once said that his television work was like cottage pie, flambéed in expensive cognac. Poor Jeremy. She knew that her leaving him would embitter him too. But he would draw comfort from the fact that he had long ago divined the nature of human beings. Her desertion would prove to him that he was a perceptive man. He had a talent for placing himself in the middle of the action.

When he read the Sunday papers, he took the stories personally: 'Rushdie's cottoned on at last. I said exactly three years ago, in *Distant Rooms, Dark Secrets*.' Once he said that the Prime Minister had stolen his exact words about race in Britain, but that he had perverted them. 'We do not look at the colour of a person's skin; we look at the value of their contribution to our country.' What Jeremy had written was: 'In Britain today, the colour of a person's skin cannot be separated from the question of his deeds.' Hardly a black person had ever been spotted in Hartfield in living memory.

Sophie had eaten all the brazil nuts and two of the cookies.

'Will you tell me what I should say to Stan? When you're ready of course.'

'Sophie, I'll talk to Stan and then I'll try to talk to Richard, then I'll talk to Jeremy, then I'll call you. Just hold everything until tomorrow.'

Joanna stood by the window. This was what happened. You found yourself standing by a huge panorama, desolately taking part in a play for which you'd never auditioned, and for which there was no script. This was the price you paid. Richard wanted to resign after he was stabbed, because he felt that, in some way, he deserved it.

'He called me a posh cunt,' he'd told her in hospital. 'I was pompous. Maybe I was too pleased with myself, I don't know.'

'Richard, some little National Front yob stabbed you, you've got nothing to feel ashamed about.'

'I don't feel ashamed. I feel dislocated. I never asked for this.'

I never asked for this either. Richard's withdrawal, she saw now, came from a knowledge that more would follow.

'Your agent's downstairs.'

'Ask them to send him up.'

Stan's arrivals and departures were always accompanied by an atomic commotion, as though he disturbed the air as he moved through. Delicate objects such as glass began to tremble and oscillate as he passed. Joanna thought that Jews were more in touch with elemental things. They were more firmly in this world, more human.

He embraced her. Recently he'd taken to wearing a little goatee which made him look old and rabbinical, rather than young and savvy, as he intended. The goatee was shiny and resilient, but surprisingly soft.

'This is Sophie, who's doing the publicity, and this is Stanley Blumberg, my agent.'

'I'm just off,' said Sophie.

'What is it, whenever I come into the room, beautiful girls leave?'

'Give it a rest, Stan.'

But Sophie was pleased. 'Nice to meet you. I'll call tomorrow, Joanna.'

'Good.'

It was the first time Sophie had used her first name, Joanna. Stan ordered tea.

'Don't bring me the oatmeal biscuits or scones and jam, or salmon sandwiches cut by brain surgeons, just tea, okay? Indian tea.'

'You've been here before, obviously,' said Joanna.

'Once or twice. Now, how deep in the shit are we?'

'You're not in the shit.'

'Whither thou goest, I go.'

'Quite deep. A journalist from the *Express* asked me some questions about Richard.'

'Fishing type of questions, or serious questions?'

'I don't know. Somebody was in the village last week taking pictures of Richard's horse and our place.'

'Can I ask you what you and Richard want to do?'

Questions can be too simple. There was also, hiding behind the question, the wraith of resentment. There was nothing that Stan would ever promote to the status of jealousy, but Joanna knew that Stan loved her still in his way, despite his burly worldliness.

'Can we start nearer the beginning, Stan?' she said. 'Can we find out from the *Express* if they're going to run the story. I'm sure it's all going to come out, but I have to speak to Richard and to Jeremy. I need a few days, maybe a week.'

'I could call the editor. The problem is that if I call her she will know immediately that something's going on. She's not going to pass on a story like this with her circulation. Richard would have far more clout. He could get Downing Street on to her.'

'Richard is in the sticks.'

'Even in the sticks they have phones. He has a phone. Ring him.'

'I promised not to ring him until he came back.'

'Maybe you should reconsider.'

'Maybe I should.'

She knew that Stan was thinking how silly it sounded: a pact not to phone. She was in some kind of idiotic Gentile self-denial. Richard looking at horses, having donned blinkers himself, and she prattling to journalists and TV interviewers about what fun it had been, and what a privilege it was working with Joel Mannix on *Half in Love*, and how well the new film was doing in America, and telling her little actressy anecdotes about the Oscars, and all the time longing to speak to Richard.

All the time she was in the television studios and all the time she was talking to journalists, she was longing for Richard.

'I'll call him later,' she said.

Stan drinking tea, Stan looking out of the window without interest, Stan exploring how this could be announced to the studio – Stan's presence – calmed her. Sometimes she thought she had never been suited to the life of an actor, because she wanted a calmness and a peace which acting denied. But the truth was, she wasn't sure where that calmness could be found.

She certainly didn't want a dull and domestic life. The impulse to act was probably a search for assurance. And it was true that her awards and acclaim had given her a feeling of solidity that she had lacked.

The journalist with closely cropped hair had given her a push when she had been afraid to jump.

'Are you really up for this?' asked Stan.

'Stan, why are you trying to modernise your vocabulary? Say what you mean.'

But she knew what he meant. He was referring to the pain she was going to cause Jeremy and the recriminations and the uncertainty which lay ahead.

Stan began to make phone calls. The phone was his natural medium. On the river now, two tourist boats were passing on the tide at surprisingly high speed. She could see tourists leaning over the side, looking in her direction.

She was fourteen when her father died. He was shot as some Argentines surrendered in the Falklands. She and her brother were picked up from the boarding school by her mother and a Ministry driver. Her brother liked sitting in the front of the car with the driver, because he hadn't grasped what the news meant. She sat next to her mother, who was weeping quietly, and they drove home, where tired, faded Granny was waiting. Joanna went back to school after two weeks. Her father was a hero, awarded a posthumous medal, and the other girls for a while idolised her. Her eyes, she believed, acquired their depths then in some inexplicable way. She felt herself becoming an English heroine. The direction of her life seemed to have been drawn from the films of Noël Coward and John Mills. Sometimes she thought that her public — her new, vast public — saw her in softly filtered monochrome. In *Half in Love* she was the cool Englishwoman in the New York inferno.

3

Richard McAllister was taking breakfast at the Wagon Wheels Hotel in Mafeking and reading his great-uncle's account of General Stonewall Jackson's horse, Fancy. Fancy had been bought by the General for his wife, but 'was promoted from ladies' hack to charger, by an accident, namely upon the General's finding that he preferred Fancy to his own horse. Fancy was no more than a pony, but upon this plebeian beast, General Stonewall Jackson was mounted at the Battle of Bull Run in July 1861.' After the war, Fancy became a household pet until he died at the age of thirty-five. His remains were stuffed and are displayed at the Robert E. Lee camp, adorned – his great-uncle noted proudly – with a British Army saddle and bridle, presented by an English admirer, Lieutenant-Colonel John Fremantle of the Coldstream Guards.

Richard was happy. He was conscious of feeling something close to bliss, sitting here in the long, silent dining room with the drying toast and the coarse marmalade and the huge pots of railway coffee, designed to test your tolerance of heat as you picked them up. His great-uncle had stayed here, and Baden-Powell had made his headquarters near by. All this he had discovered at the little, rarely visited museum. He had found his great-uncle's name in the original hotel guest book, preserved there, and noted that he had ordered a case of Cape wines to be kept for his use. The cost was thirty shillings. But Richard's happiness arose not from nosing around in his great-uncle's life, truffling up a few forgotten fragments of an Army veterinary officer's routine, but from his own sense of weightlessness. What he was doing here in this obscure, dirty town, reading about horses, following his great-uncle's trail, was a quest (no, quest was too strong a word) without purpose, without any connection to events in the world. What was called the real world. He had a sense of swimming in obscurity, although his presence in the hotel, with his rather English clothes and the scar on his neck, had caused curiosity. He was no dandy, but he could see that his clothes might look sumptuous in this sun-bleached place, where the raiment was as faded as the landscape. Government encouraged the wearing of stripes and silk ties and loudly discreet shoes. At Westminster he had discovered a whole range of small vanities, at first with amusement.

Baden-Powell had developed his scouting ensemble here: broad hat, innkeeper's breeches, later to give way to shorts, stave, lanyard and so on. Baden-Powell had also given the order to start to eat the horses as the siege progressed, so his great-uncle wrote. A soup was made from the horses, which B-P called 'chevril', and the tails and manes were used to stuff mattresses and pillows at the hospital. The horses' oats were pounded to make a porridge. The skin, hooves and head were boiled to make brawn. Richard's great-uncle had been overseeing the landing of the horses from Australia, Argentina, Britain and Ireland but entered Mafeking to complete his study of the care and management of horses in warfare a few weeks before the siege started. Of course what he didn't know was that horses are not going to take part in too many more cavalry charges, even though the cavalry training manual said that *the rifle could not replace the effect produced by the magnetism of the charge and the terror of cold steel.* The magnetism of the charge must have meant the hypnotic effect, the stampeding effect, of a thousand horses galloping, rather than their charm and beauty. And Richard saw that, in many individually small and cumulatively final ways, the past had sunk below the horizon, out of view.

His great-uncle, Major Dick, wrote without any apparent malice that he had acquired an assistant who was good with horses, a man who had a pleasant, ugly face which reminded him of his family bulldog. This man was called September and developed 'a dog-like devotion' to his great-uncle. His great-uncle, he discovered, had met Kipling in Lahore, and Kipling had made reference to him in *Plain Tales from the Hills* as an expert horsebreaker. For the past three years in the Government, he had wondered, despite his affection for the Prime Minister, whether he or any of his chums realised that their principles and their beliefs were as subject to fashion as Major Dick's. Or Major Dick's friend, Colonel Baden-Powell's? Baden-Powell had written to a friend, a schoolmaster, saying how much he wanted to see his collection of photographs of naked boys again. Baden-Powell discouraged his scouts from taking an interest in girls: he disparaged 'girlitis'.

A young and different waiter, whose hair was standing straight up in short rows, like newly risen carrots, approached him.

'The menja want to spek met jou, seh.'

The manager, a Portuguese whose eyes were excessively liquid and deeply recessed, said he had a message for him. He handed Richard a piece of paper that requested that he ring Pretoria, urgently, to speak to the High Commissioner. The manager had had trouble with the word 'Commissioner'.

Richard went to his room, his heart beating lightly with apprehension; his happiness, his contemplative life, had gone up in smoke. The High Commissioner said that he had been asked by Downing Street to find him in Mafeking and to ask him to speak to Talfryn Williams, and supplied him with a phone number.

'How's Mafeking, Minister? Enjoying yourself?'

'I am enjoying myself. Least I was. As you know, I have been on leave for a few weeks.'

'Absolutely. If there's anything you need, ring me on this number. Are you coming up this way?'

'Don't think so.'

He started up his mobile phone and dialled Williams's number.

'You haven't had your phone on,' said Williams.

'That's true.'

'I had to get the Ambassador out of bed. Last night.'

'Did you enjoy that?'

'I did actually. I was thinking, why should this bugger be sound asleep while I'm working.'

'What are you worrying about?'

'There's a story in the *Express*, or there will be a story in the *Express* tomorrow, that the real reason you are having a rest is because you and Joanna Jermyn have been having a ding-dong.'

'Oh fuck, poor Joanna.'

'Very unfortunate choice of language, Richard. The PM is concerned, both for you personally and in case you were hiding something when you took a rest. He would like you to run your side of the story before me, just so that we're all reading from the same hymn sheet. He told me to say that you have his full confidence and support, whatever.'

Under different circumstances, he would have known for sure that his career was over. He told Talfryn Williams that he would call back after he had spoken to Joanna. She too had tried to phone. It seemed that while he had been wandering in the grave-yards and the old brick fields and the care-worn savannahs, and the drying stubble and the railway yards, many people were trying to speak to him, politicians, journalists, friends – and Joanna.

She was back home. She had spoken to Jeremy, but his reaction had been strange and unexpected. Her voice, her famous voice, perhaps because of their two cell-phones communicating over thousands of miles, was tremulous.

'He said I was quite justified if I wanted to leave him, he was a failure, and perhaps we would both be happier apart. I was so ready, so ready to defend myself against a storm of abuse. I was expecting him to say that I was being predictable, opportunist – is the word opportunistic? – that in the bad times he had supported me and so on. To tell you the truth, I had the strange urge to tell him to shut up and read the script again. Jesus, I don't know, it was a frightening experience. Like encountering a complete stranger.'

'Where are you now?'

'I'm in the garden. But he's gone. I'm in the garden just in case. What am I going to do?'

'I'll come home as soon as I can. It's only a few hours to Johannesburg. I'll be home in the morning. Joanna, I love you, and maybe this was meant to be, if that doesn't sound corny. What I mean is that it had to happen.'

'Did you leave town because of us?'

'I think I did, if I'm honest. I wanted to clear the decks.'

'Richard, I love you. Please ring me when you get to Johannesburg, when you can. I'm in complete turmoil.'

When they had finished speaking he could still see her in the garden, perhaps under the apple trees, the remains of an old orchard which she had under-planted with spring flowers. He hadn't really told her how much he loved her. He was, after all, English. He found such things easier when they were naked. He had never liked casual sex: for him, sex with someone he did not love was almost impossible. He knew from other men that he was freakish. Some of them even preferred sex with people whose names they hardly knew. For him, sex was the desire for human intimacy, to inhabit one skin. And how could you do that with someone you hardly knew or hardly cared for?

He called Talfryn and told him that he had spoken to Joanna, that Joanna had spoken to her husband, and that there was no more he could say.

'The Prime Minister is concerned that there are no nasty surprises coming.'

'Are you concerned, or is he concerned?'

'I'm concerned, I'm concerned on his behalf. That's my job.'

30

'Talfryn, I have been seeing Joanna, but I can't say honestly what she will do. We don't have a love-child or any skeletons in the cupboard. Please tell the Prime Minister that as far as I know, that's the whole story.'

'I have to ask you how long it's been going on?'

'A year.'

'It's unlikely to be the whole story in that case. It's not going to be pleasant, but I don't think there's anything they can pin on us.'

'That's what concerns you.'

'I'm afraid so. You know the score, Rich. I'm so fucking tired of being painted as some Machiavelli. Are you coming back tonight?'

'If I can get a flight.'

'I'll fix it up for you.'

'No thanks. I'll turn up like any other member of the public.'

'Don't get mugged in Jo'burg. That might be too much.'

'Thanks.'

Talfryn Williams had always liked him. Talfryn had gone with him when he gave his first minor interview to the BBC and seen how he reacted to the make-up girl's attention.

'Make-up is the big test. It tells me a lot about politicians,' said Talfryn. 'Some of them want to spend the rest of the evening in full make-up.'

'I look as though I've been to Marbella.'

'Enjoy it. Like success in politics, it fades away.'

Talfryn was a television journalist for twelve years, but he had come into his own as Press Secretary for the Prime Minister. He told Richard that when he was writing stories he was never really interested in issues; he was always looking to see how his stories would play. It was a case, he said, of being more interested in the effect of journalism than the substance. He had found his niche in Downing Street, where he had – everyone said – an extraordinary ability to help his master express himself in a frank and appealing manner. It was a kind of talent, and one which was now required by all politicians. In his three years, Richard had seen that politicians, the heavy hitters, the big beasts, didn't have time for abstract thought or time to write detailed speeches. They must rely on their lieutenants. And that is why the Prime Minister had brought Richard into Government, to have another trusted friend to lean on.

His old friend had called him in and explained it to him with charming frankness: the mistake of previous governments had been that they were in thrall, both to the unions and to some very dodgy ideas. In their hearts they believed that government was there to take the rich down a peg or two. They believed that the powerful exploited the weak. They believed in, even nourished, the class system while blaming it for all ills. You only had to look at council housing: it was a fiefdom. It had all gone, the establishment, the class system, the financial hegemony. The power of the unions. All gone. And it was on this green-field site that Jerusalem would be built. He knew, said the Prime Minister, with his not-too-formal grey suit and his slightly raffish haircut, that they would make enemies. There would be charges of cronyism. Cronies, he said, would come in for a lot of flak. But the people understood, even if the Party faithful didn't, that success can only be built on pragmatism. To put it baldly, he said, tax revenues will fund the new society, not dogma. Richard believed him.

Downing Street, despite its moribund decoration, was pulsing with a force he recognised, immediately, as power. The Prime Minister was throbbing with conviction. When he left to consider the offer, he felt that the world outside the gates was sickly. The Westminster schoolboys, in their fustian, looked like nose-picking Dickensian clerks, civil servants passing were drones, cars appeared to be on aimless joy-rides, the tourists were lurid nobodies, the policemen were waiting his bidding. Oh Jesus, I will have to accept.

An elderly MP was dying and the writ for the bye-election was delayed a week so that he could meet his potential constituents.

'You didn't realise up here in Smallfield that my whole life up until now has been spent in preparation for the honour of representing you. Nor did I.'

Talfryn had written the speech for him, and it was well received, except by one member of the executive, a National Union of Teachers' representative, who resigned. That was how he entered politics, on the promise that there would be fulfilment. It had occurred to him more than once in the three years since that power was the promise of fulfilment. It could be bestowed in just the way that Popes gave blessings and dispensations. Power, he came to see, is not a ritual thing at all, but a desire for divinity. Jerusalem had to be builded. At first he kept these thoughts to himself.

The assistant manager of the Wagon Wheels Hotel helped him with his luggage. No porter was available. He explained that since

1995 it had become impossible to get these people to work. They were always off, and if you tried to make them work harder, some fat bastard in a suit arrived from the ANC to threaten you.

'That's the new South Africa,' he said. 'They want everything, but they don't give fuck all.'

Richard set out on the straight road. You left the town behind in moments. In a treeless, flat, brown field he saw some horses standing, stunned by the featurelessness of their surroundings. It was the end of summer here. Now beside the road there were unexpected stands of chocolate and pink and blue flowers, tall things with large lacy leaves.

One skin. Joanna and he. One skin. That was all that mattered to him. His own skin had been punctured by a fat, pale boy. At least he had believed it must have been the fat boy who had sprayed him with saliva and randomly fired abuse at Wembley. He had told the police he could not identify his attacker. His *assailant*. The police still had a fondness for sonorous words, as if they needed to lend a literary authority to their reports.

He felt his scar. It prickled to his touch. He wondered if the hidden static in there was because of a stitch left behind by the doctors. Since the stabbing he had seen Joanna only twice, when she came to hospital, a celebrity in disguise, and once when they had met on Ashdown Forest and made love against a wet tree, which had turned her thighs to verdigris, and caused alarm to the first tentative squirrels of spring. His scar, still lightly bandaged then, had felt as though it were going to burst open. He had the mad notion that she had come quickly to relieve mounting pressure. Damp bark, the mushroom smell of fallen tree trunks, the thick vapour of dead leaves, the slight bruising around the mouth, Joanna's cries, as clear as if she were playing to the back row of the stalls, the dumbstruck hurrying squirrels, the fear that anorak-clad ramblers might appear, the giggling walk back to the car, the tea served by a gloomy woman who made her own scones. He remembered it all as he drove towards Jo'burg, as you always remember what is precious.

The savannah rolled and unrolled as he drove. It reminded him of scenes in plays, where they use a huge sheet of fabric to simulate the sea and blow air under it. There were farms with wind-pumps, and sometimes small villages of shacks with mud walls and tin roofs. Some had pumpkins drying on them. But where were the people? It was a mystery. The countryside was asleep, perhaps shocked. He saw a tall bird with long legs picking its way fastidiously through the grassland.

A little fear entered him: what had happened in the damp forest would not happen again, not in the same way. Whatever they decided, whatever they were allowed to decide, circumstances had changed. Jeremy knew; the world knew. A love affair had become gossip. Their love, which had seemed to him Olympian, had been directed down to street level. They might have the outline, the way that palaeontologists discover vertebrates in stone, but they could never know the warm, familiar flesh, the intoxicating urgency, the almost insane urge to be one, to achieve communion.

Once she said to him: 'The intensity frightens me; what is it?'

What is it? If you knew, you couldn't experience it. If love was comprehensible, it wouldn't be love. But he feared that now the innocence had gone. The ideal of true and enduring love was so powerful because it was impossible, although you could have intimations of it. There is a period of delirium, but it is made more urgent by the knowledge of its inevitable decay. Love is a play, when you know the surprise in the third act. Love is death speeded up.

We are condemned to see death in Arcadia. *Et in Arcadia ego*. The human predicament in four words. There are no votes in death. Nowadays you couldn't appeal to our boys to go and get themselves killed out here on the veld. Only Muslims saw any virtue in death these days. Joanna's father was killed out in the windy Falklands, shot by some Argentinian waving a white flag. That was the kind of death which almost every family would have been familiar with fifty or a hundred years ago: a relative catching a bullet. Now it was freakish. Joanna had been awarded an anachronistic distinction: she was the daughter of a war hero. Sometimes when they were naked he looked at her body and his own (although you get a strange perspective on your own), and saw the two of them dead. Occasionally he was too conscious that he was lying next to someone many thousands, perhaps millions, of men desired.

He passed a dam, merely scooped out of the savannah, and drinking there in the care of a man on a sturdy, hairy pony were about twenty or thirty steers, of a lustrous brown. He waved at the man, who waved back. He wondered what it was like to live out here in this vastness herding cattle. The emptiness was probably deceptive, not as elemental as it looked. As if to confirm his intuition, he was now passing the gleaming towers and ducts of an aluminium smelter, a small town enclosed by high fences and from some of the chimneys, lizards' tongues flicked the sky. He had never seen a sky so deep. In England the sky was a canopy; here it was an invitation to consider the notion of infinity. He declined.

In his stomach a knot had formed as he thought about what tomorrow would bring. In his three years in Government, he had woken so often with this feeling, that he had begun to wonder if there was some physical obstruction, some sort of accretion of chemicals forming a ball in his thorax. The peace he had felt reading Major Dick's advice about feeding horses on board ship, and the right flooring for the horse boxes — he had preferred coconut matting because it gave the horses some purchase in rough weather — this peace had gone. His hope that he could publish some extracts from his great-uncle's journal, with his own observations on Mafeking, perhaps even a short, charming bedside book, had gone too. From recuperating young politician — a high-flier, a favourite — he had now become just another predictably sleazy opportunist.

He stopped the car and walked down into a culvert for a pee. He rang his home telephone. There were thirty-seven messages. It had started. He peed deliberately onto a column of red ants, which dispersed and then regrouped.

Piss ant. He said it out loud.

4

Joanna told her mother what had happened. She called her from the orchard because reporters and photographers were camped outside, and maybe they had friends at BT who could divert her telephone convesations. You couldn't tell. Her mother had already seen the *Express* and there had been shots of Richard on the news hurrying into a car at Heathrow.

'Why didn't you tell me dear?' she said.

Her mother believed that they had a very close relationship, more friends than mother and daughter.

'I couldn't, Mum. I wanted to, but it wasn't possible.'

'Not possible to tell your own mother?'

The question was so weighed down with reproach that Joanna felt a familiar leadenness. Her mother introduced into their every conversation a hint of her dereliction as a daughter. Mothers required constant attention, yes, but the attention was of a ritual sort, as though by giving birth they had achieved a religious status. Mothers were semi-divine. They were like the goddesses in Euripides, able to behave with human pettiness, but also licensed to take refuge in their divinity when it suited them.

'He looked very nice. Not at all crumpled.'

'Who?'

'Richard McAllister, your lover, dear.'

'Mum, I'm ringing to ask you not to speak to any reporters or have your photograph taken. They are such bastards. But they only go away if you don't say anything.'

'Why would they want to speak to me? If they do, I'll just tell them the truth, that I know nothing.'

'It's better not to speak to them at all Mum. They twist everything.'

'All right. You probably know about these things.'

She was disappointed. She lived in a little house near the River Test, and the boredom, which she described as peace and quiet, was oppressive because it came dressed up as something superior and tasteful. Joanna promised to see her at the weekend, hoping that this would end the conversation, but her mother opened a new front: 'How has Jeremy taken this?'

'He's left. I don't know what he thinks really. He just left.'

'Does he want a divorce?'

'Mum, honestly, I don't know. I'm completely confused. I've got to go. I have to get things sorted.'

'Are you going to do the film?'

'Of course. I have to anyway. Bye for now.'

'That's a horrid expression . . .'

'Bye Mummy darling.'

'Now you're being sarcastic.'

She stood in the orchard, amid the apple blossom. Early apple blossom came in nursery colours, begging for approval. The whole half acre was stippled with infantile supplication. And through these sturdy apple trees she saw Jeremy's study, built from the old granary, paid for by her as a fifth anniversary present, even as she had known she was falling in love with Richard, and Jeremy's study stood empty with the early clematis around the door, named after a French countess — they were all named after French countesses — waiting for Jeremy to return to his work, his mission to help people understand the real issues.

At times she had looked through the window at him and watched his important earnestness unobserved and felt some, though not enough, of the love she had once had for him, and walked away unnoticed, often thinking of her lines, which to her had a physical form at first, just lines of type, hostile and cold, and it was only when she had them under control that she was able to turn them into sense; and it was this way she had of appropriating words and giving each one the imprint of the character that had raised her out of the crowd, and it was true that there were lines she was given that would not take on any human properties because they were not really speakable, and Jeremy's lines, she discovered with a gradual but sickening certainty, were of this sort, and Jeremy had been so sure and so convincing when she met him, and it was this that had appealed to her because after her father's death and their anxious wanderings she had mistaken Jeremy's bold assertiveness for a kind of truth, or at least an artistic map she could follow with him; but instead she found that the certainties were sometimes banal, so that she, who had not had much education, began to think them facile and smug, although she resisted, and soon after his way of making love, lying on her heavily, and sometimes wanting her to bend over the bed, nothing wrong in principle, began to annoy and even disgust her, so that she slept with the cameraman, Miklos, on *Half in Love*, but it was really in anticipation of Richard.

Richard riding his horse along the lane towards the forest. Richard introducing himself in his very natural way. He had just become a Member of Parliament. He was said to be a friend of the Prime Minister. He sat on his horse, which snatched at the grass, without any of that overbearing quality that the local horsey men adopted. Richard sat easily and humbly on the horse, not too concerned if it ate grass or fidgeted, as horses do. Richard said later that he loved horses but hated horsey people. This was not completely true; he liked jockeys and grooms and he had friends who rode, but what he meant was that he didn't want to be part of the horsey world. He said later that he felt sorry for horses: they were born into servitude.

Richard knew who she was; he had seen her in two plays and in a television drama. She invited him to dinner. The whole scene – him on his horse, she picking up some apples, the insistence of autumn, the fermenting dampness – was English. Even giving the horse an apple – 'Is it all right?' 'Sure, go on, she'll love it.' – the horse's amiable impatience, the way of feeding apple, the gobs of horse saliva around the bit, was shot through with self-awareness, as though to be English in a country lane in autumn was to be in a travesty. But Richard said that day how wonderful it was to be here, and how much he enjoyed the village and the forest. He was only renting, but had to get away from London from time to time. The horse lived at a stable near by. She was called Mimosa; she snuffled all over Joanna's flat out-stretched hand in an amiable way. Delicate hairy lips. Richard dismounting easily, apples falling constantly, plop plop in the orchard (although probably no more than two or three made the descent). Dinner would be fine. Jeremy would love to meet him. He would love to meet Jeremy. Did he have a partner, as they say? No, not at the moment. Did that mean he wouldn't be long without? Who knows. For a moment she wondered if he was gay, but she knew a lot of them in the theatre and he lacked those wounded too-bright eyes. Gays are ever alert to sounds on their private frequencies. In her experience, some thought they were blessed by this super sensitivity and some thought that they were cursed. Richard said, I've often wondered what it's like to be an actor. The horse stamped impatiently: time to go. He smiled. He was good looking. Yes. Almost conventional, dark hair, dark eyes. His manner was easy, very unassuming but also content. His eyes – she remembered now, standing in the same orchard – were guileless. It was a strange thing to notice, nothing you could articulate. There was just an openness, and perhaps kindness. Back in the house she told Jeremy about the dinner invitation and she noticed that his little eyes were reddened, light-pained, tender, chafed by the big issues which coursed behind them.

A photographer with a ladder was trying to get a picture through an upstairs window. She called the police. She didn't want to sound overwrought or self-important. She could tell that they were not going to take this too seriously, unless there was breaking and entering.

'But he's trying to take a picture of my bedroom.'

'All right. I'll send a car over,' the duty sergeant said wearily.

They're thinking, you wanted to be famous, so what are you complaining about? She drew the curtains and made herself coffee. The kitchen had just been redone with granite surfaces. She wondered if she would be able to keep this house. There was a knock on the door, but she ignored it: if you opened the door they got a horror picture of you looking aggressive or foolish or baffled.

A voice said, *Joanna, darling, please come out for a quick photocall, then we'll go away. We're just doing our jobs, darling.* And it was true. The picture editors sent them out and they dared not go back without something. A bedroom window, a note to the milkman, a neighbour's disapproval, a solicitous friend's visit. A cuckolded husband returning for his books.

People don't love actors without reservation. They envy them, but also they don't believe we have paid our dues. We've skipped some of life's important lessons. We're the people who have escaped. So any little difficulties, any big difficulties, are terrific fun for the watchers. How could you explain to them what you really are? How could you explain the terror, the fear of forgetting your lines, the constant uncertainty? How could you explain that you had wanted success, but you hadn't solicited this new life. When you went for a job as a young actor you offered yourself up for humiliation. But with success, it was worse. Now there was a sort of Dow Jones of popularity: if you took this part you would be seen as unglamorous; if you took that one, as a bimbo; if you worked with that director you would win an Oscar, with that one you would be a laughing stock. You never knew exactly who the jury was, but they were sitting in judgement, that was for sure. It was so important to make the right choice, it seemed. You don't want to be too English after *Half in Love*. Maybe you should do an American part. Maybe a comedy, to show that you aren't just an icy English bitch. But then, why not corner the market: there is always going to be a demand for the English bitch in every acting generation.

She could see the police car now, through the curtains. It was a small harmless car, perhaps a Vauxhall, and the young policeman who got out was large. A lot of young men around here were big and formless, as though the diet had changed without warning to something with a high protein content, laying mash or horse nuts. Their faces were rubbery like a seal's, and they tortured their hair. This one's hair stood straight up. He put his hat on to lend himself some authority. He was talking to the photographers, but she could see already that it was a man's gathering, bit of a laugh, not too serious, you do your bit chaps, give a little, and we'll all be okay, know what I'm saying? The policeman approached the front door through the parterre of box trees, which fomed two jays intertwined, for Jeremy and Joanna. She opened the door without showing herself, and he came in clumsily. He put his hat down on the table where the letters gathered. His upstanding cornstubble hair was released. The tulips on the hall table were shedding their petals in accord with the prevailing mood. Large petals, like mussel shells, lay on the rosewood. She remembered her father's hat – which he always put down on a table by the front door – the khaki, the badge of a gold lion, the red band, the braid. The tulips were the colour of veinous blood.

The policeman spoke with a slight rural accent, a wheedling tone as though he were coaxing reluctant animals into pens: 'Unfortunately, as the law stands, I can't do anythin' unless they actually trespass. But I've asked them to behave theirselves. It's a pity the front of the house is so close to the lane.'

'Bit late for regrets,' she said.

Before he left he asked her to sign an autograph for his wife who had seen *Half in Love* three times, although it wasn't his kind of film. He furred the word: 'fil-im'.

As he left she could hear the camera motors whirring, and she could imagine the picture captions. She waited sitting on the bottom step of the stairs with a coffee for Richard.

Even Richard, she shought, would not be prepared for this. After he was stabbed he went away because he wanted to avoid attention. Being stabbed was to find without seeking. The small, livid scar on his neck, which had become engorged when they were making love in the forest, was a calling card from another world; it was a souvenir of a trip he hadn't wanted to make; it was an opening through which all kinds of things might enter.

Above all, being stabbed was shameful: 'Don't be crazy Richard. It was random.'

'Nothing is entirely random.'

'That's very new age.'

'No I don't mean it like that. I mean that there I was at Wembley, rather self-important, free tickets, man of the people, all that shit, and this fat boy just felt me giving off a scent. He knew I was patronising them. He knew I was thinking, Jesus what a shower, what a load of revolting, yobs. When he called me a posh cunt, it wasn't just random.'

'Oh, so you deserved it?'

'At some irrational level, yes. I was just completely off kilter. I never really wanted to be in politics, but now I was beginning to enjoy all the wrong things. Am I making sense?'

Half in Love

He was lying in a hospital bed with a drip in his arm and an oxygen line attached to his nose. She knew exactly what he meant. It was essential to live in a fit, appropriate fashion; that was what he meant. His grandfather or great-uncle or whatever had written about horses, an honest, homespun work, and Richard had the idea that he could do penance by publishing this little book. He wanted to lower his sights. He was like T.E. Lawrence in *Ross*, wanting the impossible, to lose himself in the ordinary. She knew that in the acting world, the ordinary is the hardest part to play. Being ordinary demands skill, or it becomes pastiche, or even parody. As in Jeremy's plays.

Her phone rang.

'Hello?'

'It's me.'

'Jeremy, where are you? I was worried about you.'

'Worried as in, how's poor Jeremy, has he topped himself, or worried as in what's Jeremy going to get up to?'

'Just worried. Where are you?'

'In London, at Alex's flat. Where are you?'

'At home.'

'At home? Doing?'

'Doing nothing. I am sitting on the stairs.'

'Are you waiting for Richard?'

'Please, Jeremy, don't.'

'Yes or no?'

'Yes.'

There was a pause. She had no idea what to say. The enormity of what she had done, and done so blithely, rose up between them.

'Jeremy, I'm just terribly sorry.'

She tried to say the words as they were, words, not a line of dialogue, but she saw now that in this situation, a situation which had been played so many times on film and on stage and on television, there were no unfamiliar lines. What a strange, discomforting thought. Jeremy would now say: 'Sorry? Sorry? Is that all you can say after seven years?'

But he said, 'You are a cold deluded bitch,' and he put the phone down.

That word, 'deluded', what did it mean? Was he saying that in general she was deluded, or in relation to Richard? She longed for Richard now. She wanted to speak to him because she wanted to be reassured that what they had done was not just selfish indulgence, but something more. *Somos más.* Maybe she was deluded, and maybe all the time she had been nothing more than an actress, caught up in a part.

Last night Stan said, 'Don't worry, professionally it's not going to hurt you, not professionally. The punters expect this sort of thing from stars.'

The punters expected it. And she had delivered. Big time. Big time was a phrase Stan had adopted. Stan believed – many people in England believe – that American English was more suited to the task at hand. It was stripped down, adaptable, practical, where the English were still trapped by their prissy, out-of-date let's-not-get-to-the-point ironies. Stoppard and Pinter were the theatrical gods, and look at them. Jesus. It was a crime to say anything that wasn't steeped in ambiguity or stuffed with allusion.

She had delivered big time. She was doing what was

expected, teetering between banality and tragedy. Richard would never use the word, but in his heart, in his fibres, he would see the whole business as vulgar. The notion of vulgarity is something which no middle-class English person can ever quite extirpate, the lingering certainty that there is a right way to behave which has a set of rules running from how to drink soup to how to say hello. It was not as pervasive or as obvious as it had once been in her parents' time. In the ordinary world of people of her age, it was fading fast, to be replaced by other, better disguised snobbisms. But in the Army criticism had been merciless: officers were pilloried for their wives' vowel sounds; furnishings, food, wine, cars, schools, all had a place on an invisible index. Her mother suffered from the certainty that she had never quite lived up to expectation as the Colonel's lady. She was held back by a sort of conventionality, a suburban timidity. She was also prone to consider herself as a victim, which in turn was judged to be bad form. Officers' wives, young heroes' wives, were supposed to be dashing and carefree and unconventional. In the Army there was an unbroken thread to aristocratic values; the truly aristocratic were above convention.

And she? She had learned too well the nuances of the life. Now, at thirty-three, she was in danger of being cast forever as the kind of Englishwoman whose day had, in real life, long since gone. Stan wanted her to do a comedy: 'Not Oscar Wilde or any shit like that, but a warm, Meg Ryan kind of thing. Or Shakespeare, kind of contemporary, I'm not talking baggy-tights Shakespeare.'

Stan had a very Jewish fondness for the bitter-sweet, for the wised-up tragi-comedy of life. He told a joke – too often – about a young boy who comes home from school: *Did you get the part, his mother asks. Yes. What part? I got the part of a Jewish husband, he says. I think you're better than that. A lot better. You could have got a speaking part.* Even sitting on the stairs, she smiled. Stan was hopeless at telling stories, but he plodded on with an endearing earnestness. Nobody could refuse him the laugh.

She decided to call him, although she had said she would call him later, after she had seen Richard. But his number, his special number known only to her, was busy. Her mother didn't really know any Jews. It wasn't that she didn't like them. In fact she thought they were very clever, but perhaps they were a little too pushy for their own good. She wouldn't say this to anyone else, but Stan was a bit brash, wasn't he? But anyway Jews made the best agents, she had heard, and the best lawyers. It was a world – she might have said a souk or a bazaar – in which they were at home.

It was almost midday now. Richard's plane had landed at seven. Last night from Johannesburg he had said he would call her as soon as he could. He was off to see the PM. Talfryn was arranging for him to be driven straight to Chequers.

She had no idea what to do. She sat on the coir matting – Jeremy's choice – beneath the stairs. She wondered if she should tidy up. They had a new cleaner from the village and a part-time gardener now. The cleaner, Maureen, was a lesbian. This middle-aged woman, a divorced grandmother, came to clean every day to finance her apparently active sex life, which demanded excursions to specialist clubs in Brighton, and even further afield. She was in love with Joanna, Jeremy said. Jeremy approved of different sexual choices. He felt far too much was made of hard and fast distinctions. In Greek times there was absolutely no idea that homosexuality was wrong. And lesbianism? He wasn't sure where the Greeks stood on that, although of course in Greek, homosexuality means same sex, not homosexuality as we understand it. And Joanna had thought, what a strange people we are. Everyone, even cleaning ladies in cosy villages, believes in the importance of the self. The self has become the only authentic truth. It's your own irreconcilable property, and there's not another one the same anywhere. People were probably always just as preoccupied with their selves, but they didn't realise that it was such a desirable and healthy subject. Now the self had official endorsement.

She peeped through the curtains. The gang of photographers had thinned. Two men in Barbours were still standing there, holding polystyrene cups. But ladders and camera boxes were scattered along the verge of the road. The rest of the gang were probably in the Barley Mow.

Her phone rang.

'Are you alone?'

'Richard. Yes. Yes. Where are you?'

'Look out of the back, towards the forest.'

She rushed to the window. She could see the horse, the faithful Mimosa, cantering comfortably down to the stream, vanishing for a moment and then appearing again. Richard waved. She could see him open the gate of the orchard and trot up the path, past Jeremy's barn. She ran to the back door, out into the loud orchard.

'In moments of danger the master gives his life into the keeping of his horse,' said Richard as he dismounted. 'Xenophon.'

Mimosa was turned loose in the orchard, under the apple trees. She whinnied loudly, looking for company in unfamiliar surroundings, as horses do. Richard and Joanna lay naked on her bed. It was a deliberate betrayal.

The photographers outside, no more than a few yards away, were drunk now. Their voices had a raucous, derisive tone. Soon the deadlines would have passed and only the freelances would stay. There was that little man in a rat's beard and the fat man, as gingery as a Viking. These two had photographed Diana and Dodi Fayed, and were said to be very rich as a result.

Richard and Joanna lay close, sharing the unguents and sweat and earth scents of sex, and yards away, across the parterre, the photographers were unaware.

They lay flat out on the bed like victims of an accident, which in a sense they were.

'I was worried that you would be having second thoughts. It's one thing to, you know, have an affair . . .'

'Don't use that word,' he said.

'Everyone else is, apparently.'

'That's true. But it doesn't apply to us.'

Outside they could hear the horse's cries.

'How were my famous tits?'

Once when he was kissing her breasts he said, 'I can never forget how famous your tits are.'

'Perfect.'

'Am I allowed to ask what we are going to do?'

'With your tits?'

'Yes, and what's attached. Apparently rather loosely, in your opinion.'

'Joanna, I want to marry you. I have no other plans at the moment.'

She began to cry. It was true that you could cry with happiness. This unstoppable stream of tears seemed to her to drain from a deep bottomless sump.

'Oh God, Richard, oh Jesus, I love you.'

'Don't cry.'

But she couldn't stop Why stop?

'I'm sorry.'

Now she was tired. All her human essences had flowed away, leaving her strangely calm, as though she had left the animal world to join the vegetable kingdom.

'Tell me everything, darling,' she said.

'Everything?'

He seemed to be considering this task gravely.

'The lot. What you have been doing and thinking. It's all I care about.'

One skin, he thought. We will inhabit one skin.

'The Prime Minister sends you his love,' he said. 'For a start.'

5

The air on the plane was thin. They did something to it which impoverished it, leaving just enough there to keep you breathing okay, but without any belief that the air had ever seen the outside world of plants and sea breezes and ruminating beasts. He had tried scuba diving once and the air you breathed while marvelling at the coral, the friendly fish, and the waving tentacles of urchins, was of the same dead formula.

The static in the air made his scar tingle. The stewardess was solicitous. She knew who he was, treating him with a kind of complicit discretion. No doubt there'd been a briefing by way of Talfryn Williams to British Airways. A car would be waiting; he would be escorted through the special exit. Generations of politicians have been made to believe in their importance in this way. In every era a few hundred people have to be found to fill the vacancies. Richard had seen former Members who had lost their seats hanging around Westminster, forlorn figures, working for PR companies or charities, suffering political cold turkey. And nobody was interested in them any longer: the privileges had been withdrawn from them in a mysterious way which was still painful to them.

When he had told his father three years ago that he had been offered a safe seat, his father said 'as long as you understand that it's all balls in the end'. He wondered if his father was talking about politics in particular.

Some of his colleagues loved this proof of their vitality, evident in the small attentions, the briefings, the television interviews, the endless smooth lobbying, the Tussaud's civil servants with their self-effacing superiority, the matiness of the bars and dining rooms where women from a lost tribe called Doris and Eileen and Elsie attended to them with blowsy flirtatiousness, and they loved the amateur dramatic gothicness of Parliament, the Pugin wallpaper and portcullis curtains and hectoring carpets and leather-bound books, and monogrammed bottles of cheap wine. They loved it. They swam in it. And they found an audience, beyond the scepticism of family, free of the restraining ropes of the quotidian, an audience which apparently wanted to know what they thought. They discovered something which had not been apparent to them before: all the time they had been harbouring important thoughts which now, after burnishing, could rub shoulders with the universal truths. They had new haircuts – political haircuts – and small affectations, and they acquired aldermen's pot bellies from all the important dinners. Their tailoring became more statesman-like. They had to think more carefully what they were seen in at weekends or on fact-finding missions if cameras were present. They had to decide if they were to be traditional or forward-looking, country gentlemen or faintly bohemian, and the women began to wear suits and their faces became shiny and they too adopted management jargon using words like 'resources' and 'delivery' and 'sourcing' and this is where Talfryn and his chums came in, with their ears to the ground and their fingers on pulses. The pulses, a wag said, were too often the sort eaten in fashionable restaurants, but never mind, these boys lived amongst the opinion formers; they brought the latest news from the front across the moat to Westminster. And the news was that people – the people – wanted emotion and sentiment and feeling. They were fed up with facts and dogma; they abhorred ideology. But was that news documentary fact itself, or was it feeling? You could never tell with Talfryn and his friends. Richard wondered if they really knew themselves, or whether they were simply responding to a demand to appear to know what was going on. Politicians were preoccupied with the idea that the people had a collective mind which they must plumb in some way. This collective mind couldn't be understood by talking to individuals, because individuals were like the dots in pointillist paintings: on their own they conveyed no meaning at all. Every week constituency meetings and surgeries demonstrated this truth.

Richard knew that important work was being done. As a minister he himself was in charge of huge budgets for transport. But he had soon begun to see Westminster as a cult, with its own rituals and fetish objects. It was a cult into which he had not been properly inducted. Friendship, matiness, were no substitute for the proper blood rituals of a political life, which he had missed. The Prime Minister had told him that he would get to love it, that he would see that behind what he called boyishly 'the bollocks' (unconsciously echoing Richard's father) was a serious and effective system of government. But

Richard had begun to believe that the cult was self-serving, and that at the heart of all politics, even democratic politics, lay something ignoble and the hypocritical. And now by loving Joanna, he had fallen victim to its hypocrisy. In the name of public interest he and Joanna were about to be wracked.

Through the back alleyways of the airport, and in a car driven by a woman in uniform, and out into the spring-stippled countryside. Last night approaching Johannesburg the air was cold and still; clouds of smoke hung beside the hills and in the hollows rising from the shacks and townships, trapped there like mustard gas. Somebody from the embassy had taken him to a special entrance to the airport where a black man, who appeared to be a little drunk, escorted him to the plane and gave him a friendly slap on the back as he mounted the steps all alone to the plane. 'You're a lucky chap my bro,' he said cheerfully.

Now the English countryside was passing the windows of the Rover. It was looking fine: blossom, narcissi, daffodils, but it depressed him. He thought it was like a middle-aged lady at a wedding wearing a new dress that nobody cared about. Near Marlow he saw some horses with foals and they were pampered innocents, the mares in their New Zealand rugs and the woolly foals straight from Hamleys. The Prime Minister was waiting for him at Chequers. He had delayed a meeting with the Bosnian President who was kicking his heels in Claridge's. The driver said the police all the way were on alert, in case of traffic. She said it with pride, and he again saw something of which he had become aware over the past few years, that power creates fields of energy which the acolytes, however humble, find invigorating.

Half in Love

The car was waved through the gate of Chequers. A few photographers and cameramen were waiting as they swept past, and even from inside the car, he knew exactly how the picture would look in the papers: dark car, tense face. *Summoned by Prime Minister. On the carpet. Glittering career. Beautiful actress.* If he could have stopped the car and spoken to them and told them how simple it was, told them that he loved her, they would have thought he was mad, but he would have meant it. Although it had very suspect chemical origins, love was an overwhelming fact. To be in love and to be loved by Joanna was enough. His brother used to say that to write one perfect sentence was all he needed in life. Then he became a journalist.

As the car rolled down the long drive, thickly outlined by super-fit daffodils, he conjured and inhaled her warm and life-giving fragrance, to fortify himself for what lay ahead. In the event it was not difficult. Valerie came to the door. She kissed him. She knew about human frailty and susceptibility. She said breakfast was ready; the PM would be along in a moment.

'She's so lovely, Rich,' she said. 'Nobody's going to blame you.'

'Is that official?'

'Oh, I am just the consort. I won't be joining you for breakfast, I'm working today.'

She was dressed for court, in a dark suit and white shirt.

He went to the guest lavatory, just off the front hall. Little bowls of dried flowers and spices and embroidered hand towels were in place to soothe him. Englishness was everywhere, but with intimations of a Soviet spa behind the scenes, behind the panelling and the herringbone brick fireplaces and the oak furniture and the famous Titian, which had been touched in by Churchill himself. Some of the servants gave the appearance of having had an earlier career in the armed forces. It was in the way they walked, plumped up and purposeful.

There was a knock on the door.

'Come out, what are you doing in there?' It was Talfryn Williams.

'Just thinking.'

'He's ready.'

Talfryn was smiling happily. The Welsh seemed to come in two broad types, the bony dark ones and the rounder reddish ones. Talfryn was a hybrid, red but thin.

As they walked down the corridor to breakfast, Talfryn took his elbow lightly.

'The main thing is to get it out in the open, and to stick to the plan.'

'What plan?'

'The plan which you and the Prime Minister are going to agree.'

'This wouldn't be the plan you have already put to him, I suppose?'

'Richard, Richard, there seem to be a number of options. It's prudent to consider them. There's no plan, not yet anyway.'

Talfryn had framed the options, of course. In these options there had been no consideration given to the turbulence of the human heart.

The Prime Minister was waiting in his shirt-sleeves behind a huge cafetière of coffee and a jug of orange juice. A waiter arrived with a basket of croissants.

'Richard, how are you? Was the flight okay? Good. Coffee or croissant?'

Richard knew that almost all the Prime Minister's waking moments were plagued by a certain consciousness. He looked relaxed but business-like at the big table, behind him the spring-green garden glowing through the many-paned windows.

Talfryn placed the *Express* on the white linen, unfolded it: *Minister's secret affair with Joanna Jermyn.*

'I've seen it,' Richard said.

'In my view, speaking now entirely dispassionately, I can't see this being a problem,' said the Prime Minister.

'Unless there are revelations to come,' said Talfryn.

'For example?'

'Well, these things have a habit of popping up where least expected. Photographs, neighbours, husbands.'

'What Talfryn is trying to say, but is too polite, is that in our experience it's best to tell all now, up front. Nothing looks worse than grudging admission and grubby stories.'

'There's nothing grubby about this.'

There were flakes of croissant lying on the table beside his Wedgwood plate. He studied them.

'I'm not saying there is. Far from it. But what's the husband going to say?'

'Obviously I don't speak for him, but he's not going to be happy.'

Jeremy, the deep thinker. Joanna said that he was behaving erratically, blaming himself.

'The Prime Minister has to meet the President of Bosnia in half an hour. What I suggest is that you think clearly about what you want to do, speak to me this afternoon so that we can release a statement. In the meanwhile I will say that you have had talks with the Prime Minister and you have his full support.'

'I want to resign,' said Richard.

'No, Richard, not now.' The Prime Minister's voice was sharper than it had been.

'Isn't that what you want?'

'Falling in love is not a crime. You aren't married. She obviously isn't happily married. If you resign it will look as though you've done something wrong.'

'It would also look,' said Talfryn, 'as though the Prime Minister's chucked you off the ship. As you know we're trying to draw a line between personal and political life.'

'So you must be sure that there is nothing which could come up later.'

'Like?'

'Well, the stabbing couldn't have been related in some way?'

'As far as I know, and as far as the police know, the stabbing was entirely random.'

'But you were not willing to identify the suspect in the police line up.'

'No, because I didn't see who stabbed me.'

'As long as there is no connection. I have to go. Arrange with Talfryn the statement. Be happy. I'll be best man. Give her my love.'

Before his old friend had reached the door of the dining room it opened and he was borne away. The helicopter outside began first to whine in anticipation, like a spaniel behind a door, and then to roar. The helicopters have introduced a harsh, modernistic music to politics and warfare. He caught a glimpse of the Prime Minister and his wife, hand in hand, crouched slightly as they hurried past the window, as if they were expecting fire.

'So, tell me all, as our leader suggested.'

How could you tell all? How could you describe love? How could you explain to this friendly but amoral man the impulse to risk yourself in a sort of unrealisable state. To merge with another person. Instead he gave an account of how and when he had met her while riding, how they'd fallen in love and how they'd continued to meet in secret. Talfryn asked if they had discussed her leaving Jeremy. Of course. They'd decided to wait until after she had finished her new film which was taking her away for three or four months.

'Talfryn, why did the PM ask me about the stabbing? There's no connection.'

'The Met had the impression that you were uncooperative, you didn't want to help them.'

'I told them all I knew. They wanted me to finger the boy who I'd told to shut up. I couldn't.'

'The Commissioner looked at the papers and he seemed to think you were hiding something. He thought you might be trying to keep something quiet.'

'It may be that unconsciously I didn't want to be exposed to too much scrutiny because of Joanna.'

'Yes.'

'And the truth is that I somehow felt that I deserved it. I had behaved like a pompous prick.'

'And then you set off to Africa to recuperate? Or to get away?'

'Both.'

'But with no intention of giving Joanna Jermyn up when you came home?'

'No.'

'So you see, Richard, there are two or three routes through this minefield.'

He said 'through this minefield' with particular emphasis on the word 'through'. He hooted the word: *throuough*. The Welsh vowels sounded like a train in a tunnel.

'There are several ways through, but they all depend on what you decide.'

'And what's your preferred route?'

Talfryn's skin was freckled and his hair, thinning at the temples, was delicately red. It was the colour of the rocks around Mafeking, which were rufous with iron ore. Red hair really was a strange thing: Richard thought it made people look more ethereal, as if they were not wholly of this world, as though they heard Celtic sounds, perhaps flutes and mountain streams, undetectable to Anglo-Saxon ears.

'Richard, you are suffering from the popular delusion that people like me make policies and that we are really running the Government. All I do is try to offer our lords and masters some alternatives and some advice. Do you know those tick birds, egrets, in Africa? Well that is what I am. I wander along beside the big beasts and perform a little service.'

'So I am a tick?'

'They usually eat grasshoppers as it happens.'

He laughed in his attractive, quick, economical way.

'Anyway, if you want me to advise you I would say to declare

yourself, say it's true, say "we're in love, and it's my business".
As for my political career that's completely separate. But if I was
advising the Prime Minister . . .'

'Which you are.'

'Which I am, I would say give Richard your full support, but
if there's anything which comes out later which suggests he has
not told you the truth, cut his fucking legs off.'

Talfryn poured him another cup of coffee amiably.

'We'll speak at four sharp, so I can brief the press. Okay?
And meanwhile I'm going to say you've met the Prime Minister
who has the greatest confidence in you and believes this is an
entirely private matter . . . blah, blah . . . and we will be issuing
a statement after you have had a chance to talk to your nearest
and dearest. How's that sound?'

'I suppose it's fine. For the moment.'

'No wild talk of resigning, please. The PM particularly
asked me to stress that. I've got a car waiting, shall we head
for town?'

'Sure. Can it take me on afterwards?'

'Of course.'

So Richard arrived in mid-morning at the stables. He couldn't
go back to his cottage, because photographers were waiting for
him there. And anyway he longed to be on his horse.

Her coat was still rough. He helped the stable girl, Jenny,
brush her. If Jenny was surprised to see him, she didn't show
it. Her smooth face was strangely composed, encased in a
rural reticence. The rituals of grooming, largely just rituals,
pleased him. He faced the horse's tail and worked with the

coat, starting at the head. Mimosa's nose always became a little ticklish when he reached the stomach. Jenny picked her hooves quickly, scraped them out, and they saddled up. He put his hold-all in a crib.

At first as they left the stable yard out on to the road that led to the forest, she was fractious and nervous, snatching at bushes and starting when a panicky pheasant bolted across the road, but she soon settled into her steady, eager walk. He bent down over her neck and briefly, like a lover, brushed it with his cheek.

'I've missed you.'

Through the gate where he had to bend down again to unlatch it, and the horse stood rock steady, they went into the forest. They always cantered down to the bottom of the hill; he only had to cluck once and she was off. He breathed this rich forest air eagerly. It was mushroom-scented. He found the air of politics, like the air in the plane, starved. He saw himself in the landscape: a horseman. What was the point of riding a horse? There were people who didn't have a television or who were vegetarians, and congratulated themselves on their distinction. It made them believe they were connected to higher things. Riding a horse was no different, just self-indulgence. But every time he got on a horse he felt happy. He had tried to explain it to Joanna: 'I just feel more myself. I feel as though I'm in the right place.'

'You can be quite soppy, can't you?'

It wasn't that he was a countryman. Farmers and country people were often deadly boring; a deep vein of tribal solidarity, like seams in a rock, ran through them. Their tribe was shrinking and they felt compelled to utter inchoate and ill-directed derision and defiance. Joanna told him that when she and Jeremy moved down here, the local farmer's wife, a Lorna Stiffkey, had looked at her hands and said, 'You don't look as if you've done a day's work in your life.' Acting is not work.

He slowed Mimosa to a trot as they rose up out of the valley into an open area called Hundred Acre Field. She was blowing lightly. The gorse was coming into bloom. The colour of Dijon mustard. He rose and fell gently, finding the right rhythm. From a very early age he had known how to sit on a horse. You couldn't learn it in later life. They slowed to a walk. She had a long striding eager walk, just on the verge of breaking into a trot, which he loved, as though she were keen to see what was over the next rise.

It's all balls. But balls sounded, in his father's mouth, quite good fun, frivolous, meaningless. The old boy (actually he was only sixty-seven) had been out of the swim too long. This wasn't a game: it had taken a very ugly turn. The police suspected, maybe the security people suspected, that he hadn't been quite on the level. He had told them the absolute truth as far as the facts went: he had no idea who had stabbed him, because he didn't see him, and he could not even speculate if it was the fat, foul-mouthed boy. In truth he no longer saw the goose-pimpled boy as a neo-fascist member of the underclass, but as somebody who he, Richard, had insulted. He hadn't told the police that. But they had seen that he wasn't exhibiting the proper outrage, not displaying the appropriate enthusiasm for pulling in the fat boy. The fat boy, who was easily traced by his seat number, had a history of violence and had once been charged with possessing a knife. All it required was a little lie, *yes I saw him out of the corner of my eye for a moment*, and he would have been banged up, as the police put it.

Even in this landscape – the blasted trees, the rolling open patches of mustard gorse, the folded valleys, the portals of a distant farmhouse – even here he again felt his stomach contract as he heard the Prime Minister: 'Well, the stabbing couldn't have been related in some way?' The Prime Minister's eyes, a smoky delft colour, had seemed artlessly childish when they were no more than friends, ordinary people trying to make their way in the world. Nowadays they appeared to be bathed in some clear spirit, so that they were disturbingly refracted. What connection did they imagine? That Jeremy had paid a hit man? The connection, if there was one, was of a different order, a question of mortality and consciousness and their proxy on earth, love. Nothing you could tell a policeman or a prime minister, nothing you could explain to anybody except – perhaps – Joanna.

And now down below he could see her orchard, and the brick and tile of the house, whispering.

He urged Mimosa on and they cantered down towards the stream, through this little patch of England.

6

Who decided that the world had to be arranged? It was a mystery. Politicians had assumed the burden. They were obliged to interfere in the natural order. The universal suffrage gave them the power of judgement. They made a list of things which had to be done. They said that these things conformed to some natural law, or religion, or the great false science of Marx. Because, if you think about it, it is an incredible presumption to set about ordering the world. The Masai, from what he had read, wanted to live in an unchanging universe. Ditto for the native Americans. What would the role of a politician be in these societies? Would the politicians be offering them a more humane way of slaughtering buffalo or drawing blood from cattle or educating women? It was a new phenomenon in history, this idea that a manifesto should be drawn up. The manifesto was what the politicians offered the public; apparently this was a list of the important things that had to be done. And each party list conformed in some way to its personality and its beliefs, but these beliefs were no longer so easy to discern. The edges had been knocked off, so that they were generally about feelings: you contacted the voters, after all the beneficiaries of the manifesto, through their feelings, because they no longer had any coherent beliefs of their own. During his rest and recuperation following the stabbing, he was supposed to do some deep thinking about the manifesto. It needed some time. It needed some new ideas, which chimed with natural expectations. Or possibly even led them: the Prime Minister believed that the public needed to be presented with some fresh options. It was too easy to get into a rut. He hadn't put it this way, but he meant, get their eyes out of the trough, the gutter, the sink of self-indulgence. Get them thinking about higher things, like civic duty and education. It became known that he, Richard, was the Government's designated thinker. A wag had named him Minister Without Manifesto.

And then the public suddenly found him glamorous. Nothing he had done to try to repair the chronic state of public transport, nothing he had suggested about a weekly civics lesson in schools, in fact nothing at all in his three years in politics – not even being stabbed – had aroused an interest compared with the attention that besieged him after it became known he was having an affair with Joanna Jermyn, Oscar nominee and winner of a Golden Globe. It was clear to him that the public felt that he had been touched by something numinous. The public believed, he saw, more fervently in the reality of illusion than the reality of everyday life. They could imagine something sacramental in his relationship with Joanna – as a matter of fact, so could he – a relationship which had elevated him to a more spiritual plane. This was the incredible thing: he, the Minister of Thought, had become in their eyes somebody far more interesting and important. The people who decided how the world was to be arranged, people who were in charge of the human enterprise – including scientists and ecologists and professors of profound learning – were not as interesting as the people who performed in highly artificial films or the people who made simple music.

> Chin, chin, Chinaman, Muchee muchee sad!
> Noee jokee, brok-ee-broke, makee shutee shop.
> Chin, chin, Chinaman, Muchee muchee sad,
> Me afraid allee trade, Wellee wellee bad.

He held this note from his great-uncle's papers. Major Dick had seen Colonel Baden-Powell performing the role of a Japanese teashop owner in *The Geisha*. It had been performed to an appreciative audience of locals and transients— including Major Dick who was in Mafeking on horse business. Baden-Powell was Wan Hi, Chinaman and proprietor of a teahouse. The chief geisha, O Mimosa San, was played by Winston Churchill's aunt, Lady Sarah Wilson. The Prime Minister's son, Lord Cecil, played one of the officers from *HMS Turtle*, visiting China, and a Captain Kenneth McLaren 'later captured by the Boers' played the romantic lead, Reginald Fairfax, light tenor. His great-uncle had also noted 'The Amorous Goldfish' ('not as good as Marie Tempest, but quite a praise-worthy effort by Lady Wilson') and he had copied the lines

And she sobbed. It's bitter bitter,

He should love this critter critter,
When I thought he would wish
For a nice little fish,
With a frock all glitter glitter.

He tried to imagine Major Dick humming that one or *Chin, chin, Chinaman, Chop, chop, chop* out there in Mafeking a week or two before the Boers let fly with Long Tom, and his beloved horses were doomed to the soup kettle and their oats made into flour. He tried to imagine these people led by the little colonel, and he tried to re-create for his own use the sense they had that they were doing something useful and valuable, in fact that they had a mandate to interfere in the natural order out there. Less than twenty years after his great-uncle was fretting – with some justification, in view of their bouillon potential – about the horses, less than twenty years after Baden-Powell was dressed up as a Chinaman singing *Chin, chin, Chinaman*, Nelson Mandela was born, and Nelson Mandela was still alive although he had retired from his great task.

Richard's great task was 'to introduce some idealism into the manifesto, while taking account of people's genuine feelings and legitimate aspirations', but the feelings had proved to be as inscrutable as cuneiform. People's legitimate aspirations were to lead a life of increasing material comfort, attested by appliances and brand names, and their genuine feelings were directed towards themselves. The self was the recipient, in handy form, of the necessary religious and spiritual content of their lives. The self was the household god, the supreme object of veneration. The self had to be nurtured and encouraged in its aspirations. Politicians were there to deliver the goods, emotional and electrical. And the prescient PM had seen that this was a blind alley: if the economy turned down, if things went wrong in an unpredictable but inevitable manner, they needed to have something of substance to point to, some beliefs that were not ideology, but were none the less a little more substantial, a little deeper, than mere feeling. The PM wanted a second term, and a second term entailed philosophical staying power. He couldn't accept, and no politician could accept, that he was just a little Dutch boy with his finger in the dyke. And then there was the question of gays and lesbians. Richard was supposed to suggest more sympathetic but not wildly permissive ways of treating this tricky question. The gay lobby had a habit of racking up their demands. They tried constantly to elevate their sexual habits to universal principles. The Prime Minister wanted to know, in not so many words, where to draw the line.

Joanna had gone. With her agent she had decided that it would be better to leave for New York for readings and rehearsals and then to go straight to the location of her next picture in Phoenix, Arizona. 'Picture' described a big movie. 'Picture' was the top classification, above 'film' and light years away from 'British film'.

Joanna was gone and he was left here holed up in his brother's flat arranging the world. It had been announced that his recuperation was not complete and that he would be taking a few more weeks' leave before returning to his duties. He was working on policy. The truth was that he had been driven into hiding by this madness. The stories about him and Joanna, the parties where they had met, the hotels where they had spent nights together, the anguish of Jeremy Wolhuter, the playwright and unsuspecting husband, the fabrications – he had given her his mother's ring; she had removed a tattoo from her inner thigh which offended him – had multiplied, building on each other like the combs in a beehive, and the only press conference he had chaired, on a new proposal for the ownership of London Underground, had become utterly anarchic as claret-cheeked and bouffant-haired social correspondents had asked him if he knew who had stabbed him, if it was true that he and Miss Jermyn were going to get married, if it was true that she was pregnant by him. His attempts to talk about the benefits of a joint venture between public and private money (on which he had no strong feelings, in reality) had been hopeless. A senior civil servant had taken over the briefing, but all the journalists left immediately, except for the editor of the road hauliers' magazine who wanted to expose the issue of hidden subsidies.

In all this commotion there was a tune that he could discern increasingly clearly, a hymn to celebrity. As the Prime Minister's wife had predicted, nobody blamed him. He was touched by grace. He had had a near-death experience; he was loved by a goddess. He and Joanna had made a joint appearance before the press, and she had told the world that she loved him. Her declaration was made to no one in particular, only to a wall of indifferent camera flashes. He had mumbled, upstaged by a professional, of his love for her and his determination to serve the country and the Prime Minister.

She had said, 'Unfortunately in all human relations, in all affairs of the heart, pain is caused to others. It was never my intention to cause hurt, but I am powerless in the face of love on this scale.'

The way she said it, her eyes so intense although blinded by the lights, her voice warm and natural, her hand seeking his, was devastating in its simplicity as he realised when they watched the news together later.

'I was wonderful, wasn't I?' she said. She added, 'Because I meant it. It was just what I had to say.'

Now, as he read Major Dick's notes, he wondered if with actors you could ever separate the performance from the reality. Major Dick said that Baden-Powell had 'a wonderful aptitude for musical comedy, and a commendable voice (a light tenor)'. Richard pictured these light tenors and deep contraltos trilling and warbling unaware that they were about to be besieged for two hundred and seventy days. Major Dick wrote 'Colonel Baden-Powell and I conversed for about forty minutes. He was extremely interested in my theories on the use of cavalry. He believes that the Boers will never stand still long enough to be engaged by our regiments. They have quick, hardy ponies. He believes that we should develop irregular units and units trained in scouting. He himself wears an extraordinary get-up of his own design, sort of Tyrolean breeches and a broad-brimmed hat from the American West. He professes to dislike what he calls high-collared and kid-gloved officers. He is also a great believer in the cold bath, which he describes as "the cold tub for the soul". He is a remarkable man and much loved. He is not a passionate horseman sadly.' As it turned out nobody could have depended on the horses more than Baden-Powell, even though it was as foodstuff rather than cavalry.

Through English history, he thought, there runs a thread of absurdity.

Teach them citizenship. Tell them that Baden-Powell was gay, that he loved cold tubs, and naked young men, hangings and whippings; tell them the Boy Scout movement was started by a sado-masochist with a taste for dressing up but with a pleasing light tenor voice. Tell them that our history, lives, institutions are – like every other country's – a mixture of farce, delusion and self-interest. No wonder nobody believes there is any such thing as historical truth. The fact is nobody believes in anything much and the manifesto was already overstuffed with meaningless good intentions and pointless generalised statements. In Baden-Powell's day, and Major Dick's day, it was known beyond question that the English way of life was superior to all others, that the English gentleman was at the cutting edge of evolution. And yet, despite Baden-Powell's absurdity, and Major Dick's limited, horsey horizons, they were both caught up in the grand enterprise of life. The deluded idealism, the restless activity, even the easy benign racism, contained a sort of nobility which had been booed off the stage.

His father, no fool, knew that this old world had passed; in fact he put a date on it: '1961, a year after you were born. One day women were wearing twin-sets and pearls and boys were wearing suits and jackets, and the next day girls were walking down the Kings Road wearing handkerchiefs.' But it hadn't gone away. It was hiding, biding its time, laughing at itself, and ready to make a comeback. The problem was that none of the receptacles – the Prime Minister preferred the word 'vehicle' – for this lost idealism was in working order. Patriotism, the Church, Parliament, the

Monarchy, had all taken terrible knocks. The Prime Minister believed that a new concept of nationhood was being forged. What was it exactly? The old one was founded on antipathy and notions of superiority. Richard thought it maybe needed suffering and antagonism; maybe life was a chiaroscuro. But of course things changed: it was one thing being out in the Empire, or opposing the Vietnam war, quite another thing working yourself up about fox-hunting or gay soldiers. What the people, the points in the pointillism, cared about was the personal odyssey through this vale of emotional obstacles.

He couldn't think of a single new idea. He was truly the Minister Without Manifesto. Perhaps they should make a virtue of their lack of ideology. They should try to elevate lack of conviction to the status of universal principle. That was certainly a new idea.

Joanna was in New York. She was having daily meetings with the director and the writers. There was some question about the cameraman, and his ability to light women. She called Richard every morning when she woke, and he longed for these moments. Until she rang, just after midday, his mornings were distracted. His brother's flat, a half-completed loft near the City, was empty and clamorous. The bed was on a platform up the staircase of glass slats. There were no blinds on the skylight above, so that at night he lay looking up at the woolly tapestry of clouds, lit by the city beneath. Last night a police helicopter had passed into his skyscape and hovered for a few moments. He had begun to think of this frame as a painting, so he was startled by the urgent lights and violent motion.

He hadn't gone out for three days since Joanna left. His private secretary sent him sheaves of papers and urgent briefings every day; mounting up on the unfinished work surface which was half covered in zinc and they were going native among the unwashed coffee cups and pizza boxes. His brother's new flat was evidence of his desire for a more glamorous life after he and Jill split up. Richard had liked Jill, but Tim said that she was stifling him. When his novel, which was supposed to free him for journalism, sold only one thousand copies, he blamed her. She had cut him off from real life by erecting a wall of dull friends around him. He didn't want to know any more people with incredibly gifted children, or any more chubby lawyers, or glazed people who sang the 'Mass in B Minor', or the people who had country cottages where they were planting old, rediscovered varieties of roses. He was only thirty-four for Christ's sake, and he wanted to live in Cuba or write a play or explore the upper reaches of the Orinoco. This flat, this building site with its immense, unstoppable windows, was his first step on a new road. But the newspaper had sent him to Berlin with a better salary. Every night in Berlin he went to language classes and he was falling in love with his teacher. A new novel, much less conventional, was developing in parallel. It was set in Berlin and involved a young English writer. Tim, too, was half in love with fame. He hoped Joanna would be staying in the flat; he hoped to find it charged with her presence.

Houses, apartments, had become an expression of yourself. You were encouraged to believe that you must demonstrate something of your inner self, your reality, by decoration. This apartment – half finished – demonstrated something unintended about his brother, the fledgling novelist, Richard thought, and that was a super-sensitivity to the little breezes blowing around the edges of society, the eddies created by the passing of bigger ideas. Modishness and savvy were not the same thing as understanding. We are plagued by the Platonic idea, the myth of the cave, that we are seeing only the shadows of real things. After three years in Government, he could no longer tell the difference. If there was one. So interior decoration, the manifesto, life style, politics itself, seemed to have fused, in the same way that cooking had become eclectic. The loin shall lie down with the lime.

His father had insisted on coming round to see him. He saw himself as an emissary from a more rational age. Possibly even from Athens, about 100 BC. He'd appear, bristling with advice, but also issuing disclaimers: 'Of course, what I believe is completely irrelevant. I'm a fossil. Ever since Mick Jagger peed in that garage I appear to have been exiled, like the wretched Albanians, in my own country.'

The facts did not support his assessment of himself. He had lived very much in this world, with keen worldly appetites. Richard's and Tim's mother had died nearly twenty years ago, and since then his father had been married twice. That did not disqualify him from giving advice on affairs of the heart. Far from it; he was an expert. Richard had the strange feeling that he himself was composing the conversation which was to come. His father would look up the stairs, preparing his knees – the defiant victims of his vigorous life – for the ascent; his eyes – small, dark, vivid – giving a signal of the imminent delivery of his assessments and judgements and bons mots. His grey hair, which had once been curlicued and fed with tonics made of rare tropical oils, had become thin in the last few years so that only a defiant coxcomb stood up in the middle of his forehead. He hadn't adjusted his demeanour, however, to the straitened circumstances of his hair; it was still, in Tim's phrase, full on. His ferocious charm continued to work: in restaurants and cafés he commanded attention and sycophancy. Even accompanying his older son, the Minister of Thought, he gave up the limelight only grudgingly. Richard had the impression that his father believed that his sons shared a portion, the lesser portion, of his own ineffable substance. They were the paring from the Parmesan; they were shavings from the marble bust, and they were snippings from the clan tartan. The tricky part, the fascinating part, was that you could never discount him or his views. Richard was looking forward to seeing him even though he knew the way the meeting was destined to go.

The phone rang. He picked it up exultant.

'Hello, Richard. It's Jeremy. Remember me?'

'How did you get this number?'

'Joanna told me you were at your brother's. It wasn't difficult.'

'Why are you ringing, Jeremy?'

'What a strange question.'

'Jeremy, I deeply regret any hurt. I can imagine how you feel, and I'm very, very sorry, but I can't talk to you.'

'You can't imagine how I feel.'

That wasn't true; because he loved Joanna he could imagine Jeremy's sense of loss in direct relation.

'Jeremy, what do you want to say?'

'I just think you should know that you aren't the first. She's an actress, in case you hadn't noticed. You're the new romantic lead.'

'It's not worthy of you, Jeremy. Goodbye.'

He put the phone down. Why would Joanna tell Jeremy where he was living? It was supposed to be a secret. He wanted to ring her in New York but it was only 6.30 in the morning there.

Major Dick wrote that Baden-Powell thought that horses were doomed in modern warfare. Baden-Powell thought that the War Office was crazy to continue to emphasise the role of cavalry. The Boers had German rifles that picked off cavalry from two thousand yards. What would the cavalry be charging? A few rocks. Baden-Powell said that the piles of rock were 'kopjes', and that he told Major Dick they were the Boers' natural fortresses. But Major Dick's conclusion was that Baden-Powell, not being a natural horseman, had failed to understand the horses' full potential except in the culinary department.

His phone rang. This time it was Joanna.

'I love you,' he said, and then, 'Good morning. I adore you, how are you?'

'I'm going through the motions. I'm hoping you will be able to get away.'

'Joanna, Jeremy rang me.'

'Oh God. What did he want?'

'How did he get the number?'

'I'm not sure. He said that there were all sorts of things that had to be settled, and that he wanted to write to you, so I said I thought you were at your brother's, but I have no idea how he got that number. I was trying to fob him off.'

'Oh well. How's New York?'

What he meant was, are you making a life without me, however rudimentary? Are you going out to the park and to the delis and the restaurants? And are you talking to people and living without me?

'I'm half alive,' she said. 'There's plenty to do. I do it, interviews and so on and script discussions, but I spend all day longing for you. What did Jeremy say? He's become awfully creepy, sort of sanctimonious.'

'Jeremy wanted to chat, but I told him it wasn't appropriate.'

'What did he want to chat about?'

'I don't know. I wouldn't allow him to talk.'

'Do you know, now that it's out in the open, I don't feel sorry for him at all. I just feel a great relief. It's almost as if I was trying to keep my dislike of him in bounds, trying to be positive. Now that he's running around all Uriah Heepish, I really feel nothing for him. I just want never to have to see him again.'

'Something tells me it's not going to be that simple.'

She had instructed lawyers. These days you could be divorced in three months. The picture was due to finish at the end of the summer. They could be married in the autumn. He had promised the Prime Minister he would give it until the end of the year before he made any decision about resigning.

'Jeremy didn't say anything about me, did he?'

'No, not directly.'

'He worries me. He's up to something. Even though he probably doesn't know exactly what.'

'We can deal with it.'

But at that moment the door buzzer rang. He picked up the entry-phone and heard his father below saying, 'Anybody there? What's going on? Let me in, I want to see Richard McAllister, my son.'

'It's my father,' said Richard, 'he's come to see me. When can we speak?'

'Later.'

'I love you with all my heart and all my soul.'

'I love you.'

'Goodbye, darling.'

'Goodbye? Goodbye? I've only just arrived,' said his father's voice now becoming blustery.

'It's me, Dad, Richard. I'll let you in.'

He pressed the release button, but his father charged the door just too late. There was a muffled crash from below.

'Bloody hell, what's going on?' His voice was oddly strangled by the crude phone.

'I'll come down.'

'Where are you?'

'I'm coming.'

Richard opened the door and ran down the concrete steps two floors to street level. He hoped nobody had followed his father. The journalists had been hounding Joanna's mother down in Wiltshire. As he opened the door to the emissary from an antique land, he caught the familiar scent of Jamaican Limes by George Trumper. His father peered in, his small dark eyes eager to penetrate the mysteries of the industrial twilight within. His eyes had always seemed to be the wrong fit for his impressive, strong face, like buttons on a child's plaything.

'I've been dying to see a loft. It's a sort of kick in the face for people who live in houses with nice furniture, isn't it? It's a statement. How are you, my boy? Aloft.'

'Two floors up, this way, Dad.'

'Aloft we shall go. Strange part of the world, vee strange.'

They set off up the stairs. The climb was going to take some time. His father was fit, but his knees weren't keeping pace with the rest of him, he said. From behind him, Richard could see the way he leant forward, like a sherpa on an ice wall, so that his torso led the way, encouraging his weak knees by example. He wore a tweed jacket, the sort that the French and Italians had adopted, the checks a little too attention-seeking. His shirt was of a pure sea-island blue, rakishly cut away at the collar where a soft knitted tie reposed comfortably. His grey flannel trousers were bunched around his bottom, loosely. There was nothing there to support and comfort them any longer. Richard felt a stab of pity. He remembered his father when they were at the seaside and he was about seven; and his father had solid, meaty, hairy thighs and strong buttocks which were outlined by the wet swimming trunks, as firm and rounded as piglets'. He remembered how his father carried Tim on his shoulders and him, Richard, on his back as they went out and took on the waves while his mother watched from the beach. Once his father fell and they had to fish around in the surf for Tim, and he pretended it was all part of the game, although Richard could see that he was briefly panic-stricken until Tim was coughed out by a retreating wave, his ears full of sand and small pebbles, reproachfully silent.

Now his father stopped for a moment, holding the handrail, which was a piece of painted pipe.

'Lucky for you you haven't done any serious sport,' he said. 'You may be spared this wear and tear.'

Honourable injuries. War wounds, scars from a duel, a duel with life. At the moment the score was about even, a number of hits for both sides. They reached the flat, and Richard was alarmed by the heaviness of his father's breathing.

'I like it. I may buy one myself,' his father said as he slumped heavily onto the only serviceable chair. 'Loft living.' He said the words as though he had stumbled on a forgotten language.

'It's a way of saying houses with rooms and little gardens at the back and curtains and so on are bourgeois. Boring. Don't you think?'

'Tim was trying to tell the world something, yes. How are you, Dad?'

'I'm fine. But you don't want to waste your time asking me questions. You're the man of the moment. Are you coping?'

'I think so.'

'Actually, I'm quite pleased. There were times when I thought you might be queer. Gay.'

'Really?'

'Not deep down, but you showed a certain restraint around girls. Lovely girl, Joanna. When do I meet her?'

His father had displayed no restraint. Looking back over the years he could see now that sex had been his leitmotiv. Even now there were women, some of them reasonably young, who responded to his primal bellows. He occupied a lot of male space, a sort of territory which he took with him like those rams and bulls in nature films. Women had to acknowledge it if they entered.

'Joanna is in New York starting on her next film, and I'm going back to work in a few weeks. Not that I am on holiday now. I am working on the manifesto.'

'The manifesto. Another load of balls. People aren't interested in the manifesto. They want leaders to lead. And that's what your chum is good at. Although I must say when I first saw him I thought he was a dreadful little creep.'

His father believed that his relationship with political figures, with newspaper articles, and with the occasional film or play, was somehow seminal. The world was waiting for him to endorse, to deliver judgement, to offer the definitive opinion.

'I wanted to go, but he asked me to stay,' said Richard.

'Of course he did. You need a few kindred spirits in any enterprise. You're his man.'

'Not altogether. He's moved on. He thinks my stabbing and Joanna's husband may be connected.'

'There are all sorts of connections of course. The older I get, the more I see the fine wires which string us all together. Got anything to drink?'

'There's a little white wine in the fridge. Or coffee.'

'I'll have coffee.'

When he drew close to give him the coffee, Richard saw that his father had missed some straggling clumps of hair under his chin and on his cheek. He was fastidious, even vain, about his appearance, so this remissness seemed to indicate, as the laboured scent had, that his father's essence was dribbling away. When was the moment that you became certifiably old? The handsome, assured, middle-aged man was about to be replaced by an older, more frail figure, a figure whose outlines he could now see within, like a pupa about to hatch. And the implacable, cyclical, nature of existence mounted a sudden assault, in this bright, uncurtained, unfinished loft.

7

Central Park was beautiful. It wasn't true that you could learn nothing from scenery. In amongst the scenery, she could see the hurrying, improving, preoccupied figures of New Yorkers. They were rollerblading and throwing footballs and jogging determinedly and – now a glimpse – playing tennis. She was riding with a little Guatemalan man from the stables off the West Side. Her horse was called Thunderhead, and his was Chiquita. Like a lot of professional horse people, the Guatemalan didn't seem to like horses much. The horses were afraid of him; their eyes showed it. As they rode along past the wild landscape of the lake, he chided the horses, which were chronically tired, and spurred his own horse as soon as its head dropped. There was a painting in the Met or somewhere, of Indians after a defeat returning home to the forest on horseback, the horses' heads low, the landscape, if you didn't look up at the towers and turrets, similar to this.

Horse people were in a state of low-level war with their horses. Horses were backsliders. Horses were opportunistic. Horses learned bad habits. She was riding because she had a horseback scene in her new film. But she felt she was riding because Richard loved horses. She wanted to ride with him when they were together. She hadn't ridden since she was a young girl, when she had briefly hung around some stables near the base. When her father died, they moved and horses left her life. The fatigued Thunderhead was hardly a ride, but she enjoyed the distinction of being mounted on a horse; and she enjoyed the sense that every shambling stride brought her closer to Richard. She felt protective of her fly-blown, angular, but tough, old horse as it began to trot reluctantly after Chiquita, whose eyes were rolling in anticipation of the Guatemalan's reminders of who was boss, of who was sitting on top. Strangely, New York was quite horsey. There were piles of horse shit on Central Park South where the tourists' hansom cabs waited, which lent an antique perfume to that part of the city, and there were mounted police in the park, as well as the livery horses. There were also polar bears and other beasts in the little zoo: the place was heaving with animals.

She remembered how uncomfortable trotting could be on a horse that was barely lifting its legs. The horse was so reluctant to trot that it was practically skating.

A policeman called to her from his horse: 'You were great in *Half in Love*,' he said.

Policemen are trained to see through disguises; she was wearing huge sunglasses and a hard riding hat.

'Thank you,' she said.

'Need an escort?'

'No, we'll be all right.'

'Okay, m'am. Have a good one.'

The Guatemalan looked at her more closely. His eyes were Indian, black, deep set in the sockets, speckled with soot and cumin.

'Who jew?' he asked.

'I'm an actress.'

The horses had slowed, gratefully.

'Movies?'

'Some.'

'What jew name?'

'Joanna Jermyn.'

'I never heard jew.'

He became silent again, slapping the horse with his whip.

Joanna Jermyn. She had chosen the name in a panic for her first audition, which was for a part as a maid in Oscar Wilde. By choosing that name, she had started down this path. As an actress you needed something to lift you out of the crowd, said Stan. She was marked as the cool Englishwoman. She was becoming rich playing a type that no longer existed outside films and plays. The English were being parodied and exalted all at the same time. Americans couldn't make up their minds if the men were charming gentlemen or sinister perverts; the accent could tip it either way. And the women were beautiful upper-class bitches, or eccentric frumps. Perhaps this confusion and ambivalence were the product of the literature, which had colonised the world, leaving these characters stranded in the imagination. The characters had bred film versions of themselves, and they merged with the actors who played them, from Vivien Leigh to Maggie Smith, and from Diana Dors to super models, so that it was no wonder that the wider public, if they cared at all, were confused about Englishness. Englishness had become a self-parody. The truth was the English had no coherent idea of what they were, although they saw that they carried a bigger burden of history and expectation and derision than most, if you could weigh such things.

When the fat boy had stabbed Richard, Richard said that he deserved it; he meant that he had been living in a world entirely separate from the people he was supposed to be representing. He thought it was a kind of hypocrisy, but Joanna could see it was not that easy to be true to any simple ideal any longer. As an actress, was she on a mission to portray some national virtues? Probably not. Richard thought that in politics, into which he had been drawn, he must discover what it was that people wanted. He had discovered that they didn't know: they'd given over all responsibility for their philosophy to their feelings. Their selves were like sea anemones, with the tentacles testing the water to see what nutritious particles stuck. But Richard had still tried to find some nobility, some pattern of decency and rationality, that he could respond to. In his heart he believed in goodness, and she loved him for it. She loved him so much that she was riding with this surly Guatemalan on a close, late spring day in Central Park.

She tried to remember: toes up, heels down, firm but light contact, back straight. The Guatemalan sat on his horse like a jockey. He perched there. Richard sat on a horse in an easy, natural, matey way. This man was a little incubus; the relationship between him and the horse was not healthy.

They had almost circled the park. She could see the Dakota Building now, and remembered that she was in the car with her father when Lennon's death was announced, and her father – war hero to be – cried, and she cried too onto her school uniform. A year later her father was dead, shot on a miserable rainswept, sheep-cropped hillside by a trigger-happy sixteen-year-old Argentinian. They asked her about it at every interview. If you were interviewed often enough, you refined your answers as you saw what played best. She said, 'It has made me realise that life is a precious thing, and that nothing is safe and secure. It has also given me a slight wariness, perhaps a distance. And I believe that this has made me a better actress.'

The truth was, naturally, much more complicated. At times she hated her father for abandoning them in this way, for getting himself shot in some windy cold islands nobody could locate on a map. At other times she felt that her father had left her a precious legacy, a kind of sanctity which was for ever perfect and imperishable. It was a chipping of immortality. A few years ago she and her mother had been to Goose Green and stood together in the small, windy cemetery. A bugler had played the 'Last Post'. She stood there, a chill wind blowing up off the sea, sea birds protesting, sheep huddled in pockets and depressions, wiry little grasses barely acknowledging the wind, the desperate notes of the bugle flying away in the direction of Antarctica, flying away individually, all team spirit lost, the music torn away, like those calendar pages in old movies. And as she stood there she felt blessed.

She had never tried telling that to an interviewer.

The stables were like crates, down a side street where the upper West Side began to crumble, but her horse was perfectly happy to be back, calling to its listless friends, snatching at a hay net, shaking itself as the saddle was removed. She gave the Guatemalan a twenty-dollar tip. On the ground he was small, with horse-disfigured legs that let in light. He pocketed the money in the way that Third World people do, furtively, as though it were already earmarked for a needy relative.

'Thank jew,' he said. 'Jew come some more?'

'Maybe.'

'I give jew nice horse.'

But he wasn't in charge. A very fat Hispanic woman with a Bronx accent was in charge. She wore immense blue jeans, which were meant to suggest a familiarity with the equine life, but only served to emphasise that major engineering would be needed to get her onto a horse.

'Francisco say you ride good. You wanna make another booking?'

She booked for the same time tomorrow.

'You like Thunderhead, or you wanna change?'

She pronounced the horse's name 'Tunderboid'. Out of loyalty, Joanna opted for the same horse, whose knocked-about head was now poking out of the battery-hen stalls. She went over and stroked the head. There was a very pronounced bone running down below its large, dry eyes. The horse gave her no sign that it cared what she did. It certainly wasn't thinking about recent, shared experience.

A limousine was waiting to drive her back to The Plaza. She would have preferred to walk. She felt lonely in the back, a vast space full of useless junk; a folding cocktail cabinet, a television which didn't work properly; a CD player; a telephone. The car was meant to flatter you: you are the sort of person who needs all this stuff, even if you are just going a few blocks. But it was like being in a nightclub during the day. Dead. She tried to call

Richard on the phone, but of course there was a problem; it couldn't dial out of the country without some code or card or something. All show. All plastic junk.

Jeremy had put the house on the market. He said he had no money. His last play, a dramatisation of a strike at Liverpool Docks in the Sixties, had closed at the Everyman after ten days. Despite its contemporary resonances, there were no plans to pick it up anywhere else. So far he hadn't mentioned her money, put away for her by Stan, but no doubt that was coming. She had barely left the country before he phoned the local estate agent, Buckhursts. It was vindictive but she didn't protest.

One of the producers, Michael Berkovsky, was waiting for her. He wanted to have breakfast with her on full view in the main restaurant. It was important for producers to be seen with actresses. He wanted to discuss the choice of cameraman, because he felt that on a picture like this the DP would be vital. He wanted her opinion, and she had agreed to breakfast. She didn't have time to change, but she tried to scent herself to suppress the smell of horse. He was sitting at a table ostentatiously tucked away. He had that look about him she had come to recognise, the accountant from the suburbs who could not disguise his origins with a tieless Armani suit and a few days' growth. He was reading *Variety* and occupying several waiters at the same time.

'You look gorgeous,' he said. 'How was your horseback riding?'
'Good fun.'
'I know from nothing about horses. But I tell you what, there are whole buncha people from my neighbourhood who have moved to the mink and manure belt. My dad used to say Poland to polo in one generation. Sit down. Sit down.'

He was trying too hard, but his nervousness endeared him to her. He ordered a health breakfast with so many extras that any health benefits were vitiated. In the film world there was a mania for individualising your order. Food was one expression of your individuality and a proclamation of your intentions, particularly in regard to mortality. She ordered coffee and a Cantaloup melon, while Berkovsky was still pondering the implications of Canadian bacon with a fat-free blueberry muffin.

'You know what Lenny Bruce said: bacon is the only part of the pig which is kosher.'

He had prepared this little witticism well in advance.

'Lighting,' he said. 'Lighting is important. If *Half in Love* had a fault – God forbid I should find fault with one hundred and five million dollars – it was the lighting. I don't think Miklos handles big scenes well. I think we should use Peter Suchitsky. What do you reckon?'

Did he know that she had had an affair with Miklos Sandoz? Probably. Producers believed in some way that they were professional people like gynaecologists or lawyers, who needed to know intimate details of actresses' lives. She'd only seen Miklos once since, and that was for lunch in Paris, where she had told him about Richard, although not by name. He understood that the time you were all confined together in a studio or on a location was different. In truth, she had tired of him before the end of the filming, but the relationship was sustained by the knowledge that they would be returning to the real world. Now she discovered that there was no real world. What happened was that you were exiled from the familiar world: you became a character in a life which bore some resemblance to what had gone before. If she and Jeremy had had children, she felt sure that she could have returned to a more recognisable landscape. But everything had changed.

'I thought Miklos did a good job,' she said.

'Little too artsy-fartsy for a big movie.'

'Maybe.'

'There's that scene in the store where I don't think he did you any favours.'

It was one of her favourite scenes, where she is confronted by her ex-lover in a Seven Eleven, and Miklos captured perfectly the sinister quotidian, exaggerating the frozen neon effect, and making the whole scene more intense by a very limited depth of field, so that she and Linus seemed to be isolated amongst the extras.

'Perhaps you're right,' she said.

Her melon arrived couched on chunks of ice in a silver-plated holder made expressly for the job. Berkovsky's plate was brimming with uncompanionable items and it was escorted by a basket full of muffins which had been impregnated by segments of fruit.

'This is the fat-free, right?' he asked.

'Yessir.'

'So you have no objection to dropping Sandoz?'

'It's not my decision, obviously. I believe it's up to the director. I must put my trust in his judgement.'

'He wants Suchitsky.'

'That's fine by me, as long as no one says I vetoed Miklos.'

'No. There's no question of that. He's acting a little high and mighty, as though he's got the franchise after *Half in Love*.'

'He was nominated for the Oscar.'

'True. But Jim's worked with Suchitsky and trusts him.'

'Okay. I'm just an actress.'

'You're a lot more than that, honeybun.'

His upper lip was slightly moist as he ate. She was aware of the family at the next table studying her closely. Above her head the long-stemmed and expensive flowers arced outwards from a giant display. They gave off a strange scent, part decay, part tropical fruit.

In truth she was glad Miklos would not be working on the movie. Because she loved Richard so intensely, she could not bear to be reminded that she had slept with Miklos in strange hotel rooms for six weeks. She no longer wanted to remember the intimacy she had had with his body. She wasn't ashamed, but she had no doubt that if he were on the movie he would assume a certain intimacy again. And there were things he knew about her, which perhaps even Richard didn't know. Between men and women who are having sex, there are understandings and accommodations; these understandings contain an acknowledgement of weakness, because sex is an activity like no other, that dramatises the precariousness of our hold on the rational world.

Berkovsky was telling her about his summer house being built in the Hamptons. He had found an old house with a sea view and was having it extended around a concealed courtyard. He wasn't proposing to bring up his children in Los Angeles. That was a definite no-no. The family Berkovsky were moving to Manhattan. At the end of the day kids were the single most important thing. Know what I'm saying?

She thought how often the truth is hidden within clichés. Sex with Richard seemed to her to be related in some way to the continuation of human life. Richard had said to her that to have a child with her would be the most wonderful thing he could imagine. He said it as though he'd already imagined it fully. There was a straightforwardness about him, a kind of directness which at first she had assumed was a front. She was so used to people like Berkovsky who were always trying, with various degrees of subtlety, to paint themselves attractively: the summer house was designed by a fashionable architect; the children enrolled in an expensive upper East Side school; LA with its tawdry paper-thin glamour was repudiated; the dropping of Miklos was dressed up as something aesthetic. And then there were the high-minded egotists, like Jeremy, who took easy refuge in social awareness. Everything was an issue for Jeremy, and of course, miraculously, he was always on the right side. His politics, very left, were self-congratulatory. He always knew what was important. At any dinner party he could be relied upon to trump everyone with his support committees for exiled writers, and his knowledge of CIA-sponsored torture, or his intimacy with murderers on Death Row in Texas. He described in detail the effects of sodium thiopenthal, pancuronium bromide and potassium chloride, the drugs used in executions, and the penis and anal stoppers. He played these chords with a skill which his writing did not match. The first time she had introduced Richard over dinner, Jeremy had been keen to put him right when Richard said, mildly, that the Prime Minister placed his hopes in a growing middle class. Jeremy was ready to sneer. All politics was based on conflict, he said, particularly British politics. To him politics was the play of forces, the progressive against the reactionary. It was a tragedy, which she was compounding.

But she was helpless. Love made you helpless. How strange and wonderful it was, this sense that you did not own yourself, the feeling that your body, which had been yours, was now mortgaged to somebody else. She thought that maybe nuns — not that she had ever met a nun, knowingly — gave themselves to Jesus in this way: they were in love with the pale, broken body and they surrendered themselves to this love. She tried to talk to Berkovsky. He was looking for some sign that she liked him. She knew that she intimidated these associate producers, because they saw her as cultivated and cool. Miklos had been able to draw on his long experience of actresses, from the Danube to all parts west, to see what she was in reality. But to the movie-buff accountants, like Berkovsky, films seemed to be more real than life: they longed to share in its illusions, so that they wanted to believe more in her screen self than her real self. Real life was long and often boring; movies were fleeting and engrossing.

Berkovsky left eventually. He seemed reluctant to go. Perhaps he expected her to invite him to her suite. What he wanted was not sexual, but intimacy. He was a plump, moist CPA, waiting for the studio on budgets, and he wanted to make friends with the classy, English actress. So she made a small fuss of him, even wiping some crumbs from his dark bulging suit, when they parted, and kissing him in the European fashion, twice, as they left the circus-ring dining room.

She was in the bath when Jeremy called.
  'We've had an offer for the house. The full amount.'
  'Are you pleased?'

'It's not a question of being pleased. Freedom is the recognition of necessity.'

'Nobody gives a fuck about Hegel, Jeremy.'

He'd often used the phrase, but now she couldn't bear to hear it. He wanted to sell her house, because she had met Richard there. And the last time they had made love was there, in the marriage bed, although he didn't know that. She loathed Jeremy. He was ringing partly out of prurience and partly out of spite.

'Jeremy, why did you call Richard?'

'I just felt that with my experience of actresses, I should give him some tips. He's from a more sheltered world.'

'Jesus. What did you say?'

'Just general pointers.'

'You're being very grubby, even pathetic, Jeremy. Have a little self-respect if you can.'

There was a silence and she could hear him gulping for air.

'Jeremy, goodbye.'

'I just rang to say that the house is virtually sold.'

'Jeremy.'

But he rang off.

The bath had cooled as though time had been accelerated. Jeremy's choking sobs – there were just two, deep upheavals – lingered on, fugitives in this room, this marbled and chromed and polished bathroom. Her father was spartan in his tastes. The furniture issued to officers, the dull gardens thinly planted with azaleas and standard roses outside the boxy little houses, the standard ribbed sweaters he wore, the cheap cars, all this was fine by him. He regarded luxury with suspicion. God knows what he would have made of this bathroom. The soap and bath gel and shampoo and Q-tips and scents and mending kits were ranged along every surface. What was the meaning? Perhaps it was just a competition that every hotel was obliged to embark on, an arms race of toiletries, spiralling out of control. Jeremy's sobs, gushing from his deep wells of superiority, made her feel queasy. She could hear herself speaking in her father's brisk tones: get a grip man, have some backbone. Have some self-respect. Now Jeremy would be rooting around in his collection of truisms to find some comfort. But they would all be self-regarding. He was not capable of looking at himself honestly. If his plays failed, it was because the audience was seduced by forces unknown (to others) into a material world; that ideas were no longer valued in education; that the Conservatives had started a Gadarene rush to selfish individualism – and so on. That Joanna had left him was because she no longer cared for art; she had sold out to fame and glamour. Art was a difficult pursuit. Art was uncompromising. He, Jeremy, would never give up the heroic struggle. *L'homme n'est rien sans l'étude.* Even his television work contained important ideas.

But now she thought the art he believed he was pursuing was just out of his range. He liked the idea of art, but he was incapable of creating it. She remembered him explaining to Richard that first night what was wrong with the London theatre, and Richard listening politely, even eagerly. She remembered thinking, for Christ's sake Jeremy, stop banging on, you've only just met him. She thought then, that first day, that Richard was a decent, charming, but probably rather boring person, but he said to Jeremy after the lecture: 'You're very privileged. There's nothing I'd like more than to have some true creative talent.' And he said it with a sincerity which she found appealing. Now she wondered if she'd fallen in love with him already that evening. How do you know with love? It's not just a simple question of fixing on an object, but of feeling that between you there is something that has never existed before. Art and love are related. They exist in a realm which is beyond understanding, but very real, too real. She had read somewhere that they were intimations of immortality. She saw now that people looked for immortality in art as much as in religion, and also in love.

And women, particularly women, saw her as someone who offered at least an idea of what perfection could be. Women were said to be romantic: in truth she believed that they had a far greater yearning for perfection: they carried a model within them of love and contentment; it was a powerful sense of rightness. And that was why they were so seldom content, and why they took refuge in romance, which was this doomed quest for perfection. She, Joanna, was sometimes alarmed by what she had come to represent. After *Half in Love* she received a thousand letters from women praising her attempts to run a magazine and bring up children in New York after her publisher husband was unfortunately killed in a skiing accident in Aspen. In some ways it was laughable: out there in Ohio were school administrators, divorced bookkeepers, ex-cheerleaders, who found solace in her fictional character, Becky Browning, an English woman who had come to New York to get married and been widowed so soon with two young children. Underneath her cool exterior, warm geysers of humanity were found to be gushing. It was this that her fans found so moving.

All during the location filming she had been having sex with Miklos. In a heartbreaking scene she had told her lover that, for the sake of the children, she would not be able to see him again much as she loved him. That night, in the hotel room, Miklos said to her: 'I thought you were talking to me when the camera was running.' 'I was,' she said, although it was only half true. Miklos had a hairy, brown body. His hair was long and greying, and his beard was slightly darker. She never took him completely seriously: having sex with him was as easy and natural as eating or drinking and he made no deeper demands. Sex with actresses was part of his life, carried out on film sets for the last twenty years. He had been married twice, and spoke of both of his ex-wives with affection. He appeared to have freed himself entirely from any guilt or any need to justify himself. Everything was simple: do the work properly, take the rewards. She was one of the rewards. He'd fucked many actresses and make-up girls and production assistants. So what? That's the way things were ordered in his world. He liked scuba diving, old English cars, antique hand-wound watches, baggy expensive clothes. He didn't want to penetrate life's mysteries any more deeply.

How did this happen? How did one person become so obsessed with meaning – with ideas – and another so happy to enjoy the objects littered on the face of the blankness? In the space of eighteen months she had slept with three men. Richard saw ejaculation, the transfer of his vital body fluids to her, as something extraordinary, even mystical. It was truly a strange thing, to propel your essences into somebody else. For Miklos, this act was entirely recreational. He'd like to come all over the place, and she had gone along with his whims quite happily in that spirit.

Jeremy's sobs, which had escaped the phone lines, had faded

away now. She thought of them as fugitives, as intruders. She was shocked by how much she despised Jeremy. He had said that he had to give Richard a few pointers in that supercilious fashion of his. And typically generous, Richard had not told her any details, because he didn't want to humiliate Jeremy. Jeremy had once said to her, if you were not so beautiful you'd be a nobody. She felt a surge of loathing for him, and she hoped that this hatred would make the road ahead clear.

8

Landscapes are postcards, self-addressed.

In just a few days he had passed through a countryside of brown grass, the famous veld, arriving in an English spring, and now he was in this urban brickworks. You made each landscape for yourself, because landscape was nothing until you brought yourself to bear on it. His great-uncle described the veld around Mafeking in September, just before the rains. Rain was in the air, he said; he was thinking of the horses. The supply lines were extended and the right food was not coming through. Officers' horses had a better class of feed, as did officers. Officers were like their horses — better bred, less able to survive on basic rations. They needed to shine. They had servants and grooms and silverware and glossy boots and thoroughbreds. The men lived on bully beef and biscuits, and their horses had to get by on hay. His great-uncle wrote that this hay was called 'teff' in South Africa. It was extremely dusty. He recommended that it be given a good shaking before being fed to the horses. He reported one trooper being blinded temporarily by the venom of a spitting cobra hiding in the teff. The cobra had become understandably angry when it was shaken. They had bathed the man's eyes with milk, a Boer remedy.

Justin Cartwright

There was a grudging admiration for the Boers in his writing. The Boers were tough, resourceful, direct, God-fearing. Major Dick said nothing about the Boers' relationship with the black people around them. He appeared to see black people only in relation to horses: grooms, stable hands and occasional riders. Their hands were not good when they rode, they tugged savagely at the bit, and the bit could be made from anything from a bent nail to a piece of watch chain. Major Dick saw horses as a thread on which history was hung. Sometimes talking to lawyers – there were plenty of them in Government – Richard thought that lawyers too saw the law in this way, the spinal cord running through all human life. Richard had come to see the law as a secondary activity, a sort of waste product of the human condition. When he first met Jeremy, he had been impressed that Jeremy lived in the world of ideas, very different from the world of lawyers who were always qualifying and noting and circumscribing. Reading Major Dick's work, he saw that while horses were relatively straightforward, there was nothing straightforward about the people he dealt with in the Army. Veterinary surgeons were often ignored or treated with arrogance by cavalry officers, who were impatient with science. The horses died of starvation, colic, and the African Horse Sickness. Major Dick knew from the Boers that grazing horses in the early morning, when there was dew on the stubbly growth, caused the sickness, but when he advised feeding only on teff, he was ignored and the horses, shipped from India, Australia, Argentina and Ireland, died in their thousands. Baden-Powell listened. 'The Colonel is a great one for learning from the Boers. He admires them and their makeshift ingenuity. He talks sometimes of setting

108

up fast-moving, mounted, irregular units for reconnaissance and scouting purposes.'

Major Dick was more interesting in what he let slip than what he said. His ideas of history and warfare, and the nature of the local people, were full of assumptions which now seemed ridiculous. Perhaps we are all prisoners of our times and popular beliefs. Richard had seen that politicians are captives of the prevailing mood, and worse, that the prevailing mood is itself completely artificial, confected out of journalism and polls and sensationalism, which then become a political reality.

When Richard was stabbed, Talfryn saw only a political problem, a sort of cancer that had to be treated decisively. This other reality depended entirely on the prevailing mood, but – and here was the extraordinary thing – the prevailing mood depended entirely on what was perceived to be the reality. No wonder people like Talfryn had become so important: they were both creating and responding to the public mood. This mood was like a horse: you had to ride it, you had to control it, but you also had to understand the nature of the herd animal. It was a follower, but it could stampede in entirely the wrong direction. This was the nightmare scenario, that public opinion would run out of control.

Richard's thoughts were running out of control here in the brickworks of Clerkenwell, where he was waiting.

Last night Joanna rang. She had been riding in Central Park. She said she was doing it to bring her closer to him; it was the only thing she could do. His heart lurched. And then Talfryn rang to say that the police had new information about the boy sitting behind him. A friend of his, arrested by chance, had grassed him up in the hopes of lenient treatment. He had seen this boy follow Richard at Wembley. He had heard him say he was going to do him. The boy was carrying a knife with a thin, sharp blade. He wanted to get the posh cunt. It was these words that convinced the police that the second boy, now in custody, was telling the truth.

'We can't stop them, Richard, it's gone too far. They're going to arrest him in the morning.'

Richard fingered the scar on his neck. It still had a life of its own, and now it was pulsing gently.

'You'll have to give evidence. The Prime Minister agrees. Apart from anything else, we are trying to be tough on crime. You can't adopt some sort of unique philosophical position that applies to you only, Richard.'

'What do you mean?'

'You've got to tough it out. You'll have to give evidence, you can't be ambiguous.'

'Ambivalent.'

'Whatever. You can't piss about.'

'What will happen is that the defence will try to prove provocation: I'll be pictured as some sort of pompous idiot and everyone will have a good laugh. On top of that it will just remind everybody of Joanna.'

'Not if he pleads guilty. It'll be over in a minute.'

'You can fix that?'

'I couldn't, even if I wanted to. Luckily it's not going to be a problem.'

He said the police would drop attempted murder and

substitute a lesser charge, assault with a deadly weapon, if the suspect agreed.

'Talfryn, I don't want some deal done on my behalf, or on the Government's behalf.'

'No deal is being done. The Commissioner has already given his opinion that it would be impossible to prove attempted murder. Apparently he just wanted to cut you, but something went wrong.'

He attempted a little Cockney with the words: 'e jus wanned te cutcha'.

'Oh, Jesus.'

'Richard, why are you so damn reticent about this? Some yobbo stabbed you, he might have killed you, the police have him now. What's your problem? You didn't do anything wrong.'

'Talfryn.'

'Yes.'

'Don't tell me that the Prime Minister is right behind me or I won't sleep.'

'He is, but I won't tell you. Good night.'

He had lain staring at the orange-stained sky – the close, slovenly, matey sky – through the uncurtained square. Sleep was a strange thing. It was unpredictable. Sometimes sleep itself was the issue, as though there is nothing so important at that moment as to seize some sleep, to appropriate a length of sleep and wrap yourself in it. At other times sleep was simply a force which overtook you, a natural event. Last night he had woken in starts until early morning. Outside in Clerkenwell there was not much activity although he could hear the rumble of the meat trucks heading for Smithfield. In each one hung huge, powerful carcasses. When steers were killed and skinned like this they became human: the view into one of these trucks was like a glimpse of large commuters shoulder to shoulder, raw and headless, true, but not unpleasant. Not long ago there used to be a still life in most butchers' shops: a pheasant or a hare or a few mallards all cheerfully garrotted and hanging there. The public mood had changed: you hardly ever saw them now. Now only fish were attractive in their entirety. Fish corpses, gleaming and fresh, spoke of health and vitality, but meat meant heaviness and mortality. This was the diktat of the public will. And in this restless night, he knew that he didn't want to be painted as the victim. For all the press's hypocrisy and fake concern about unfair dismissals, sexual harassment, fatal and protracted illness, domestic violence, police brutality and so on, victims still made people feel uneasy. Victims had a contagion that could spread its effects, causing fine crazing and powdery mildew on the souls of happier people.

He wanted to be rid of all this; of looking over his shoulder, of the public mood, of Talfryn with his suspicions. He didn't care that much if he never saw the Prime Minister again. His old pal had transmogrified into something different. He was proof that reincarnation was possible. But Richard stilled himself with the thought that Joanna loved him. When she had told him that she was riding an old nag called Thunderhead around Central Park as a way of expressing her love for him, he thought that it was almost a miracle. In truth, despite his father's barely contained fears, quite a lot of women had loved him. He had sometimes been reticent because of his father's prurience. The old boy gave off a manly, bristling sexuality and he had probably adopted a less stentorian approach to sex as a result. Now, this masculine gas his father leaked, disguised as Trumpers' Extract of Jamaican Limes, was beginning to thin; soon there'd be nothing there to sustain him.

When his father left to find a taxi, Richard had walked with him into the Clerkenwell night. He hadn't wanted to leave him alone on these streets although, for all his new frailty, his spirits were high.

'I like it. Will you get me the names of the local agents? Loft living. It could be for me.'

But he was heading back to parts of town where carefully groomed and expensively suited old fellows like him could still talk loudly without fear of public derision. They were a dwindling band.

At least if the boy in the seat behind was the one who stabbed him, it put to rest any fears that there was a connection with Joanna, something which Talfryn had seen, as he put it, as a definite plus.

He wondered how his horse was getting on. The stable girl, Jenny, said she was exercising her every day. He wondered how long it would be before he could ride his horse in peace and live honourably. What did that mean? He wasn't sure. He didn't want Talfryn working out scenarios, and Jeremy threatening him with something, with some revelation, some opening of the veins. Jeremy, the thinker, was proving to have the same base passions as other, non-thinking, people. But Jeremy must know that once this dark blood was allowed to flow, there was no going back. It was a kind of murder of the self, a wilful self-destruction. Richard had seen it in fated marriages, where the women — more often than the men

— humiliated themselves and scared off their friends and lost their humanity by becoming obsessed with the injustice of the situation. At least there were no children involved. Because of the intense involvement of parents with their children, children had become the prize and the capital of failing marriages. Children were the only substance of marriage; the rest, as everyone knew, was insubstantial, a hangover from the middle ages and hunting and gathering, or peasant collaboration. And yet he wanted to marry Joanna. Talfryn had said he wanted to occupy some unique position that applied only to him. But that was not true, he wanted the opposite, he wanted like Aircraftsman Ross to lose himself. He had been singled out by his old friend, and look where the attention had got him. The point that Talfryn was making was that he expected him to be a team player, to sing off the same hymn sheet, to remain on message.

In the night, in the brick lanes of Clerkenwell, he saw that the message itself was nothing, just a mantra, just words disappearing into the woolly stained sky above him, to merge possibly with the last words of Bevan and Bevin, and Wilson and Macmillan, and Heath and Thatcher and Kinnock. Oh Jesus, it was all so ridiculous and maybe even dishonest. He wondered if the uttering of political purpose was of itself dishonest.

He and Joanna were lying so close that their skins were breathing and sighing together. She liked to be held tight, swaddled. They were fused as if they had been surprised by Vesuvius. Although she moved in her sleep, it was only to adjust her marsupial closeness to him. He had the feeling that she was drawing vital supplies from him in some unknown fashion; he was pleased to be the donor although one of his arms began to tingle. Reluctantly he unwound himself from her and she turned, still asleep, and curled herself into a cochlea and, without a pause, drew his hands around to her front and pressed them as if she had wounds that needed stopping. And so they lay until morning. He was exhausted, but exhilarated, while she seemed to be renewed and refreshed. She said: 'If I loved you any more, I would be dead.' He saw that you could die for love. Late in the morning a car came for her and she left for New York and he moved secretly to his brother's, here in this brickworks.

Major Dick wrote that the horses began to cough, then their breath would begin to rasp, and then they would be dead. He wrote: 'They came here in their docile way, submissive to the end, and we killed them by ignorance and neglect. In all my life I have never seen such a waste. On one transport ship,' he wrote, 'glanders had been wrongly diagnosed by a sergeant-of-horse, and two hundred and fifty horses were shot and thrown overboard. The carnage was caused by the contempt of the Army for proper veterinary science.' Richard read through all Major Dick's prescriptions for the avoidance of colic, laminitis and farcy. He specified the amount of hay and bran to be given, how the hay nets were to be hung, what the matting should be made of, and how to avoid diseases of the feet and hooves. He was a meticulous man, trying to do his duty, but disappointed Maybe he had become a nuisance, a man with an obsession.

Talfryn appeared downstairs. He rang the bell.

'Come on up,' said Richard.

When he arrived at the top he asked, 'What have you decided?'

'I will give evidence, but it won't be very different. Is he going to plead guilty?'

'We believe so. How's the manifesto? Any blinding flashes of inspiration?'

'I'm not sure I'm the person to be dreaming up a new moral order.'

'Morals and sex are not the same thing. You may be a sex machine, but that doesn't disqualify you from knowing what's what. Anyway, you dream it up and the Prime Minister will take all the credit. The best of both worlds. By the way, the boss thinks you should delay your rest and recuperation until we see how things pan out.'

'It could take months.'

'True.'

'I should resign. I should just resign quickly.'

'Can't be done. You're one of his oldest friends. You shared a room with him at that public school of yours. You've seen him in his Y-fronts. The storm would start: you know — "Old pals fall out", "Was he pushed or did he jump?" — Christ, I could go on all morning. The line is that we're looking forward to the return of this valued member of the team, when he's ready, but in the meanwhile, he — that's you Richard — is doing valuable work on fundamental issues which the Prime Minister believes he is uniquely qualified to tackle.'

'I'm writing a short account of my great-uncle.'

'The horse doctor?'

'That's the one.'

'I'm not sure horses are part of our manifesto, except in a peripheral way in relation to fox-hunting, but still. What we really need is to get all the skivers off the dole, without appearing to be harsh on the deserving. What do you think of the "Family Credit"?'

'I think it's bollocks.'

'Is that your considered opinion, after three weeks of meditation?'

'My problem is that I have ceased to believe, if I ever did, in social engineering. I just think there are deep currents, myths really, which govern societies.'

'Your plan for the manifesto is what exactly? Excerpts from *The Golden Bough*, *Unexplained Mysteries of Our Time*, the use of healing crystals in public, or aromatherapy in politics. Or what about "Our party will consult leading astrologer Russell Fucking Grant and play the fucking ouija board"? Brilliant, I like it.'

Talfryn was enjoying himself.

'That's the sort of thing.'

'Richard, what are we doing in politics? We only got in to take the piss out of the others, and now we're talking about Family Credit.'

'Just like New Deal, Back to Basics, In Place of Strife.'

'Why don't we just say, don't worry, we've got it sorted. You just keep on pissing your beer up against a wall and supporting Manchester United, leave the serious stuff to us.'

'That is more or less what we are saying.'

'Richard. You've given me an idea. How about "You never had it so good"?'

'Brilliant.'

'Got to go. It's all right for some.'

'You're breaking my heart.'

'Nice place,' said Talfryn, as Richard showed him to the door. 'Just needs some wallpaper and curtains and an Aga. And possibly, a carpet, some rooms, a ceiling, and some plaster. Nothing more. Oh, perhaps some furniture.'

Richard held him by the forearm as he opened the door.

'Talfryn, I love Joanna.'

'I know.'

'Are you sure you have taken it on board?'

'I think so.'

'Good.'

Richard felt his loss minutes after Talfryn had gone. It was true that they had been happy in preparing the way, when they were working on the campaign. The other side seemed preposterous, as though a job lot of bores and freaks and mediocrities were pretending to be the Government. And they had talked about how ready the electorate must be for some reasonably sane, intelligent people in Government, namely themselves.

This morning when he woke finally, the loft was being bombarded by cold, granulated rain. Now the rain was over but Clerkenwell was seeping. The skylight above him was awash so that for a moment he thought he must be under water. His brother had mournful music, Leonard Cohen, The Smiths, Bruce Springsteen. He played Leonard Cohen. Rain music: *Your famous blue raincoat is torn at the shoulder.*

He had told Talfryn that he loved Joanna, because he knew that Talfryn wanted to draw him back into the fraternity. But he had also told him because he wanted to make it clear that he had left the rational world. He knew that they relied on him to give substance to their endeavours: he was the thinker, the honest and likeable one who could talk to trade unions and head teachers and City people, who had an alarming – to himself – surfeit of charm. A charm which was accentuated, in the eyes of his colleagues, by his obvious lack of ambition. High office meant little to him. As a politician that made him unique. It was a characteristic he apparently shared with Major Dick, who was reluctant to accept promotion, fearing it would remove him from the company of horses. When he died of yellow fever in 1914, he had just been gazetted as Lieutenant General, much to his surprise, but still he liked to be known as Major Dick.

Giving me head on an unmade bed. What a felicitous phrase.

Talfryn did not understand something very simple: you could not alter a society like this one, hell bent on reaching consumer heaven. Once the unemployable and the uneducated were released from their mental shackles – a sea change which happened about thirty years ago, and which was given a boost by Mrs Thatcher – blind forces were at work. In reality, only war, death, deprivation and disaster changed societies. Fiddling around with the Family Credit, the school term, fox-hunting and public transport were small potatoes.

Talfryn was right, what they had been good at was deriding the Government. World class. It had been heady. They had talked late at night, they had laughed at John Major and his pals. They had amazed themselves with how simple it all was. How did this happen? Only he seemed to think it might have been a little too easy, but of course he kept this opinion to himself. Once he had lectured to undergraduates on elites and how they came to power, using the Kennedys as the example. He had mixed in some Frank Capra movies and political gossip, and even suggested that there is little difference between a democracy and a totalitarian society. It was simply a question of how elites were chosen. The ballot box could be seen not as an expression of the people's will, but as a tool for achieving power, which the elites could use. *Es schwindelt.* But his old friend had said to him at the time, there is no other way, we have to use the means that are available. And then when the leader died, there they were trembling and ready. He hadn't realised that the Prime Minister had been ready for years. Now Richard saw that to be a successful politician you needed to have credulity. The PM believed that the public needed some fresh thinking.

Richard had thought of O'Faolain: 'We are at the mercy of uncharted currents of the heart.'

The phone rang. A reporter from the *Mail* asked to speak to him. 'This is his brother speaking,' he lied, 'I have no idea where he is.'

'Come off it, Minister, it's you. Let's be grown up shall we?'

He would have to move. They must have trailed Talfryn.

'I just want a reaction to the PM's statement that you are going to give evidence at the trial of Carl Panky.'

The doorbell rang.

'Just come down for a quick snap, Guv, won't take a mo'. Piccie. Wife and kids. Mortgage to pay. Just give us a couple of minutes. You know the game. Please, sir, come on down.'

It had started again.

9

Miklos had been drinking in the Oak Room. Now he wanted to have sex with her. He thought that this would even the score. He stood with his back to the park, which was turbulent, and not yet ready to admit spring. The new leaves were taking a beating, a lesson in the dangers of presumption. The buildings around the park were witness to natural forces which couldn't be suppressed.

Miklos blamed her: 'You didn't want me because of your new man. You know I don't care about that.'

'It was nothing to do with me. I promise.'

'Did you fight for me?'

'Oh shit, Miklos, you know how it goes in this game. The director wants someone else, but he doesn't want to tell you himself, so they dress it up as something different. I had no choice.'

'You could have insisted. Thanks to me, you're big enough.'

'Thanks to you, I looked good. Yes. But there was some acting involved, in case you've forgotten.'

'And a lot more. I hope you haven't forgotten this.'

'I haven't forgotten that, or anything else. You're a star, Miklos, and it won't kill you to be bounced off one movie; you've probably got ten more lined up. But if I'm totally honest, I'm glad you're not going to be on this one, because I'm in love with Richard and I don't need or want any undercurrents or demands.'

Miklos's proud, ravaged, boyish face was subject to seasonal turbulence too.

'It's always the same, on the way up they fuck anybody, and then they become ladies.'

'Who are "they"?'

'Actresses.'

'Don't be cheap. We had a wonderful, uncomplicated relationship and now you're making nasty remarks because your professional pride is wounded.'

'Nasty. So English. To you English, "nasty" is just bad taste. We don't do that. It's not on, old boy, pip-pip.'

'Miklos, nobody says "pip-pip". Nobody ever has and nobody ever will. Don't try and do accents. Just keep looking at the spotmeter. Although, by the way, there's a rumour out there that you don't look at it enough.'

'Is that what Berkovsky said?'

'Berkovsky, no, I'm just kidding. Lighten up.'

He stood there for a moment, looking like a Magyar, wounded pride, blood up, centuries of hurt, aeons of pig-headedness. Then he moved forward and put his arms around her.

'No, Miklos,' she said.

'Lie down.'

'Miklos, no, don't, for God's sake.'

'You fucked me, now I fuck you,' he said.

He's been rehearsing this line, nursing it, she thought. He pushed her towards the sumptuous bed.

Half in Love

Oh Richard, Richard, Richard, Richard, Richard.

She understood what Miklos was doing as he loosened his trousers. In his world he was simply marking defiantly.

'Lie down,' he said. His face was congested. His breath was an awful mixture of tequila and something medical.

'I can't.'

'I want you to.'

'I can't. Miklos, you're making a fool of yourself.'

He slapped her face.

'You're a fucking bitch.'

As he reached for his trousers his legs looked thin and old. Mere twigs supporting the canopy above.

'It was fine and dandy, when you were unknown.'

His face was wild with hatred. She feared he might spit on her as he left the room. She lay very still, her face hot where he had struck her. Miklos was right, she had betrayed him; she could have insisted. She hurried into the bathroom. She looked at herself in the mirror. Her face was flushed. A stain, like a continent in an old atlas, was spreading down her face. Miklos had turned out to be no more than some kind of East European bully-boy whose sense of injustice was intimately linked to his maleness.

She turned on the torrential shower. As the expensive water sluiced over her, she longed for Richard. She remembered how close they had slept and how he had apologised for moving his arm which had gone dead holding her. She had slept a profound narcotic sleep, her thighs sticky and lightly crusted. She could never tell Richard what had happened, and this saddened her too: she wanted to have no secrets from him, but it seemed secrets were not so easily disentangled.

Actresses will fuck anybody on the way up, then they become more selective. Was this true? Was there even a grain of truth in what Miklos had said?

The water coursed around her, a thick insistent Niagara. At home, she and her mother, horribly alone after Goose Green, had never been able to have more than a six-inch-deep bath in their tiny new home. The Army seemed to take pleasure in its familiarity with death. Death was, after all, its staple product. The cruel formalities which accompany death had been in place for a long time: they were dusted off like skeletons in a biology laboratory after a holiday. There were interviews and forms to fill and bank statements to be produced. Death was a serious business.

Her fingers were beginning to pucker. She had been in the shower for too long. She poured the whole contents of one of those little shower essences over her head and shoulders. What actresses see is how things play. Like writers, who can see some redeeming feature in every domestic horror. Perhaps Jeremy was even now recycling his bitterness. She turned off the shower and smothered herself in towels. There were more towels in this bathroom than she and her mother had ever owned. Her shiny little body had been rubbed with something resembling a damp dishcloth as she jumped from the tepid, fatherless bath water into her mother's tense arms. Maybe she was the last child in England to feel the rigour of being English. All around them, the English were exploding like ripe figs into indulgence. This knowledge of another world had been imparted to her by the cold cruelty she and her mother had been offered, even as her father became a hero with a posthumous Victoria Cross, awarded for being shot by some snivelling, freezing teenager from the barrio. Oh Jesus, how the generals in their scarlet epaulettes and snug tailoring had enjoyed the solemn ceremony, the band thudding and screeching its morbidity. This was what it was all about, death.

'Greater love hath no man than this, that a man lay down his life for his friends.'

She felt so lonely. Outside, the park was being lashed into an intemperate frenzy. She tried to call Richard, but his special phone number made an unsettling noise, as though small suffering animals were nesting there.

She was famous. She couldn't walk down Central Park South without a minder. She couldn't stop at Macy's or eat at Union Square Café without being stared at. And yet life was still sending her little notes of admonition. Miklos and Jeremy both wanted to remind her that actresses were only out in the real world on parole. They should never forget that they were on lifelong trial. Actresses, too, were the creation of powerful men, men who masqueraded as directors and producers and financiers and cameramen. Actresses should suffer for the ignorant adulation they receive. You sacrifice your individuality by becoming an actress. The downfall and misery of actresses produces *schadenfreude*: this is the price you have to pay for flying too high or forgetting who helped you. They all believe it, and maybe it's true. She lay on the bed. I'm not going to spend a lifetime looking at my face and turning to the plastic surgeon on their account. When my tits begin to sag, I will not be looking for silicone implants. And yet, and yet. She knew the deal she had made and understood the way it worked. Miklos understood too: there was an element of whoredom in it, dressed up as something finer and more artistic, but she knew, she knew that there was a redemptive power in art. Her ability to make audiences weep, or to imagine themselves being represented and championed by her performance, or inspired by the words she uttered, was a magical thing. When she was performing, when she saw herself on film, she knew that she had that magic.

Richard had said, when you act I believe.

When Miklos left the room, his greying long hair was bunched and sticking out at angles, so that he looked ridiculous. She wondered what other little scenes from life's tragi-comedy had been played in this room. It stood to reason that the people who could afford to live here, above the whirling-dervish park, were alive to their own importance, their own destiny, their entitlement to sex, to happiness, to expensive food, to self-expression. Scott and Zelda, near the beginning of their descent into hell, had danced in the fountains one night. God knows what had gone on in here. Whatever it was, whatever folly, whatever passion, it was charged with the knowledge that there was an entry fee just for getting here. You weren't licensed to look down on the park and the hansom cabs and, over there, the Met without some cost to the human soul. She tried Richard's number again. The squeaking was still there. She rang her agent, but his wife Cynthia said he was at a meeting, something to do with work, she added as a rider. He would be back soon, should he call? In the background Joanna could hear the music of a television serial involving doctors in the

Lake District. She had once had a part in it, as a young district nurse.

'Is that the *Lake Practice* in the background, Cynth?' Joanna asked.

'Yes. God knows why I still watch. You were in it five or six years ago.'

'Yes I was. Don't tell anybody, for God's sake.'

'Any message for Stan?'

'Just ask him to ring. Tomorrow. I'm going out now.'

'It's only five or six o'clock with you, isn't it? Bye-bye, take care.'

Did Cynthia know her husband's feelings for Joanna? Probably. Her voice was so English, so comfortingly North-London-Jewish-English, the telly on, the kids tucked up, something fattening waiting in the oven for his return, a few cookies or perhaps the cheesecake the children didn't finish. *Take care. Take care.* She emphasised the first syllable, almost plucked it.

Joanna rang her mother.

'What's wrong?'

'Why should something be wrong? I just rang to say hello to my dear old ma, that's all.'

'It's quite late.'

'It's not late here. It's early here.'

'Are you all right?'

'I'm fine, Mum. We're in the nervous period, started but not really started.'

'I'm not sure what that means.'

'We haven't begun filming, and once that happens as Buñuel

or somebody said, the express leaves the station. We're in the station.'

'What's wrong, darling?'

Her mother was ready for bad news. The anticipation flooded back down the line all the way to The Plaza.

'Nothing's wrong. I just wanted to say hello. To tell you the truth, I couldn't speak to Richard, so I rang you instead.'

'He's going to give evidence. Did you know?'

'No.'

'It was on the television news. Some youth has been arrested and Richard is going to give evidence.'

'He wanted the whole thing to be over.'

'I don't blame him. But anyway, it seems pretty cut and dried. His friend split on him. Grassed. Grassed is the term, I'm told.'

Talking to her mother, Joanna quickly lost the comforting illusions, already in tatters, of her position, whatever that might be. To her mother, she was a girl without judgement, a girl who couldn't dry herself without help.

'Your husband rang.'

'What did he want?'

'He didn't seem to want anything. He asked where the grandfather clock came from. He's trying to separate all your possessions. He was quite charming.'

She could see Jeremy practising his cut-rate charm on her mother. She was so desperate for the company of men that she was easily amused.

'And did you and Jeremy have a heart-to-heart?'

'Not really. He just said he was so sorry, but your work had driven you apart.'

128

'Did he mention Richard?'

'Not really.'

'In other words, yes. What did he say?'

'He said Richard was a decent chap, a little out of his depth.'

Joanna began to shake now. She couldn't speak immediately.

'Joanna?'

'What a cunt. What a fucking cunt,' she gulped.

'Joanna! Joanna! Language! Are you all right?'

'No I'm not. Tell that manipulative little creep Jeremy, if he dares to ring up again brown-nosing, that he isn't fit to lick Richard's arse.'

'Joanna!'

'All right, lick his boots, if you prefer. Goodbye, I've got to go.'

'Is he a homosexual, was that the problem? A nancy-boy?'

'No, no. I'm sorry. Don't listen to me, I'm fine. Just a little fraught.'

'He is a bit of a nancy, as daddy . . .'

Joanna put the phone down. She hated to put the phone down on her mother, who would be unable to rest until they had spoken again and she delivered herself of some comfort and advice. It was strange, this mutual advice. For nearly twenty years her mother had lived a life a church mouse would have found stultifying, and yet she believed that as a mother she had the final word. She seemed to regard Joanna's career as a separate entity, which had only slender connections to life, like a dream or a work of fiction. Yet she was inordinately proud of Joanna. In the local butcher's shop, Fox and Nash, they had put up a sign saying: 'We are proud to meat the requirements of Joanna Jermyn's mother.' Her mother said she was embarrassed, but in fact she was thrilled. Two weeks after the Golden Globes the sign was down.

There had been one or two men, but they had not flourished in the deep shade cast by the deceased Colonel. Her mother was not giving off the right signals, said Jeremy. It was the sort of glib remark he made, but there was some truth in it. She was a beacon of selfless suffering. It was she who was laying down her life for her country, and the country didn't give a fuck. If anything, the country regarded sacrifice as faintly perverted, like chastity or religion.

The maid came in, scuttling in a furtive forest manner, as though she were afraid to snap a twig. A few days ago she asked shyly for an autograph. She brought water and flowers and more lotions and soaps. She had a chariot of these things outside. Joanna watched her as she removed the bedspread. Passions produce human evidence. Blood, sweat, tears — and semen. Chambermaids were trained in the code of silence. She smiled her small, wan, lemur-like smile as she was leaving.

'Do you have children?' Joanna asked.

'I got four.'

'At home?'

'Yes, in my house.'

'Where is that?'

'In Ecuador. Not far Quito.'

'Boys or girls?'

'One boy, three girls. Tomorrow I bring photo. Show you.'

She was edging to the door, where the perfumed cart was waiting.

'Jew so beautiful,' she said, and vanished, leaving her crumbled-tooth smile lingering for a moment.

I am so beautiful. I am so alone.

She longed to sleep tightly, swaddled by Richard. Her longing was so intense that she felt it as pain. She lay in the bed which the maid had neatly plumped up, and tried to sleep. She could not. The side of her face was hot. She tried to read the script. She loved scripts. This one still bore traces of the writer's intentions, the over-literary reference to states of minds and unspeakable thoughts, which the viewer would never be able to detect, however hard the actors tried. Film people often derided the writers whose improbable dialogue they had to bring to life and whose good intentions they had to make real. And yet, Joanna thought, the directors and producers live in a state of delusion too: they have a fantasy about popular success. It's the philosopher's stone. Gold could be manufactured by an alchemy which only they know. For a while, when they are successful at this, they become shamans and then they are the dangerous and overbearing ones.

The paper of the script was rough and artisanal. She liked that. She looked at the scene she was supposed to be reading tomorrow with Case Stipe. She had met him once. They were of not quite equal stature in the business yet, but they could go in together. Mismatches – heavyweights with bantamweights – were not permitted in big pictures.

She tried to read the words. It was a scene outside a courtroom, with her lawyer. She and the lawyer, who was representing her against her husband, a senator with presidential ambitions, were about to embark on an affair. In this scene, he is talking to her about the offer her husband has made, to delay the divorce until he has won the nomination. If she won't agree, he will take the gloves off. He says he has some evidence which can be used to show that she is an unfit mother. Her daughter, Kimberly Jane, will be taken from her. The lawyer wants to hear what this evidence could be. They are alone in court for the first application which is due at any minute.

The directions read: 'The clock is ticking.'

JED: Why didn't you tell me about this? [troubled]
HELENA: Some things are too personal.
JED: Did you withhold this information from me as a lawyer, or as a friend?

(There is something grammatically wrong, thought Joanna.)

HELENA: As a friend. I couldn't tell you.
JED: You've got to tell me now.
HELENA: I can't.
JED: Are you serious?
HELENA: What happened was just a small thing, an aberration, but it would sound terrible in court.
JED: Like?
HELENA: Jed, I can't tell you now. When the time is right I will. Maybe soon. So just accept the offer. Tell the judge we've settled.
JED: After all we've been through, Jesus fucking Christ Helena,

this bastard has put you through hell, and now we're going to nail him.

HELENA: Don't underestimate him. Accept.

[HELENA walks slowly but deliberately down the echoing halls of the courthouse. JED pauses for a moment, his mind still troubled by the revelation. Or perhaps by the fact that she has secrets from him. Then he rushes into court.]

Joanna put the script down. *I can't tell you. When the time is right, I will. Some things are too personal.*

The most banal songs and obvious sitcoms (like the *Lake Practice*) contained at least a portion of verisimilitude. But now she found herself thinking that these lines, still somewhat rough, were about her. Jeremy was not finished yet, that was for sure. And Richard had to go to court to give evidence. Why does success have a price? He is stabbed by some little Nazi and he has to pay a price because he is in Government. They fall in love and they become fugitives. No good explaining that when she first met him she was almost unknown and he was just a new boy in political life. Miklos reminded her that nothing came without a price.

Outside the park is growing dark. She sees the films that Miklos has lit: the haunting black-and-white of his early film, *The Stationmaster*; the beautiful African scenes of *Savannah Song*; the edgy, almost documentary feel of *Streets of Gotham*; and her own shimmering scenes in *Half in Love*.

He can create such beauty, so much illusion, just by moving the lights around. His electricians adore him. They are members of a hairy, beer-bellied, down-to-earth nation, and he is their prince.

Perhaps they have sent him to The Plaza with a message from the real people. Poor Miklos. As he left the room he looked like the stationmaster in his own film, an elderly man confused and out of place.

She sees now that nothing can easily be laid to rest, as in scripts. Her father is dead, but her mother is still paying. Yet she cleaves to the certainty that with Richard she'll be happy, no matter what.

10

His friend Igor's mother was Russian, an elderly Princess, who lived in Venice. It was a mystery: there was a certain type of woman who is always accompanied by men on life's journey. Igor's mother was apparently one, married for the third time to a banker, who had been brought in to clean up the Banco Spirito Sanctu, and was now retired to a palazzo in Venice. Igor was no longer invited there. After they'd left university, Igor became a psychotherapist. Now he was living in a village near Oxford, and from there he practised among the affluent deranged. As he entered his forties, Igor's face seemed to be settling into a very Slavonic look — long and pious. His hair, also long, had become rather thin on top, so that the more luxuriant side bits emphasised the north–south axis of his features.

When Talfryn said they had lined up a place for him, Richard had refused. He didn't want to go and live in some John le Carré flat in Pimlico or a safe house for visiting spooks. He said he would find his own place. When he considered all the possibilities, he rang Igor, who was in the middle of a group therapy session. As they spoke, he could hear a kind of female keening going on in the background. Igor was used to crises.

'Ricardo, come now, immediately. I'll get something for dinner.

Come down, dear Ricardo. Come as soon as you can, my dear
Ricardo. Don't worry, the loonies will be gone.'

Igor spoke with an extraordinary outdated swooping accent,
almost Edwardian, Richard imagined. The loonies were not
so mad, but they were mostly women who lacked men or
purpose and needed solutions to their problems from Igor.
These solutions were drawn without discrimination from many
cultures and religions and New Age sources. Some involved
physical objects like crystals, and others required only chanting,
in tongues. Igor didn't appear at all surprised that a Minister of
the Crown should want to come and hide with him. He had seen
many stranger things.

A car picked Richard up at his brother's flat. The driver was a
woman he recognised from the Cabinet Office. She greeted him
politely, as the photographers sprang to life. Once they were in
their car she said: 'We're going to change cars, sir, so this lot
don't follow you.'

They drove off quickly in the direction of the City. Just past
Finsbury Square a policeman waved them through a barrier and
then put out a sign, 'Stop For Police', in the road. Behind a
Marks & Spencer they changed to another car.

'Are we going to the Oxfordshire address, sir?' the driver
asked.

'Yes.'

She doubled back, past the policemen and a knot of waiting cars.

'Do you do this sort of thing often?' he asked her.

'Once in a while, sir. When I'm asked.'

She smiled at him briefly in the mirror. He wondered if

she was specially trained for this work. Perhaps she carried a weapon. There were people — how many he had no idea — who lived a parallel life to ministers, trained to drive high-speed cars, trained in first aid, equipped with special phone frequencies, and perhaps even trained to kill. He didn't know exactly who was in charge of them, but you could always recognise them by their air of elaborate and unnatural calm. They were members of a sect, who had been passed information denied to the rest of us. Their election could be read in their ordinary English faces. (Actually some of them were Scots or Welsh or Northern Irish.) They were made of less volatile material than their masters. They should have been sitting in Parliament instead of the strange and etiolated products of democracy and back-room dealing. They should have been there in a Parliament of yeomen (and yeowomen), representing the people, like Cromwell's New Model soldier-preachers, stolid, certain and saved.

He dialled Joanna's number in New York. He was connected immediately to her voice mail. 'I miss you, darling,' he managed to say, 'I miss you. I've had to change my number. I'll ring when I can.'

The driver glanced at him briefly in the mirror, perhaps reproaching him on behalf of women for not speaking more warmly.

The car was warm, and the driver — her name was Jacqui Braithwaite — was fully in charge. He felt the relief of someone admitted to hospital, into a world of comfortable procedures. He fell asleep as they passed the towers of St Pancras and the new library, abutting it like a grand cowshed. Once he had seen just the towers of St Pancras from up the hill, caught in evening sunshine, above the rail yards and low buildings, and for a few moments he had wondered what this Mad Ludwig folly was, and how he had never seen it before.

Now he dreamed. Or perhaps he didn't dream, so much as continue his thoughts, which had been interrupted.

The three horses were walking, fly-pocked, around the small cemetery. A steam engine was shunting coal trucks into a siding. An ocean of brown grass covered the plains, as far as he could see to the west, maybe all the way to the Kalahari. The horses began to trot determinedly, the bony shoulders and rumps moving in a rickety symmetry, so that he could see their skeletons as in an East European puppet show. Another three horses began to canter into the sea of grass, and his view of them changed suddenly, so that they became small in the landscape. Small but relentlessly loping along. Dreams meant nothing to him; but he felt curiously happy as the stunted, weathered little horses escaped into the Kalahari. Dreams of flight. Dreams of evanescence. Who knows what starts them off?

When he awoke, he was surprised to see, not the endless plain, empty of human life, but instead the small neat houses of north Oxford, malarial under sodium light, as the car skirted the city. None of the dreaming spires could be seen from here. Down that road there, just beside the motel, was a lovely old pub on the river. Although he couldn't remember the name of it, he could picture the terrace, the silently importunate swans, the dark and cold water sluicing beneath the stone bridge, and the battered, amiable, brown interiors. I'm forty-one and already my life is an almost infinite collection of memories and of places and people. He had a picture of these memories, frayed, stacked like library cards, many of them never to be seen again. What do we do with all this knowledge and experience? Does it die with us? Perhaps this accumulation is what's meant by the soul. Baudelaire said, 'J'ai plus de souvenirs que si j'avais mille ans.'

The car, piloted into the night by the sturdy, imperturbable helmswoman, passed through stone villages and one or two close woods, until they turned down towards the Windrush Valley where Igor lived in what had once been a Baptist minister's modest house. Next to it was an old chapel, where the therapy sessions took place, and Igor kept a chaotic office. In this office, under piles of papers and weights and boxes of homeopathic remedies and an exercise bike, was a bed. Richard had slept there before, barely visible in the clutter. Igor thought of this as his guest room. The stone walls next to the bed leaked and seeped minutely, as if replicating their previous existence in a quarry.

He directed the driver through the village, which was completely still, as though villagers had fled the Plague. The car's headlights swept the barns and cottages and stone walls. They pulled in to the gate of the chapel. Igor peered, his head wrapped in scarves like a Berber in a sandstorm. Only his eyes were visible. In a muffled voice he greeted them.

'Come in, come in. Are you staying, too?'

The driver said no, she had to go straight back, but she would like to visit the little girls' room.

'Don't be so silly,' said Igor. 'After you've had a pee I'll give you some soup and chicken.'

'All right, that would be nice.'

'Go in there, the lav is straight through on the right. Ricardo. Bloodied, but unbowed. Welcome.'

He hugged Richard to him; his body had thickened over the years, so that it felt massive and solid, more arboreal than mammalian.

'Bloodied and slightly bowed, I'm afraid. What's wrong with you?'

'Sinus. The air in this valley lacks positive ions. It's hell.'

He unwrapped himself. Then he began to move some papers onto the floor. He loved papers: documents, memos, reports of psychotherapists' conventions and manuscripts of important works which would transform international relations and eliminate self-inflicted diseases, lay in drifts.

'Sit yourself down. Soup and roast chicken and a lovely bottle of Beaujolais should cheer you up.'

Igor left for the kitchen with good intentions, but he was a man who worked best in a team.

'Ricardo, could you just help me get the chicken out of the oven, it seems to have become stuck.'

Soon Richard and Jacqui were preparing the soup and the roast chicken under Igor's genial supervision. Jacqui was very adept at carving, although the chicken seemed to have collapsed of its own volition. She also retrieved some string and a plastic bag of giblets from within the carcass. Igor seemed surprised; his long, episcopal face gazed at the giblets for a few seconds: 'What are these in that bag?'

'Giblets, sir,' said Jacqui.

'A nice word, giblets, don't you think Jacqui? Giblets.'

After Igor had said a Native American blessing on their humble fare, they sat down to eat with an assortment of knives and forks and spoons.

Igor was not interested in politics as such. Politics were a by-product of poor intrapersonal relationships. They had no independent validity, and they could easily be eliminated altogether, if world leaders would learn to meditate. Or perhaps levitate; Richard could not remember.

Igor was very interested in what Jacqui did.

'So you drive my old chum Ricardo about the place?'

'And some other ministers, sir.'

'Call me Igor. I used to be taken to prep school by a chauffeur. I miss it. You would probably prefer to drive genuine members of the nobility around, I suppose?'

'I'm not sure, Igor,' said Jacqui. Already Richard's spirits, somewhat oppressed by the hasty retreat from London, were lifting.

'We were at Oxford, Jacqui,' said Igor. 'The House. To be honest, although I'm sure you won't believe this, young Richard here is a bit cleverer − more clever − than I am. He got a starred first. He could have been a Fellow of All Souls if he wanted. They begged him to come in.'

The juices of the spiced lentil soup and the roast chicken were forming a delta on Igor's chin. Jacqui leant across and mopped his chin quickly, before the trickle could reach his Afghan singlet. Igor had a way of eliciting these deep, instinctual responses from women.

'Sorry,' she said, as though she had been impertinent.

'I'm a messy eater,' he said sadly. 'I was more or less abandoned as a child. I used to forage for nettles and wild creatures.'

'Oh shit,' said Richard. 'You lived in Eaton Terrace.'

'You can be awfully prosaic. This chicken's a little tough, Ricardo,' he added reproachfully.

When Jacqui had gone – regretfully, Richard thought – they sat in front of a log fire with a glass of red wine. He hadn't seen Igor for months, but there was no need to explain or to backfill.

'Ricardo, how's your beautiful Joanna? I am longing to meet her.'

'I've got to speak to her soon. I must ring her. She's in New York. She's going to be starting another film over there.'

'Are you going to marry her?'

'I hope so.'

'I would like to get married and have children. The trouble is, I see so many women with problems, it puts me off.'

He said this as if he had reached this judgement after long consideration.

'You know my honest opinion of women, I don't think they were supposed to fly so high off the ground. I don't tell them, of course. Anyway I usually see the ones who've come crashing back to earth,' he said.

The truth was, he also had sex with many of them. He explained this once: he provided them with some needed authority, and they rewarded him. He was the missing 'male archetype'. He liked quasi-academic words. Or else perhaps some of them were just sex-starved; he didn't always know. But Richard knew that, in the short term anyway, Igor offered women something else, a kind of exotic glamour, and his wonderfully other-worldly long face (Richard noticed that the flues of his nose had become dark) always demonstrated his interest in their spiritual wellbeing. He dealt less frequently with men, but they too were drawn into this delusion that their present fate at that exact moment, and their precise standing in the cosmos, were vital matters. After all, it was what most people believed, in some form or another. Nobody wants to believe they're just a piece of soot flying out of life's chimneys.

'Do you want children?' asked Igor.

'I do. Igor, I can only say that it hardly crossed my mind before I met Joanna.'

'That's wonderful. It's something I notice that begins to happen at about forty, you realise that there's a connection between bonking and children. It may be the only real sign of love.'

He reached in the clutter for a notebook, and then dug about for a pen.

'How's the book, Igor?'

'Two thousand pages, and growing.'

As Igor was writing, Richard's phone rang. The tone was different from the previous one, and he was puzzled for a moment. It was Joanna.

'I'm having a drink with Case Stipe. He's just gone to the loo. I had to tell you, I love you.'

'Why? Is he after your body?'

'He's waiting for me to be after his. I get the impression that's the way it's arranged.'

'Are you happy?'

'As happy as I can be without you. I'm riding again tomorrow. I'll be able to come back at the weekend.'

'Thank God. I've missed you. I've had to move in with my

friend Igor. The journalists found my brother's flat. I had to escape. I'm in the country near Oxford.'

'Where can we go this weekend?'

'I'll fix something, don't worry.'

'Oh, here comes Case. Everyone's looking at him. Can I ring you in an hour or so?'

'Of course.'

'Bye my love.'

'Bye darling.'

'That was her?' said Igor.

'Yes.'

'Hasn't she got a husband?'

'Yes, it's been in all the papers, alas.'

'And you were stabbed by some fascist, too. Let me see the scar.'

Igor put his fingers on the scar. His fingertips made it tingle. As Igor gazed at him, his face tilted, Richard could see that his nasal passages were becoming quite hairy, which accounted for their crepuscular look.

They had been young until the day before yesterday.

'Can you feel anything?' asked Igor.

'What am I supposed to feel?'

'Just a good feeling, Ricardo. A little warmth, perhaps, a glow.'

Strangely, Richard did feel a glow. It was the same feeling he had had out in the veld, watching those scrubby horses, his scar throbbing gently. Richard had never questioned Igor's strange collection of beliefs. They were unsystematic, but they had one consistent thread, which was the belief in the importance of spiritual growth. No good trying to suggest that you first had to believe in the spirit, itself an unprovable notion. Igor was like a religious fundamentalist: there could be no secular answers, because God had decreed it otherwise. There were many gods in Igor's eschatology. And yet their friendship easily bypassed these logical difficulties, which in a sense proved Igor's point: the unquantifiable and the personal are always more important than the theoretical and the impersonal.

Richard felt pleasantly drowsy. The few logs were incandescent, without flame, lying on the stone hearth.

'Was it painful?'

'Yes, for a moment. But I was shocked, there was a lot of blood. Later, for a few days it hurt.'

'Why did he attack you?'

'Who knows. I made a pompous remark. I shouldn't have.'

'He shouldn't have stabbed you, though, dear Ricardo.'

'Of course not, but it's like road rage. You probably don't know what that is out here in the sticks, but there's a type who is easily triggered. They can't help it. I was deliberately provocative. Some sort of dreadful prejudice about the way he looked. He was all flabby, goose-bumps and two earrings like curtain rings and screaming all the way through the first half. I told him to shut the fuck up. God knows why. About half the crowd were shouting, fuck the French, fuck the ref, fuck everybody. In hospital I wondered if I had the judgement or the human sympathy for politics.'

Igor had stopped stroking his scar. He had fallen asleep. Richard stood up. He removed the chicken carcass so neatly sliced, and the plates, to the kitchen. The kitchen was in a parlous state. He found a corner for the plates, near the sink, but at the back of a long and disorderly queue.

Outside the air was rich and damp. He walked through the silent village, breathing this vegetable air, so thick it was almost a minestrone. Down past the church — the real one, not Igor's apologetic little chapel — he paused for a moment by the lychgate, from where he could see the Windrush, dark and bustling. The place was drained of colour; it was so beautiful that he felt the intimation of tears. It was a pleasant feeling, this confirmation that you were susceptible to beauty, to pure emotion, to . . . to what? To the inchoate sense that there was a meaning in this landscape, perhaps because it contained so much mortality. The stones were not themselves beautiful, but the impulse to lay each one in just this way, the impulse to create permanence, was itself moving. Moving, especially, because the people who created it were all dead — maybe some in the Boer War — yet they had acted as if they believed in immortality. Igor, Slavonically asleep, believed in the immortality of the spirit. The futility, the utter blind futility of human belief, was its beauty. The doomed nature of all human strivings — politics included — was its nobility. Joanna, Joanna. Speaking in her way for the human spirit.

In a field, a horse started. He walked up to the wall and the horse ambled over, exhaling nervously, as though it were blowing froth off beer. He put his hand up to its nose. Its muzzle was whiskery and warm and the animal seemed glad of his company. He put his face close to its mouth. The skin was extraordinarily soft. It reminds me of her thighs. He walked on beneath an avenue of tall trees. There was a small crease at the top of Joanna's thighs, which he longed to touch again with his fingertips and the tip of his tongue. It was important work, as vital as anything else.

Ah, love, let us be true
To one another! for the world, which seems
To lie before us like a land of dreams,
So various, so beautiful, so new,
Hath really neither joy, nor love, nor lights
Nor certitude, nor peace, nor help for pain;
And we are here as on a darkling plain
Swept with confused alarms of struggle and flight,
Where ignorant armies clash by night.

Poetry and love were cousins. Neither belonged to the rational world. That was why he could remember these lines, unread since school. He followed a narrow lane round, behind a farmyard. He heard the diffident, ingratiating bark of sheep dogs.

We are here as on a darkling plain.

The water was certainly dark. This same water ran all the way to the pub outside of Oxford. The Trout. He remembered. The glimpses of inky water marked the turning point of his little nocturnal ramble. It was one in the morning. He was in the habit of thinking New York time: only eight o'clock there. Drinks with Case Stipe. Case Stipe, such an American name, having a drink with Joanna Jermyn, such an English name. Both phoney. On his walk back to Igor's, he contemplated the question of fame. Fame is a form of immortality too. It gave hope to millions that there was joy and love and light on the darkling plain. He saw that almost everything human is tied to mortality, every idea, every principle, every aspiration. Only love promises peace and certitude. But it is also true that love contains the possibility of misery and loneliness.

Igor was speaking to Joanna on Richard's phone. The fire was barely glowing.

'Ah Joanna.' (They were already close.) 'He's here, the boy genius is back from his wanderings. It's Joanna, Ricardo. Bye Joanna,' he said, handing over the phone. 'Me too, yes.'

'Igor sounds nice,' she said. 'We've had a good old chat while you were out.'

'I went for a walk. Igor was asleep on the sofa. How's Case?'

'He's fine. He may be bonkers. He's going to pull out of this picture, at least I think that's what he was saying. I only understood about one word in three.'

'Is that bad for you?'

'It would delay the picture. Who knows what that means?'

Then she began to cry. Just as some people's laughter is disturbingly youthful, her sobs were infantile. They were little choking packages of misery.

'What's the matter, darling?'

'I don't know. I miss you. It's all going wrong.'

'No it's not. Don't worry, it's nothing.'

She quietened soon. But Richard felt a deep unease. Igor began to rub a lotion into his head, as though this was a good moment to perform some domestic chores. The room was invaded by a sweet rich smell of almonds, like an Italian liqueur. Igor placed a lot of faith in the medicinal properties of plants, specially herbs and nuts. Richard said he would arrange to meet Joanna at the airport on Saturday and he said he would find a place for them

to spend a few days alone. She said she felt better, she was sorry
that she had cried, and that she would order something from
room service and go to bed early and dream of seeing him.

'I love you almost too much,' she said. 'I ache.'

'Good night darling.'

'Good night.'

'You look troubled, Ricardo.'

'I am troubled. What are you putting on your head?'

'It's a lotion that a friend, a healer, who's completely bald,
found in a small village in Montenegro. Everyone in the village
has hair like a hedgehog's.'

'Smells nice. How's your friend's hair coming on?'

'He says it's growing fast.'

'And he's developed a taste for insects. Igor, thanks for taking
me in. I'm going to bed now.'

'See you in the morning, dear Ricardo. The bed in the guest
room is made up.'

He left Igor rubbing his head idly with one hand, and making
notes with the other, and crossed the small courtyard which
separated the modest house from the chapel. The bed had been
cleared of its usual load, although he found a hidden box file as
he slid under the duvet, which was slightly damp. There were
no sounds. The village was enfolded in a medieval silence.

It's all going wrong, she said.

Confused alarms of struggle and flight.

The moment he saw her, not many months ago, turbulence
entered his life, turbulence of the heart, but also a strange
malevolence which he had, without realising it, apparently invited
in. Here he was, hiding with Igor, because these forces had entered

his life. Talfryn said, everything passes; in politics everything passes; it's a game. If it's just a game, why are we playing? Everything's a game, Richard, wakey-wakey.

In the morning he borrowed Igor's Japanese sports car. Igor's tastes were never predictable. The tomato red of the car was faded and rusted, and it was very small, but Igor was convinced that it was the last word in style. It reposed when not in use under an apple tree, and it had suffered from a biological invasion of insects and twigs and leaves and droppings, so that when Igor insisted on taking down the roof for his benefit, Richard thought he heard a microscopic panic and scurrying from within.

The first of Igor's patients (or were they clients?) arrived as Igor was trying to fasten down the hood. It had once all happened at the touch of a button, Igor said, but now they had to wrestle the top into a small coffin. The patient looked on; her eyes were small and she was round and dark, wearing a green quilted jacket. She looked dazed and her cheeks bore the needlepoint of country living. She was leading two fox terriers. The dogs, too, had small, fixed eyes.

'Won't be long,' said Igor.

'Are the terriers barking too?' asked Richard under his breath. They laughed.

Finally Richard set off through the village. He was wearing a woolly hat and an old overcoat forced on him by Igor. It was exhilarating driving up out of the valley, although the engine produced a disturbing smell of burning. Perhaps the insects and leaves were being incinerated.

The Commissioner of Oaths in Burford was to take his

statement. He had rich embroidery on his nose, like a very detailed map. As Richard read into a dictaphone, a courier was waiting outside on a motorcycle to take his statement up to London. The process of checking and authorising his statement involved a special stamp to emboss the document where he had signed, and a flourish of expensive fountain pens and blotting paper. The ceremony also required the arrival of a cup of tea served with a Wagon Wheel. The town seemed to line one wide main street; outside the leaded windows of the lawyer's office, where the market must once have been, a quiet but insistent bustle of elderly and respectable people paraded, the English passing by with their muted but exquisite antipathies.

'I, Richard Eames McAllister, do solemnly swear that the statement I have given is a true and complete account.'

There was no such thing as a true and complete account.

He had to stop the little car to answer Talfryn's call. He pulled in at a derelict garage, which stood high above the Windrush Valley. Down below, the fields were dark green and bright yellow, looking like flags at the Palio.

'What are you doing? It sounds as though you are in a gale?'

'I am driving back from the Commissioner of Oaths in a friend's open car. I am wearing a woolly hat. I look like a twat. Altogether very difficult to hear anything. Now I've pulled in, at great risk to my life. I hope you have something pleasant to say.'

'Richard, Richard. Don't be churlish. How are you?'

'I'm fine.'

'Did the statement go all right?'

'To plan.'

'As we discussed?'

'Yes. As we discussed.'

'Just to let you know that the defence is inclined to advise their client to plead guilty, and their client is prepared to accept.'

'I'm so glad.'

Richard saw Talfryn now as in one of those old war films with the planes and ships represented on a large board, and moved about with what looked like a croupier's rake. He was plotting Richard's course on the map, checking that nothing was going wrong. But Richard also knew that if Talfryn was doing this personally, it was because the Prime Minister wanted him to.

'The office wants you to ring your brother in Berlin. They were not able to give him your new number, of course. There were some other messages, none of them important, but you should check in with Michelle. The Prime Minister asked me to tell you that he loves you.'

'In those words?'

'More or less exactly. What are you doing for the rest of the week?'

'Joanna's coming over on Saturday.'

'Is that a good idea?'

'Keep out of it, Talfryn. It's going to be a flying visit and we'll hide away somewhere.'

'There's bound to be some hack on the plane or some sneak at the airline.'

'Probably. But she'll be gone before they find us.'

'It's your life. Speak later.'

'It doesn't seem to be my life any more.'

Talfryn had gone.

Igor came out of the house wearing a bandana over his nose. Evidently there was still something noxious in the air.

'Ricardo,' he said, 'isn't she a little beauty?'

His voice was suppressed to some extent, but his eyes were liquid and princely.

'Goes like the clappers.'

'High office hasn't spoiled you, dear Ricardo. Come in. That lovely lady, with the sinister little dogs, has left us a game pie for our lunch. She cooks everything she runs over in the Land Rover. Should we heat it do you think? Any ideas?'

'Road kill is best served cold, I always think.'

'Good. Can you give me a hand? We need a few clean plates.'

'I just have to ring my brother in Berlin and my office.'

'Young Tim? How is he? Is he still a journalist?'

'He's the Berlin correspondent of the *Telegraph*.'

'Everyone's become important, except me. I just plod along.'

He sat down, still wearing the bandana pulled low, as Richard dialled. His brother told him that his father had had a stroke, and gave him the doctor's number. His voice had a metallic note to it, like a train announcement.

'I can't leave just at the moment,' Tim said. 'There's a row over the Bundestag which I have to cover. Will you ring me when you've seen him? I'm sorry I rang the office, but none of the numbers was working.'

'I had to leave the flat. If it's bad, can you come later today?'

'I'll do my best.'

Richard told Igor that he would have to go. He rang the doctor who said his father was in Chelsea and Westminster Hospital, after a stroke. It would be a good idea to visit him, although he was barely conscious.

'Can you drive me to a station, Igor?'

'Of course. Is it bad?'

'It sounds very bad. You can't always tell with doctors.'

'Ricardo, I would like to say a small blessing for your father. Do you mind?'

'I don't mind.'

So they knelt on the stone flags holding hands, and Igor spoke a language that he said was Tibetan, interceding on behalf of Richard's father, through the good offices of the Dalai Lama.

11

She rode in the park early. Her old horse, Thunderhead, moved in deliberate fashion, like a hearse; still she felt a growing loyalty. The horse had no feelings for her, but that wasn't the point. Animals, particularly enslaved animals like horses, were dependent on human goodwill because they were entirely defenceless. Also she wanted to make some small recompense for the mindless cruelty of the Guatemalan, who jabbed his horse in the mouth constantly.

When she got back to the hotel she found some flowers and a note from Miklos:

Please forgive me. I behaved in a bad way. I can only beg you to understand that I am taking Halcyon because of a medical problem, and my mind is disturbed. You said that we had an uncomplicated relationship. But I am getting old and suddenly I saw that in this business there is no relationship at all. It is all bullshit. It seemed unbearable to me. I believe that the drinks and the Halcyon produced this bad result. I beg your forgiveness. You are an angel. M.

The elaborate old-world handwriting was shaky, as though the card had been written in a taxi. The flowers were of a stateliness and waxiness that oppressed her. When the chambermaid came, she gave them to her to take, to keep or to throw in the chute. The chambermaid showed her the pictures of her children, like her, furtive creatures, faces dark and small, and the eyes red, thanks to the cheap flash. Joanna admired them, but in truth this inspection was unbearable to her today.

'Thees Juan, tree. Hees naughtee. Thees Maria, she sev-ven. She call guapa. Thees ees Pedro. He ees big man, nearly.'

She gave the maid a hundred dollars for her children. She kissed Joanna's hand.

'Jew real lady. Have you got peecture?'

'No.'

'I bring camera tomorrow.'

'I go England.'

'England, jew go?'

'Yes.'

'Sorry, jew beautiful lady.'

Joanna watched the noxious flowers borne away, nodding to the trolley's movement. She thought of her father: how he hated excuses, shortcuts and self-pity. Now everybody was in the game of self-exculpation. The worse your crime, the more credit you got for coming clean and revealing the deep forces which had held you in thrall, to your detriment as a human being.

Am I a real lady? Because of her father's strange death and because of her extraordinary looks, she had always been singled out. She sometimes thought her looks gave her an unwarranted distinction. Jeremy had wanted to acquire some of this distinction for himself by marrying her, and she had been flattered because he seemed to possess substance in the shifting world she was entering, a world of auditions and interviews and promises. The promises were always entailed. As she had seen herself on television and in small movies, she knew that her salvation lay in her ability to appeal to something very deep in the audience. Old actors called it timing, but in fact it was a kind of confidence. The creative act is an appalling thing, the offering of one's self to scrutiny. For actors the self is not just its expression, but the housing, the body in which it lives. The actual skin, bones, hair, cells and so on are on offer. She and Jeremy used to go to a market in Tuscany when the fungi and truffle season produced those strange orange organ shapes, and the true amateurs of fungi picked over them in a sensual fervour, the nostrils and the fingers and the eyes all trying to pre-figure the taste. Some kept them in inner pockets and produced them stealthily like dirty pictures. She knew she was the object of sexual curiosity and longing. Jeremy said that a million men around the world had masturbated thinking of her naked in *Half in Love*.

All she wanted now was to spend this weekend with Richard, perhaps in a small hotel in the Cotswolds, walking along deep paths, drinking in a country pub. She longed for the stillness, and she longed to lie in bed with Richard, safe. It was pathetic, really, how simple her needs were. When you got down to it these longings are primitive and basic and probably universal. Nothing fancy or intellectual or exotic.

Despite the ambling deliberateness of her ride, her legs were stiff at the junctions. She lay in the bath, which reeked with juniper essence. She regretted displacing the honest horse perfume with this tangy gin smell, therapeutic though it claimed to be.

When she finally got out of the bath, she found that there were two messages for her: there was a FedEx package for her with the concierge, and would she call Mr Case Stipe. She sent for the package; it contained the deed of sale of the house which she had to sign immediately and return to the lawyers in London. She put it aside. Case wanted her to come out to dinner. Like a dolphin, he preferred to sortie in company: a few friends were going to a new restaurant and on to a club.

'I can't, Case,' she said, 'I would love to, but I am going back to England tomorrow and I would be wrecked.'

'You would be, yes. That's the whole idea, sweetpea.'

'Can't do it, Case. Sorry.'

'No problema. See you on the set.'

'Are you in, finally?'

'Yes. I am.'

'Good news.'

'You need the break of working with someone like me. That's what swung it.'

He had probably just been flexing his muscles, as stars do. Jeremy was sending her the deeds out of spite: Look, the house is sold, this is the consequence of your unfaithfulness. For a few fucks you've lost something you love dearly. Jeremy had two very different views about sex. In his writing it was a progressive, liberating thing, a flouting of the reactionaries who were sure that the lower orders were too self-indulgent in everything, but in practice he regarded sex as a sort of Darwinian leftover from another time, like having an appendix. Sometimes when they made love, he'd seem to be concerned that this form of activity was designed to detain him. 'Did the earth move?' he would say with what he assumed was ironic charm, before dashing into the bathroom to clean himself up. His buttocks, she had long ago realised, were not made for the job: they were rather long and void and lacking propulsion. It was very hard to love someone who was so insensitive to sex, she thought, just as it would be difficult to love someone who played snooker or read thrillers, or grew alpines.

She and Richard made love with a desperation, as though they were going to fall off the end of the earth. When Richard had said they were trying to inhabit one flesh, she had understood. They made love as if they were trying to fuse their bodies. There were barriers between people and by means of sex they could be removed. It was not clear what they would become when they were one flesh. Whatever it was, she desired it. That was love, holding out the promise of the unknown.

When she and Richard had talked in the hospital about the scandal and the consequences, and they'd both understood what lay ahead, he said: 'We have to see it through. I feel that with all my being.'

'The drugs they're giving you must be lovely,' she said, but her heart – her jumpy, tricksy, actressy heart – had lurched exultantly beneath her famous front.

She opened the window onto the park. She looked onto that savage stretch of green. America, for all its fabulous materialism, was still recognisably built in a wilderness. In England, every stone and tree and blade of grass was the result of a deliberate act. She looked at Miklos's note again. Despite everything, she felt regret that he had cast such a deep gloom over their past. What had seemed innocent was now sullied.

Am I the only one, or do all women suffer this vindictiveness? She knew that there was something about her, her apparent air of aloofness, which provoked some men who wanted her to be more obviously compliant. In the early days, Stan had tried to suggest that she was giving off a sort of hauteur which prevented her from getting parts in ads and sitcoms. Her mother was living in genteel penury, and she was on the dole, so she wanted desperately to be in ads, but she was too grand. She did get a day as an ambassador's wife in a chocolate-mint commercial, because ambassadors' consorts were obviously snooty, with impressive décolleté to match. She had a boyfriend then, called Hugo, who was a painter. He had just left college. To live with him was to live in a world spattered by paint. His hands and clothes, the walls of his room, his boots and his hair were all blotched and stained with all the colours that Daler-Rowney could provide. On the chocolate-mint set they had worn dinner jackets and ballgowns, and flashy paste jewellery; back at the tiny room that night, she returned to a world of brightly coloured rags. She took Hugo to see a revival of *Peter Pan* at the National Theatre with some of her money, and Hugo said that it was fucking bollocks, but she loved it. The Indians were painted like Hugo, as brightly coloured as quilts. Like an Indian himself, Hugo had vanished silently one day.

Today the park was so calm, spring heat accumulating for the stupefying summer ahead. Old Thunderhead had stumbled along, his large, ugly head drooping ever lower. She had left him to his hairy sleepwalk despite the Guatemalan's irritation. She didn't care.

She read the script. The director wanted her notes apparently. Not on structure, of course, but comments on her lines. He believed in actors making a contribution. Happily she read a scene and tried out the lines, and carefully wrote her improvements in the margin. The scene she found most difficult was the one where she had to tell Jed, her lawyer/lover, that her husband had persuaded her to have a threesome. He was threatening to use this if she sued him. Jed was deeply upset, he lost all lawyerly impartiality,

'Jesus, I can't accept this. I just can't accept the way this thing is going. I love you, but this is way too deep for me.'

'Jed, please. It was a long time ago. It's not for you to forgive me or pardon me. It's history. At the time it was nothing, no big deal.'

'No big deal. You, Miss Fucking Perfect, married to Senator Irving P. Thalstrop, had an orgy. Jesus, what would a big deal be in your mind? Would it involve donkeys and a dwarf?'

'Jed, I'll get another lawyer tomorrow. I'm so sorry.'

'Maybe that would be better.'

Jed stands and walks to the door. He stops in the doorway for a moment, shakes his head sadly, and exits.

In life, she thought, people seldom stop in doorways, or stand with their backs pressed to doors. In real life, things drag on interminably and inconclusively.

The phone rang. As in a movie, she started and stared at the phone for a moment. It was Richard. She began to cry.

'Why are you crying, darling?'

'I'm so happy. I don't know. I'm lonely. I was reading this drivel, the script as it's known, and then I heard your voice. I love you.'

'Joanna, I'm at the Chelsea and Westminster Hospital. My father is very ill.'

'I'm so sorry. I'll come.'

'Darling, there's nothing I want more than to see you, but it would become a circus. I just want him to go in peace without turning his last few days into a freak show. Do you understand?'

'Of course.'

She understood that actresses are part of the freak show.

'Put it off for just a few days. He's had a stroke. They think he's dying. I love you, I adore you,' he was saying.

'I love you, Richard,' she said. 'Of course I understand, of course we don't want to turn it into a circus. I'm so sorry. I'll be thinking of you.'

'I know you understand. Will you be all right?'

'Yes, some friends have asked me to dinner. I wasn't going to accept, but I can't bear to be alone.'

'Look after yourself, sweetheart.'

'I'll be fine. I'll join the other gypsies.'

12

And he thought, as he took a taxi down the Kings Road, that his father was dying in the way he had lived, without proper notice. He was an impromptu sort of person; he'd never planned a holiday or made an early booking for the theatre, but he could be relied upon to turn up at the right places. His mother had found it infuriating. She said once: 'You just follow your nose around like a truffle hound.' He was pleased at the comparison.

Now death (if he was really dying) had caught him unready. He had been reading a book at around midnight when he had his stroke. Richard could imagine the terror that he would have felt, immobilised in the chair all night. The doctor had said that it was essential to avoid the lack of oxygen and the bleeding in the brain if there was to be a recovery, so it seemed his father was dying slowly in the flat in Tite Street until nine in the morning when the cleaner came, using her own keys.

His flat was a short walk to the river. He claimed to be able to tell the state of the tide by smell.

There were six photographers and two television cameramen waiting for Richard. When he had told Joanna to delay a few days before coming back, he had felt her shock, like the fierce and sudden gusting of a passing train, all the way from New

York. But he had to spare her this. And he had to avoid distraction.

'How are you feeling, Minister?'

'What's the news, Richard?'

'Is Miss Jermyn coming back?'

'Where's Joanna?'

'Look this way please, Minister.'

He stopped for a moment:

'My father is gravely ill after a stroke and I'm going to see him. It's a private matter and something which, I am sure you understand, I wish to deal with in a private manner. Thank you.'

As he walked into the hospital through the bright commercially tricked-out lobby, he caught the first gust of death. It was a fragrance, like deodorant in a lavatory, designed to hide the biological truth. The administrator came with him to the intensive care unit. A consultant was waiting. The administrator effected the hand-over. His territory extended only to the door.

'It's a very severe haemorrhage I'm afraid, Minister, said the consultant.'

He was Scottish: he said 'Minister' with a strong rolling of consonants.

'He won't be able to talk to you. He's largely paralysed, and relying on life support at the moment. Please sit with him and talk if you want to. Patients in this state do hear sometimes. It's certainly not going to do any harm. Shall we go in?'

'Can he ever recover?'

'We need to observe.'

'For how long?'

'Another forty-eight hours or so. There are measurements that we make, and various tests.'

'And then?'

'And then we make an assessment.'

The consultant led the way. Richard thought he was like a maître d'hôtel showing him to a table. His thin, raptor face, which would have looked fine tucked under a bonnet equipped with an eagle feather, was proud to demonstrate the full repertoire. The *batterie d'cuisine* was on display too: his father was wired up and plugged in to two machines which whirred and winked. Where the line went into his arm there was a huge bruise, and caked blood at his nose where other lines entered. Richard spoke to his father, 'It's Richard, Dad. I'm here beside you.'

His father's face was shockingly contorted as though he had been stilled in the middle of a cry of grief. His face was the colour of brick, in fact exactly the colour of the bricks laid outside Joanna's house to enclose the sentimental parterre. There was a bandage around the top of his head; the stain of the mustard-yellow disinfectant used in operations extended down onto his forehead. Specks of blue and specks of green flecked the deep angry russet of his face, so that it appeared to have a touch of verdigris. Oh, good God, the lack of oxygen or whatever it was, had turned the skin of his face into a rich leather, like those rococo desk coverings lawyers favour. Those fucking, awful lawyers' desks.

'At the moment we're helping him to breathe, giving him fluids and monitoring all his vital signs. The scan shows a severe brain haemorrhage. There's blood in the brain although I think we were able to get most of it out.'

'I'll sit with him for a while.'

'Call me if you need me. Just press this button here. The nurses will be in and out.'

Richard sat beside the bed. Beyond were other stricken people in aquaria, attended by nurses moving soundlessly. His father was wearing a simple shift which left his soft chest and thin arms exposed: the biceps were puckered and long grey hairs grew on his forearms. All this had been hidden by the expensive clothes. The new, tortured, cordite-burned face could never be hidden. Some miserable little blood vessel bursts, and some little piece of biological sweeping blocks an artery, and this is what happens to the temple in which the mind, and possibly the soul, is lodged: it becomes a brick that has been fired too long. An apple that has rotted prior to inviting in the worms. A cartoon version of itself, an object lesson in mortality.

He sat there puzzled. He wanted to hold his father's hand, but the hand nearest him was resting on a board and was attached to its own medical planking. His spirits sank very low. He tried to talk to his father.

He said, 'Dad, it's Richard. You're in good hands now. Just rest. I'm here and Tim is coming soon.'

But his father lay still, humiliated in this pauper's shroud of jaunty medical green with his old nipples and corrugated arms. He wanted his father to die now, to go away in peace, not to wake up a slobbering idiot. In the background, some nurses gathered around one of the hi-tech beds and consulted the machinery. He wondered what the percentages were. How many got out alive? A nurse came into the room with some flowers.

'Orright?'

'Fine, thanks.'

She placed the flowers on a wheeled tray. There was a lot of this sinister furniture in hospitals. Richard read the note, 'Darling Hughie. Please get better soon. With all my love, Adele.' He had no idea who Adele could be. But his father's musky attraction had spread far. There were always notes and appointments missed and anguished enquiries. He wondered if this battered and powerless body had been called upon to make love to these women. In this part of town there were plenty of lively older women who formed themselves into roving bands; the vain, self-congratulatory men they preyed on were a group who had never quite gone extinct, perhaps a splinter from the eighteenth century, when men-about-town were a sort of libidinous sect, with their own liturgy and high priests. To love them or to live amongst them, the women had to accept the theology.

Richard could feel his own self dragging. It was a gravitational pull, as if he too were heading for the hole in the ground. He remembered the sound but not the words of Igor's Tibetan prayer. It was the sound of falsetto, but nasal, birds. Perhaps that was because of Igor's sinus problems, which he said were caused by the vapours rising from the outwardly innocuous Windrush River.

'I'm here, Dad,' Richard whispered and put his hand on his father's wrist lightly so as not to press on the tubes. A nurse brought him a cup of tea. A nice cup of tea.

'How do you take it?'

'As it comes.'

'Sugar?'

'No thanks.'

The consultant came back. He was now in a suit with a rich silk tie blossoming under his Adam's apple. His neck was so thin, however, that the shirt and the tie were floating a few centimetres away, unsupported. He looked at the screens of his favourite piece of equipment.

'It's a wee bit early to say, but there's no change at the moment.'

'Good or bad?'

'We'd like to see an improvement, of course. There could be another stroke. We're hydrating him and monitoring the oxygen levels all the time.' He pointed at the tube where Richard's hand had recently rested; Richard saw a small chip in one of his father's fingers.

'Your brother rang, Minister, and he will be here in ten or twenty minutes.'

'Tell me, if he lives what sort of life will it be?'

'The brain is a strange organ. You can never be sure, but this is a severe infarction. He will be largely paralysed at first, but the degree of recovery is uncertain. We will need to do some more tests tomorrow. But for the moment I've done all that can be done.'

'Will he be able to talk?'

'I doubt it. I'm off now, but of course, the hospital has my pager. I won't be far away. Very good to have met you, Minister.'

'Thank you for everything you've done for him.'

'It's all in a day's work,' he said with a touch of Protestant severity. John Knox lives.

More flowers arrived and the nurses appeared and went again. His father lay absolutely still.

'Tim's coming soon, Dad, and I'm here.'

What could he see or hear through the deadened tissue? Was it that he was getting a restricted flow like a blocked drain, or was it that he was getting the lot but couldn't make sense of it? Or, worse, that he couldn't respond. Richard looked at the fired pottery face closely to see if there were minute signs of life.

'Dad, it's Richard. And Timmy's coming soon.'

Joanna had said, 'I can't bear to be alone.'

Being alone, absolutely alone, was death. That's why singing choirs of angels and utterly relaxed relatives would be waiting on the other side. As a boy he'd wondered why these relatives, who had gone before, didn't send reassuring messages back if it was all so great. Perhaps it was not all it was cracked up to be: the sun always shining, the flowers blooming, the sea the right temperature. Even when he was a boy, he had realised that the afterlife was more metaphorical than real. To this day he was not exactly sure what the religious were expecting. Were they expecting superior accommodation, or a greater peace of mind for their credulity? Politicians now acted as if there were perfectability, both of human nature and material circumstances. They were linked too. Education was the new religion of the Prime Minister. He clearly didn't mean just being able to add and read a timetable or operate a computer: he saw a whole spiritual world out there, accessible only to the educated. Sometimes Richard wondered if the people who elected them had been expecting ethical guidance and moral chivvying as part of the deal.

As he watched with deep gloom his father's face, he saw that politics too was the triumph over death by promising fulfilment here and now. His tentative slogan for the next election, 'You can feel the difference. And there's more to come', was on a shortlist of three. The Prime Minister preferred it, Talfryn said.

He held his father's wrist again. It was warm. He put his head down next to his father, his forehead on the mattress. Richard tried to resist, but he could not, even as sleep swarmed over him.

When he woke his father was dead, and Tim was standing beside him. The wrist he had been holding was cool.

'He's gone, Rich,' said Tim.

Richard took his hand away and looked at his watch, befuddled. 'He's dead?'

'Yes. You've been asleep for ten minutes.'

'Did you speak to him?' Richard asked.

'No, he was already dead. I'm not sure how long. The alarm went but the nurses didn't want to disturb you. They thought you were praying.'

'I was so tired. Thank God you're here. He looks so bad.'

'Poor old bastard. Did he speak?'

'No. He was completely out.'

The nurses removed the lines from their father's wrist and nose, and unclipped the monitor from his finger. They wanted to tidy up. It might be dispiriting for other patients to see that medical science could fail. Already what was left on earth was of no value. Mummification is probably intended to prevent this rush. His mind was working erratically.

'Come,' said Tim, 'let's go and get a drink.'

Tim was wearing a German jacket, with green flaps over the pockets. His brown hair was thinning and he was becoming plump. Although he was six years younger than Richard, he suddenly looked almost middle aged.

'How's Berlin?'

'Berlin is a building site. I never knew before I went there that it's not an old town. Not at all. There was no compelling historical reason to move the capital there. Anyway, no one asked me. I'm just a hack. Where shall we go for a drink?'

'Somewhere quiet. There are, or were, journalists outside.'

He and Tim stood by the green moulded-plastic front doors, and Richard said, 'Sadly, my father has died as a result of a cerebral haemorrhage. He never regained consciousness. We are deeply shocked and distressed, he was only sixty-seven. There's nothing more to say.'

'Will you be speaking to Miss Jermyn?'

'Did you hear me? I said there was nothing more to say.'

The hospital had ordered a taxi; they went round to the Chelsea Arts Club and sat in battered chairs in the billiard room, looking out at the garden which hadn't heard the news of death. It was lovely in the evening sun, overgrown and English. Nationality was so apparent in gardens, and cemeteries.

They could hardly believe he'd gone. This is common among the bereaved. He hadn't been much of a father, not by the prevailing standards of keen attendance and solicitude anyway, but he had been generous, uncritical, and always interesting.

'You know what was wrong with him as a father?' asked Tim.

'Tell me.'

'He put his own life, his own pleasures, above his children's.'

'We're his children.'

'That's what I mean. He liked us and he was proud of us, but at the end of the day we were monuments to him in his mind.'

It was true. When their mother died twenty years ago, his thoughts very quickly turned to how he could make himself comfortable and at ease in the world. This easement took place in the person of Fiona Plesch, who was a cook providing finger food for art galleries and publishers of art books. She had herself studied fine art. On his rare visits, Richard observed that she had spruced up the house in Fulham, putting in large pictures and colourful rugs. She exposed interesting floorboards and had them stained a Scandinavian blue. Richard didn't complain, but he was aware that his mother was being expunged. At her insistence, his father wore baggy Armani suits which looked like dinner jackets, with lapels big enough that they might have belonged to a pirate. Soon, however, he returned to his native raiment: stripes, expensive shoes, silk ties. In his circles these clothes could be read like the Rosetta stone.

Fiona Plesch was a big, strong woman. Three years ago she had left him for a man in a City bank who sponsored art. It turned out that for four years she had been having an affair with him, under the cover of serving small sticky sausage and chicken tikka on sticks. When she left, he was forced to sell the house and move to the flat in Tite Street because he had invested in her company which was supposed to organise parties.

In the garden outside, he saw two well-known writers wearing linen suits. They were laughing, hopping nervously from one leg to the other. He had seen Jeremy here once; even then he had been in love with Joanna, and he had wondered if Jeremy could detect it. Tim was a member of the club.

'Do you have time to write the novel?'

'No. I've given up. Every journalist I know is writing a novel. Are you okay?'

'I feel better,' said Richard. 'I more or less passed out in the hospital.'

'I'm not surprised. I don't know how you handle it, and now this.'

'When are you going back?'

'I'll have to go tomorrow, and come back for the funeral.'

As the afternoon had crept away behind the surrounding houses, the writers came in. They were drunk, but still laughing. Their laughter was loud, almost hysterical. Despite the heaviness of his soul, Richard smiled. He envied them their mirth. He and Tim discussed the funeral and notices and lawyers and so on.

'Do you think there's any money left?' asked Tim.

'I doubt it. The flat's a twenty-year lease, so that may be worth a little. I think Fiona cleaned him out. How's your German lady?'

'She's very German.'

'Do you love her?'

'I don't think so. Do you love Joanna?'

'I'm so deeply in love that I am sometimes afraid. Everything has changed. I don't see anything in the same way.'

His little brother who he knew almost better than himself, sat in the clapped-out chair, his red wine oiling the glass. His boyish haircut showing an underlay of skin. His eyes, which could never rest too long on any one place, were dulled but still restless. On the inside of his right leg, invisible now of course, there was a scar which was the result of a horrible fall from his bike when he was trying to keep up with Richard. His nose was slightly crooked too from a brief infatuation with boxing. Richard remembered every phase of his life, from the first yeasty babyness to the truculent teenager who smoked dope in breaks in St James's Park. And here he was with the German patches on his jacket, the Berlin correspondent of a great newspaper.

Richard had the feeling that his father's death would pull down the last, unavoidable sibling walls. He hoped so.

'Have you told Joanna?'

'Yes.'

'You always had better-looking women than me, but this is overdoing it.'

'Do you think she's beautiful?'

'I was sitting in a Berlin schauspielfuckinghaus watching *Half in Love*, which in German is called *Liebesglut*, a sort of love fervour, I think, and I was thinking my brother, my perfect brother is shagging this beautiful creature. It almost spoilt it for me. I was thinking of writing her a note about you and that blonde Annie in Cornwall in a sleeping bag, when you thought I was asleep.'

'I don't love her just because she's beautiful. Anyway you'll be pleased to hear that she is not so beautiful in the morning.'

This was a lie: Richard loved to see her in the morning, as tightly rolled as an armadillo, her face childish in sleep.

'Great tits.'

'Fucking hell, Timmy, not now.'

'Fabulous tits.'

'Fuck off.'

They were both becoming drunk. The two writers were playing snooker. They handled the cues with relish, stroking them and chalking them and pointing them at the pockets.

'Are you going to marry her?'

'I want to.'

'What about the right-on husband? The playwright? Jeremy Wolhuter, OBE?'

'Jeremy is not taking it well.'

'Are you surprised?'

'Not really.'

'And your incident at Wembley? Aren't you in danger of looking a little flakey?'

'Timmy, I didn't stab myself you know. If you read the papers you would think that I did it for publicity.'

'You have become famous.'

'Thanks.'

'Do you still have the PM's trust?'

'Apparently. So I'm told.'

'So you're told. That's worrying.'

'Don't be a prick, Timmy. I don't want to josh with you. Not today.'

'I'm sorry. We'll have to change. It's difficult to break the habits of a lifetime. Let's have another bottle. In memory of Dad.'

Richard felt mortally tired now. His father's departure had

drained him. The line into his father's arm had been attached to him at the other end.

'The consultant said he would have been a vegetable even if he'd lived,' said Richard. 'Do you remember that story about Mrs Thatcher that he loved? Mrs Thatcher takes the whole Cabinet to a restaurant. The waiter says, "What will you have, Madam?", and she says, "I'll have the roast beef." "And the vegetables, Madam?" "They'll also have the roast beef." He loved that.'

They laughed to remember their father laughing. Sometimes he would hear something so funny and tears came to his eyes. Once at Christmas his drink had reappeared through his nose as he laughed.

They were drunk now. Tired as he was, Richard felt relief. I'm drunk, drunk.

'We're alone,' said Tim, 'we're orphans.'

It sounded almost heroic.

The horses are coming back from Matjesfontein. Many have lost their riders, and the last of the team of six horses which was pulling one of the field guns are still yoked together, although the lead horse has a terrible gash on the side of its face. Richard could see that it had lost an eye. The horses come back at an exhausted walk, beaten.

He wakes.

'Jacqueline?'

'Minister.'

'Where are we?'

'We're near Oxford, sir. Near where you said the pub was.'

And he sees north Oxford again. At first he is confused, drunk, as though he has woken up on the wrong day. That way to The Trout. All those memories.

'I'm sorry. My father died. We got drunk.'

'I don't blame you, sir. When my Nan died last year there was a right old knees up round our place.'

This conversation sounded as if it were written for Baden-Powell and chums, for one of their costume parties. *We're going to have a right old knees up and no mistake, me old cock sparrer. Just you watch. Oh me goodness, lads, put a sock in it, 'ere comes the CO.*

His head was throbbing. He and Tim had played snooker against the writers, the orphans versus the scribblers. They had drunk more wine and finally he had made his way to the low cottagey front door to meet Jacqueline. He couldn't remember how she had been summoned, but Talfryn was no doubt involved.

'I'm so sorry about your father, Minister,' she had said. 'You relax in the back now.'

But he tried to call Joanna, he wanted to talk to her urgently about marriage. He fumbled with the phone and eventually got through to The Plaza.

'I'm sorry, there's no reply from that suite. Who's calling?'

'I'm not just a caller, I'm her fiancé.'

He felt foolish as he said the word. Jacqui glanced at him in the mirror.

'Sir, she went out about an hour ago. Would you like her voice mail?'

'No, just leave a message to say I called. I'll call in the morning. Nine o'clock. Your time. That's about two my time. Richard is my name.'

'Thank you, sir. Good evening.'
'I'm falling apart, Jacqui.'
'You have a nice sleep, Minister. God knows, you deserve it.'

And he had slept, but his sleep was disturbed by the tread of wounded horses, the hooves striking the rocks which resonated like anvils.

13

They had entered the restaurant, which served Cuban-Chinese food, in a cavalcade.

This is the moment, Joanna thought, when stardom is put to the test. Case's big men swept past the big men in the foyer, which was marble with an interesting rustic texture. To be detained for even a second would be intolerable. The other customers cowered against the walls. Amazingly, these customers were not resentful but blessed by this epiphany.

Soon Case and his friends were hidden away in a private room on a mezzanine, which still gave a view of the restaurant below. The waiters were dressed in tight, short jackets that his father used to call 'bum-freezers'. Mess-kit. He had often gone to the mess in his bum-freezer. There he and the other officers, all dressed in these garish jackets, would drink toasts and play boyish games. There was one game of touch rugby which the junior officers played once a year with a tightly rolled and sewn skin of a goat, procured during the Afghan campaign of 1872. The goatskin was brought into the mess on a tray after dinner by a junior chef. Her father said it still smelled of goat after a hundred and twenty years.

When she and her mother went out to the Falklands, the band

which played the laments and the Last Post had a goat mascot, with pale, unimpressed eyes and a creamy white snout. The goat was wearing a little brocaded blanket.

Almost the whole party was doing cocaine. (Nobody said 'snorting'.) Case was at the far end of the table, taking prodigious amounts. She pretended to take a little; even a half-hearted inhalation made her head suddenly become independent, as though it were going off somewhere on its own. She felt a great swooping sensation. She wanted to tell Case that she had mostly been living quietly in the English countryside. He made a space for her, dislodging two tall young girls, who didn't seem to mind. The big new idea of the restaurant was that you shared everything, said Case, offering her some paw-paw stuffed with crab. He was wearing dark glasses and grinning.

'Jesus,' he said. 'I hate acting, but I love to party. This is my true vocation.'

The cocaine was making him burn so bright. It wasn't just the drugs; he had a kind of madness, a recklessness that was hard to resist. He didn't want to be an old actor, he said, an old fuck getting a lifetime award.

Now it was four o'clock in the afternoon. She was still wearing the clothes she had been out in. A policeman was taking a statement from her at a house in East 57th Street where she had spent the night. No, she hadn't been present at a club called Viper East. She had only seen the girl briefly at the restaurant, but didn't know her name. She wasn't aware that anybody had been taking drugs in China de Cuba, or at any time later, but of course she only knew Mr Case Stipe, who was co-starring in a movie with her. He had invited her to dinner. She had no idea what to expect.

'And you stayed the night here, lady?'

'Yes. In the spare room.'

'Hey, your business is your business. I'm just trying to establish why the young girl died. So you weren't at the club and you never seen her before?'

'No.'

'Okay, that's about it. Listen, if I take a formal statement, the press will get hold of it. I believe you, so I'm going to wrap it up. I loved your last movie, by the way.'

'Thank you.'

'Do yourself a favour, stay away from those people. Get out of town.'

'To be honest, I hardly know them. Actually I don't know them at all. I was just on my own and Mr Stipe asked me to dinner. Where I come from dinner doesn't automatically mean a drugs binge and people overdosing.'

'Be lucky. You're a hell of an actress. Pip pip. There will always be an England.'

But he had seen too much to be fooled. He was letting her go with a little warning. He heaved himself up, a genial messenger from the real world. And now she thought of Richard and his stabbing and the shame he had felt. It was already ten at night in England. The house was empty. Case had gone long ago. He had houses everywhere. She had slept with him, but that was hardly the right phrase. For him, sex was just an episode, quite a brief one, in the night's drama. He had left her here at about four in the morning and gone on to the club, and it was there that the girl, Sky Waldeck, a model, had overdosed. Case came back some time and told her he was off to his place in St John — she had no idea where on the planet that was — and that there'd been an accident at the club. She had gone back to sleep, hardly aware of what he said, until a maid woke her to tell her that a policeman wanted to speak to her.

In the taxi back to The Plaza, she began to shake. If this sordid fatal night ever became public knowledge, Richard would hate her, perhaps more intensely than Jeremy had. At least with Jeremy there had been very little pretence of love. Yet she loved Richard so fervently, the thought of his distress caused her breathing to become difficult. I'm going to choke on my own shame. I'm going to die in this ratcatcher's taxi. Her lungs seemed to have seized. She had to force them to work, to inhale deeply and slowly, using voluntary muscles. Then she hoped that the fact that she had not gone to the club might be enough: she just fell asleep at Case Stipe's house, in the spare room, while he and his gang went out clubbing. Nothing more. She would have to speak to Case.

But the immensity of the betrayal, the utter stupidity and pointless indulgence, crushed her. The chambermaid at The Plaza would be surprised and pleased to see her again. She had said, 'Jew is beautiful lady.' She had no idea of the true state of affairs. But then we are all strangers, not only to others but to ourselves.

On the streets strangers were moving in the way they do in New York, as if they had urgent business a few blocks away. Only the tourists milled about uncertainly in their tennis clothes. The taxi stopped near F. A. O. Schwarz, and she saw a girl clinging desperately to a tall, thin boy. He was patting her shoulders to

console her or calm her. She looked up at him, distraught. He
tried to walk away, but she clung to him. He stopped. Joanna
guessed that he was embarrassed, but the girl didn't care who
saw her misery.

The concierge was a kindly Italian, whose dark eyebrows
formed a continuous arch over his nose and eyes. He greeted
her warmly.

'Welcome back, we were a little concerned for you. There are
messages for you, Miss Jermyn.'

'Fine, Aldo, thank you.'

'Are you okay, Miss?'

'I'm fine.'

He handed her some envelopes. She saw there were other
messages on her voice mail. A refugee, she fled through the
palms and gilt to the lifts. Once in her suite, she decided
to order a sandwich and take a bath. Her breathing began to
settle down. She wanted to speak to Richard, but she must calm
herself and see what the messages contained. By the time she had
bathed, her food was there, a club sandwich and a mineral water.
The phone was semaphoring reproachfully: *you have messages*. She
sat by the Empire desk and ate her sandwich slowly. Then she
opened the first message. It was a fax from her agent, from Stan.
'Sylvia said you rang. She said you sounded lonely. I tried to
call you but you were out on the town. Give me a call later
today if you need to talk. I have six enquiries for you, including
a Shakespeare which might be a good one to consider. Six weeks
minimum. It's the Almeida. No dosh of course, but loads of
credibility. Love Stan.'

Sylvia, the Jewish mother, has homed right in. It's the first obligation of any Jewish mother, to detect unhappiness and then strum it. Dear Stan. Maybe she should call Stan and tell him everything. He would be shocked but he would know how to handle it. The second message was from Richard: 'I tried to ring you a few times, but you have obviously been very busy. My father died while I was at the hospital. I'm going back to Igor's until the funeral, which is on Wednesday at Chelsea Old Church. Can you come then? All my love, Richard.'

She began to shake again. The person I love most in the world needed me and I was out snorting – doing – cocaine. Then I had sex with somebody just because I was lonely. She hadn't really wanted to, but it seemed prudish to refuse. No woman ever refused Case Stipe. Richard had called again. After his father died he and his brother had got drunk. He was so sorry he hadn't rung earlier, but he was very fraught: 'As you can imagine. Please ring when you get this.'

Later he said: 'Sorry to call again so soon. But I long to speak to you. It's afternoon here already, and I just wanted to tell you that I love you, and to see if you can come back. There's a hotel here I can book. If you can come with me to the funeral, I hope the press will leave us more or less alone. I so wanted to talk to you last night about getting married. Sorry, I'm rambling, bye.' His voice sounded strained and raw.

There were other messages from her mother and from Jeremy, asking her to call, but she couldn't do it. She lay down. In New York, I laid myself down; she thought of Richard on his horse, riding through the bracken to her house, which Jeremy had sold. This time the horse did not stop at the gate.

Half in Love

It is early in the morning that I saw him coming,
Going along the road on the back of a horse.

It was the poem 'Donal Oge'. She had won a prize reciting it at school. The whole school was in tears when she said the last lines:

You have taken the east from me; you have taken the west
from me,
You have taken what is before me and what is behind
me;
You have taken the moon, you have taken the sun
from me,
And my fear is great that you have taken God from
me!

When she read the poem at assembly she had been thinking of her father, and the girls knew it. Now she was thinking of Richard: the moment when he had reappeared on his horse after vanishing in a small valley. She wanted to live that moment again, but of course only in films could you re-run those scenes. (Some of her fans re-ran scenes of her obsessively. She was on the internet, half naked. She was drowning in semen out there.)

It is early in the morning that I saw him coming,
Going along the road on the back of a horse.

And now the horse and rider, instead of bobbing up, the rider's head first, the horse's brown and black ears next – horses' ears are sensitive flags – and Richard's smile, the bliss of seeing her, and the horse entering into the spirit of things by leaping over a stream, the knowledge that he loved her; instead, this time the horse was turning away, down to the dark wood:

> He did not come to me; he made nothing of me;
> And it is on my way home that I cried my fill.

She whispered the words.

> It is late last night the dog was speaking of you;
> The snipe was speaking of you in her deep marsh.

She took some pills and lay in the dark. She had told the operator she wouldn't take calls, but they rang to ask if they could put Case through.

'Hi,' he said. 'You wanna come down to St John?'

'Case. Please, don't, I'm in a terrible state. A policeman came to see me and asked me about drugs and that girl. What's going on?'

'Don't worry about that. It was a case of when, not if, for her. I spoke to my people, it's all right. It's you I want to talk about. Come and hang out here for a few days.'

'Case, what happened last night was a big mistake. I'm deeply, helplessly in love with somebody else. I was stoned. I shouldn't have done it. For God's sake don't tell anybody. Do you promise?'

'Done what? Tell what? Listen, call me if you change your mind. You can be here in three or four hours.'

He insisted on leaving a number. In the background she could hear music, the sounds of human conviviality. Apparently wherever Case went, these noises followed him.

'It won't happen, Case.'

'You can never say never, sweetpea.'

But speaking to Case had cheered her up. He was of more elemental stuff than she was. He had people. His people had sorted things out.

She rang Richard, heaving with foreboding. It was one o'clock in the morning there.

'Darling,' she said, 'I'm so, so sorry about your father. And I'm sorry I wasn't here when you rang.'

'I was worried that something had happened to you.'

'No, I just stayed over at Case's house. Don't ask, it's more of a hotel than a house as far as I could see. No, he went on to a club, I think. Richard, I had a terrible dream, I dreamed that you rode right past me on your horse. I feel so awful. God, I love you. What did you want to say about marriage? Please tell me.'

He told her that he wanted to marry her, of course, and he wanted her permission to say so.

'Yes please, but can you wait until we see each other?'

'Why?'

'There are things you should know before you jump in.'

'Like?'

'I can't tell you now, but I will.'

'Now I'm worried.'

'Don't be worried. I love you. I adore you. I've missed you so much. When I dreamed about you riding by, my heart broke. What are you doing?'

'Now? Igor's outside at the moment, sitting on the lawn in an Afghan coat he bought in San Francisco twenty years ago. I've been catching up on some papers.'

'Did you see your father before he died?'

'I was there in the hospital. I fell asleep, holding his hand. When I woke up, he was dead. Timmy found me like that. After a few drinks he said he wasn't sure how many of us were dead. Some horrible little columnist said we were both pissed in the Chelsea Arts Club and making jokes. It was true, unfortunately. I've got to get out of this business.'

'You're the blue-eyed boy.'

'If I ever was, that's over. I'm officially accident-prone.' But he laughed, as though he found the inner workings of politics amusing; as though he were only just discovering that Peter Pan was suspended on wires when he did his back-flips high above the stalls.

'If you get out, what will you do?'

'It's probably difficult, after politics. I can't go back to being an academic, or to the Foundation. God knows. We'll see. After the election.'

'That's not much of a basis for a marriage proposal: no job, no prospects.'

'True. I don't know why, but I like the uncertainty. I might take some time off.'

'I'll be working.'

'I'm counting on it.'

He didn't mean it. She knew that he wanted to make things right. He wanted to hunker down. The Prime Minister's friendship, the safe seat, the quick promotion and the mad random stabbing — all this had made him deeply uneasy. He felt that he had attracted attention by acting out of character. Politics was a trade for self-publicists and egotists. Every issue he'd ever dealt with as a Minister had to be presented as if the only purpose of his work was to influence the media. The Prime Minister had told him that it was something he couldn't run away from, like it or not, politics was about winning and keeping popular support for your policies. That had been the party's mistake in the past, to believe that policies were enough: 'The strange thing is that the public don't really want to know the detail of our policies, they only want to believe that we have some. And they judge whether they are good or not by how we present them.'

They are actors too, she thought, when Richard told her what the Prime Minister had said.

'I have a job offer in the theatre after this. Equity minimum,' she said. 'Six-week run.'

'That should do us.'

But he knew she was making nearly six hundred thousand dollars for this film. Case was getting six million, but he had made twelve pictures. She was also getting points, which Stan said were a fantasy. He was trying to sound worldly.

As they talked she felt the unease draining out of her.

'Oh here's Igor. He's finished observing the solstice, or something. Actually he believes that it's good for your hair to go out in the moonlight,' he said, almost whispering. 'Deep forces, yin and yang, moon and sun. I think I've got that right.'

'Ricardo, Ricardo old boy,' she heard Igor say, 'are you talking to the lovely Joanna?'

'Yes.'

'Kiss her dimpled bottom for me.'

'I wish. Good night, darling.'

'If only you could kiss my bottom,' she said. 'How does he know it's dimpled?'

'He's got strange powers, haven't you Igor?'

'Very strange. Would you like some Japanese tea?'

'Yes, please.'

'Hello, hello,' she said, 'I'm still here.'

'Sorry. We always have Japanese tea in the middle of the night,' said Richard. 'We're an odd couple. I'd better go. I love you.'

'I love you, you are my east and west, my moon and sun. And I'm so sorry about your father.'

She was sorry. She was so sorry.

She went to stand by the window, and from the park she heard the snipe speaking of him, above the anxious traffic of Central Park South and the more tranquil river of light on Fifth Avenue. In the morning she would go to him, she would do anything for him.

> I would milk the cow; I would bring help to you;
> And if you were hard pressed, I would strike a
>   blow for you.

The girls had cried. Some of the teachers were in tears too; in that appalling loss she had felt consolation, in her ability to touch others. Jeremy had told her that all actors are emotionally needy, in his experience. What he meant was all actors are inadequate and dependent. Including her. Especially her. But the need she felt now was to love Richard, to give him the inexpressible. Love was to want immortality, or perhaps fragments of immortality, as if such a thing were possible. It wasn't immortality for yourself, it was immortality for these feelings, this state of longing, which of course is caused by chemicals, that make you think of anything but the physical world.

It was ridiculous too. It drove a wedge between your feelings and your intellect. Jeremy had never been able to accept this. He tried to categorise every situation, even sex. He had to apply his irony to sex. At least with Case there had been no irony. She thought maybe in her own mind she could play down what had happened to her in the last few days. Maybe she could find a different, minor category for these things, as Case did. But it was hopeless. She knew it was hopeless. She would have to lie.

By lying, she would be making a breach. This betrayal was just the sort of human rubble that was used to make films, including *Half in Love*, which had made her famous.

From way up there, past Harlem, a glow, a gaseous glow, was rising up against the clouds. Maybe it was Yankee Stadium or a huge fire. She didn't mind. She felt that the threads which bound her together, the sinews of life, were tightly stretched.

She called the concierge and asked him to book her to London tomorrow.

How did it happen, that you had to tell lies to the person you loved? She thought that she must have lost something when her father died; some small but essential human constituent had gone with him.

14

It was such a pleasure to lie in the small damp room and hear outside the cows and the church bells. It was morning service, he guessed, because it was already ten. The church bells played a fierce tune, which blew across the green to him. The urgent notes resonated in his bones and made the scar, the long apostrophe on his neck, tingle. He didn't hear a harsh call to prayer, but an anthem from a lost world. The cows interjected their low, milky notes into the pastorale. Now he could hear the organ, but only in waves. Igor always went to church. There are many paths.

As he lay there, Richard hoped that his father had experienced no agony, physical or existential. He could still feel his father's thin wrist, cooling fast, as he woke. Last night, after Joanna called, Igor had told him about souls and essences. Igor said that souls were immortal — of course — and that they were composed of essences. It was nonsense, but just as plausible as the less eclectic religions' explanations. But Igor's other-worldliness calmed him. And the church bells, followed by the patchy organ, diligently underscored by the cows, soothed him and eased his loss. Religion was a conspiracy to pretend that there was purpose in death. Life and death are seamlessly interwoven. Small things, small memories, that stuck like flies to fly-paper, were all that would remain of his father: his strong, forested legs standing in the waves at Constantine Bay, his habit of carefully double-knotting his tie (which had enraged Tim), his keen animated interrogation of their girlfriends (which had enraged them both). Small things. He had been just too young for the war, but still he was the sort of Englishman who was out of time, partly ridiculous, partly admirable. Perhaps every generation produces a slippage, a boat leaving some people stranded on the quay, peering into the mist. Small things. But this kind of Englishman expected a lot from the world. In return for his manners and his conviviality, he expected a passepartout. Richard saw that the world of shared, but exquisite gradations – clothes, furniture, horses, food, of accents, a world which opened all doors – was at an end. His father, with his pantomime tailoring and his confident enunciation, had found his range increasingly restricted. He was aware of it: 'I am a living fossil. I am a coelacanth.' But he said that, safe in the belief that what had gone before was infinitely preferable 'to this cultural and racial mish-mash, which your friend the PM seems to think is some sort of wonderful renaissance for our benighted country. Which, of course, has been living in darkness and prejudice for centuries.'

Richard made coffee in the wreckage of the kitchen. Joanna would still be asleep, but later she was coming. When he was away from her, he couldn't quite believe that they were lovers, as if he too were just a deluded fan. He wanted to hold her and hear her again, to banish this uneasy feeling that he was deceiving himself in believing that she loved him.

The parishioners, less than twenty, were leaving the church. He caught sight of the vicar, his cassock brilliant under a yew tree, seeing them off. They chatted as they walked in knots towards the lychgate. A cow poked its broad, naive head over the wall and tried to reach Igor's unmowed lawn; crows screamed in the tall trees. Along the track from the farmhouse a rider on a huge horse came towards the departing churchgoers. He paused for a moment. The horse stamped restlessly. The rider touched his cap, and trotted off up the hill away from the river. And now he could see Igor, giving the vicar a hug, and perhaps some words of encouragement from his broader spiritual perspective.

Seen from here, the village idyll, the perfectly weathered and sculpted stones, the white windowpanes, the early roses (Madame Bouchard), the fat kine, the carefully planted trees, seemed to support his father's belief that there had been better times before the rot of equivalence set in. But it was all phoney. Villages like this could be read as maps of change. The big Palladian house, now occupied by a bank as a conference and training centre, the farm labourers' cottages knocked together, the weekenders' tasteful improvements, the farm subsidies, the livery stables – everything about the village was a deception. The people who lived here before the war wouldn't have had a clue what was going on. What his father really hankered for was a world where his sort were firmly in charge, and not of land and wealth, but of tone. It wasn't a closed circle, but to enter it you had to jump through the hoops. It was the ignorance of it all, and contempt for these social barriers, which had caused his father pain. It was a world which had passed.

Igor appeared, his face plumped with his thoughts. They were evidently thoughts of a profound nature, brought on by the vicar's sermon about the divisiveness of modern society, by which he meant the ban on fox-hunting, said Igor. Igor believed with the Winnebago Indians that hunting depended upon compliance by the hunted. He had promised to explain the views of the Winnebago to the vicar at a more suitable time.

'Ah, coffee. It smells good.'

Richard rose to pour him a cup. Perhaps something of imperial Russia clung to Igor, because it was impossible to resist being pressed into service, leaving Igor free to think about the big things.

'I prayed for your father,' said Igor.

'Thank you.'

'I think he is content.'

'Black or white?'

'White please. Do we have any cream?'

'We don't seem to.'

Igor's eyes were black and round, so that he looked faintly startled, as if his recent religious experience had been ecstatic.

'I'm going to give the vic a few chapters of my book to read. He needs help.'

Igor had been writing a book for fifteen years, which contained his accumulated thoughts. One day it would change the way we see ourselves. Tim's abandoned novel had also come with advance notices of this sort. Why do people believe that books can change the world? Perhaps what they really believe is that they can transform their own circumstances by writing an earth-shattering book. His great-uncle's book came with a modest wish: 'Thinking that an understanding of the role of the horse in the late War might be of interest, I have the honour of offering this slim work for the kind acceptance of the reading public.'

Perhaps Major Dick, too, had hoped to catch the public's attention in a big way, and reveal himself as a profound thinker, not merely a horse expert. There was a knock at the door.

'Could you get that?' said Igor. 'If it's one of the loonies, tell them the session is after lunch. At about four.'

'How will I know if it's one of the loonies?'

'You'll know.'

It was Jacqui, the Cabinet Office driver.

'Good God, what are you doing here?'

'Mr Talfryn Williams asked me to come and get you, Minister. He's outside in the car.'

'Where are we going?'

'I don't know, sir. He just wants to talk. Could you join him in the car?'

'I'll get dressed.'

Jacqui stayed behind talking to Igor, who was showing her tantric drawings when Richard went out of the house.

'Talfryn, why are you hiding in the car?'

'I'm not hiding. I didn't want to have to explain myself to your friend.'

'What's up?'

'Richard, a friend on the *Express* tells me that Joanna has been involved in a drugs scandal in New York.'

'Don't be absurd.'

Talfryn was wearing jeans and a golfer's windcheater, with the Nike logo. His face was very white.

'Put it this way, she was at a dinner with Case Stipe, and after the dinner in the very early morning somebody died of a drugs overdose, somebody who'd been at the dinner. She wasn't present, apparently, when the girl died. She was at Mr Stipe's home. Now I know this doesn't necessarily add up to a scandal, but when the *Express* prints the story which they got off a stringer in New York, who got it from his cousin in the Police Department, it's going to look very, very bad.'

'Is she being charged with anything?'

'No. Not at the moment.'

'Can't you stop it?'

'I'm trying. But who knows who else has the story. Our best chance is to appeal to their decency, saying, with your father dying so recently and so on . . . and hope it fizzles out during the week.'

'She's coming for the funeral on Wednesday.'

'Is that a good idea?'

'Are you asking me to postpone the funeral?'

'Of course not. I'm just asking you if you want to turn your father's funeral into a fucking circus. In a few days you have a neo-Nazi going into court to plead guilty to stabbing you, coming just after one of the world's most desirable women appearing at your father's quiet little funeral, after being accused of taking drugs with Case fucking Stipe. Wake up, boy, wake up. That would be one hell of a week. She's got to lie low. If she comes back here, all hell will break loose. That wouldn't be good. You said there were no more surprises.'

Richard knew, of course, that Talfryn meant it would not look good for the Prime Minister.

'Who said the boy was a neo-Nazi?'

'Apparently he has links to some neo-Nazis in Denmark and Germany. Stabbing you may not have been entirely random.'

'Oh Jesus.'

'Oh Jesus is about the sum of it. I'm not going to pussy-foot; the Prime Minister can't afford a week or two of major distractions.'

'So what do you want me to do?'

'Keep Joanna away. Sit tight while we try to kill the story. Let's hope the little Nazi's brief doesn't get too clever in court.'

Richard sat at the back of the car, helpless. The air had become too thin to sustain life. Outside the village was moving slowly: cows, horse, two ramblers, a fat black Labrador. They were all taking part in this pageant.

'When's she coming, Rich?'

'Tonight.'

'Will you stop her? You have to tell me now.'

Talfryn looked very tired. His skin was flaking, in the corner of his eyes a thin meandering blood vessel showed red.

'Come in and have some coffee, Talfryn. You look completely whacked.'

'I am. It's one bloody fuck-up after another.'

'Come in. Igor won't mind. He's not strictly of this world anyway.'

'Okay. I need the loo.'

He said 'loo' with a long, lingering Welsh stress, but he didn't leave the car.

'Are you going to ask her not to come, Richard?'

'I love her.'

'Look, if you love her you can't subject her to this. This will be the whole fucking horror show. At least in New York she's not going to be hounded.'

'I can't actually stop her coming.'

'You can't stop her coming, no, but you could explain the problem to her.'

'Maybe.'

'That's not good enough, Rich. Perhaps you don't fully realise.'

'Talfryn, I realise exactly. You are trying to save the Prime Minister from embarrassment. That's all you're here for. You don't give a fuck about me or Joanna. That's not your job. And of course you don't care what happens to us, as long as you limit the damage.'

'Richard, your Joanna was seen going to Mr Stipe's house at two a.m. Just him and her. At four he emerged and went on to a club. At dinner they had all been taking cocaine, including Joanna. Just about the time Stipe got to the club, the model girl was being carried out after an overdose. Stipe took a plane to the US Virgin Islands. Your Joanna left his house at five o'clock in the afternoon the next day. If it is true that I'm trying to protect the Prime Minister from the appearance of sleaze, the incidental benefit is that you will be protected. The alternative is for the Prime Minister to disown you in the way that only a Prime Minister can, saying that while no blame at present attaches to you, blah blah, it was deemed sensible for you to step down for an indefinite period. Adding, of course, that while the Government are so concerned about drugs, any fears that a Minister or his close friends are involved in any way in drug-taking must be allayed. The public would expect nothing less than the highest standards from this Government. And so on. Can I come in for a piss now. My bladder is suddenly bursting.'

Talfryn was shaking. He reached out a hand to Richard and held his wrist, in the same way that Richard had held his father's, clutched between thumb and forefinger, like a beak closing.

'Richard, I don't know if she was shagging Stipe, and anyway that isn't the point here, although maybe for you it's the only point. I don't know. The point is, we can only kill this if she stays away and you keep your head down. And if we have a little luck. The Prime Minister himself is prepared to speak to the owner of the paper, but he won't do it unless you are in agreement.'

'Singing off the same hymn sheet,' said Richard bitterly.

'Don't be a cunt, Richard. Don't be a total fucking cunt.'

'If I can't do it?'

'If the *Express* runs the story and produces a photograph of Joanna and Case Stipe at two in the morning going into his home in New York, how do you see your future?'

'I don't know. Obviously I'll think about it. I'll talk it over with her later.'

'Richard, before I go inside, just let me tell you I feel sick and ashamed.'

Talfryn began to shake again and a few choking noises escaped before he was able to control himself: 'Jesus, I'm sorry Rich. I didn't think it would be like this, did you? I'm not made for this. Not at all.'

There were tears in his eyes, as when you swallow something in haste and it gets stuck. Richard's mother used to say 'things going down the wrong way'.

Igor was explaining to Jacqui that all art is religious art. Richard introduced Talfryn.

'You're the chap who tells the Prime Minister what underpants to wear,' said Igor.

'That's me,' said Talfryn.

'He needs the loo, Igor.'

'Through the kitchen. You can't miss it. Religious art and erotic art. They're all the same, Jacqui.'

'I'll wait in the car, sir,' said Jacqui.

'Sensual woman,' said Igor. 'She doesn't know much about erotic art.'

'Do you?'

'Quite a bit. You look upset.'

'Upset. Good word.'

'I'll make some Buchu tea.'

'What's it do?'

'It soothes the troubled spirit.'

'Is it a prescribed drug?'

'No, no, it's picked by Zulus in the Mountains of the Moon at dawn. It's all natural. One hundred per cent.'

Richard stared out at the stolid cows. Talfryn said he wasn't made for this. He meant the strong-arm stuff. He had been sent down here to tell him the facts of life, but he was only beginning to see them himself. He was shocked that politics could be this crude. But Richard had known all along. Politics are crude. It was as if all the antipathies and conflicts and hatreds were capped by politics, but still from time to time there were eruptions of foul gas. Talfryn had excelled at the fun stuff, the great game, but he had never really seen that it was a lethal business. When Richard was teaching politics he had always been troubled by the knowledge that it was about very fundamental matters, things like freedom and death, which the public and many politicians thought were concepts belonging only to history. And Richard knew that if he were an obstacle in the Prime Minister's road he must be swept aside. The Prime Minister had important work to do. He was privy to massive secrets, that set him apart from ordinary people and ordinary considerations. The Prime Minister had sent his creature, Talfryn Williams, to give him the news.

Could it be true, as Talfryn was suggesting, that Joanna was sleeping with Case Stipe? He didn't believe it. He could believe that his old friend would sacrifice him, but he couldn't believe that Joanna would betray him. He would speak to her. He knew that by speaking to her everything would be restored.

Igor emerged through the kitchen just behind Talfryn, carrying three mugs of the restorative tea. Talfryn's face was drained, and his skin moist, as if he had been sick.

You didn't see it, did you? You didn't believe that the workings were so basic.

Richard was surprised by his own detachment, but he had always known the score. The history of politics is the history of betrayal and disappointment. Anyone who willingly offers himself to politics is offering himself as a human sacrifice.

Igor's sensitivity was directed to spiritual matters. He could feel agitation in the air — the energies were wrong — and he set out to help. The tea was bitter, the colour of ferns that grow in dark places, but Igor said it had been drunk for hundreds, perhaps thousands, of years in Africa. It wasn't much of a testimonial, but Richard drank deeply.

Talfryn said, 'That's good, that's bloody good,' with conviction. 'What do you do, Igor?'

'I'm a psychotherapist.'

'He's a profound thinker,' said Richard without irony.

'Thank you. No, Ricardo and I are old friends. Now I find, without false modesty, that I have a talent for healing people.'

'Oh Jesus, we need you,' said Talfryn with a semblance of his usual cheerfulness.

'Do you want to meditate for a few minutes?'

'Why not?'

'Shut your eyes. Just think about something precious to you, but don't try to analyse or probe the thought. Just let it rest there. All right?'

So they sat still, eyes shut, while Igor chanted in a low melodic voice. Richard thought of Joanna lying next to him, her legs entwined with his. And he thought of the course of her thigh where his one hand rested, and of her two hands clasping his hand between her breasts, which were never quite still as she slept her intense, dramatic sleep. He opened his eyes. There were tears on Talfryn's cheeks. What was he thinking of?

They drank some of the inspiriting tea. Talfryn said he hadn't slept for two nights. Igor explained that sleep was essential to spiritual renewal. A balance would be achieved.

'That's where I'm going wrong,' said Talfryn. 'No balance. Look, I must be off. You will ring me soon, won't you Rich?'

'I will.'

Talfryn wanted some reassurance before he left. His colour had come back, that russet look which some Celts have, and the clamminess had gone from his skin.

As they walked back to the car Richard said: 'I'll try to help you and the Prime Minister, but it won't be because of the blackmail.'

'What fucking blackmail? What are you talking about?'

'You came here, you were sent here to threaten me. How do I know if your information is true? How do I know it wasn't just some gossip columnist who was in the same restaurant? For all I know, the *Express* have no intention of running the story, if it is a story at all.'

'Why would I have come if it was all nonsense?'

'Would you know, Talfryn? After all, you're just a minion. It's the most common delusion amongst organ-grinders' monkeys, that they are playing the tunes.'

'Joanna Jermyn, your Joanna, spent most of Friday night in the company of Case Stipe. A police sergeant interviewed her; he snitched to a reporter. A waiter was questioned by the reporter. He said they were all snorting cocaine. The Prime Minister loves you and he doesn't want her to come back while he's killing the story, because he knows that if she comes back for your father's funeral none of the newspapers will be able to resist. They'll all go mad.'

'And then?'

'And then you'll find your life is hell.'

'Talfryn, I don't know if there's any truth in this, but I'm not going to act as though I believe it until I've spoken to Joanna.'

'Fine. Absolutely fine, but do it quickly.'

Talfryn looked small and frail out in the open.

'I'm sorry about your dad,' he said. He climbed into the Rover and waved weakly as it drove off up through the line of oaks. Richard knew he had been too harsh with him, but he knew that Talfryn reported the Prime Minister's thoughts with whatever emphasis he chose. He wouldn't allow Talfryn to push him into a position he would regret, just because he wanted to protect his boss.

The Prime Minister loves you. Friendship, like parenthood, is self-regarding. They were friends, it was true, but now this friendship had to serve a greater cause, and his love for Joanna had to be subject too. Talfryn feared disorder; as Haldemann said to Nixon: 'Once the toothpaste is out of the tube, it's awfully hard to get it back in.' Politicians are intimidated by the threatening elements in their constituencies, said Walter Lippmann, so that this becomes the decisive element in their decisions. It would look bad if a Minister's mistress had been at a drug-taking dinner in New York. It would look bad, no matter what the real, true facts might be.

He walked up past the church where an elderly lady with secateurs was carrying some cornflowers along the path from the gate. She smiled at him and he said good morning. It wasn't yet seven in New York. He walked out of the village to calm himself. But now that Talfryn was gone he found it difficult. He was out of the loop, as they liked to say at Whitehall. Whatever was happening there, whatever scurrying and whispering and weighing up was going on, he would only hear those muffled noises which escaped. There was no more sense in this than hearing unknown lovers in a nearby room.

Talfryn believed that Joanna was sleeping with Case Stipe. But Talfryn had no idea of what had passed between him and Joanna. He had no idea that their tears had co-mingled as their skin whispered love. How could you explain such a thing?

Trotting towards him, large feet ringing on the road, came the horse he had seen at the church. It was riderless. Richard plucked some grass, and stood in the middle of the road with his arms outstretched. The horse slowed and made no effort to escape. It snatched at the grass as he held the bridle. The bridle was of a rich, waxy leather. He walked the horse back in the direction it had come. It seemed happy to be returned to servitude.

As Richard and the horse turned a corner, they saw a man limping towards them. He was holding one arm with the other.

'A pheasant got up,' he said quickly. 'Thank you for catching Biggles for me.'

'That's all right. Is your arm bad?'

'Collarbone's gone, I'm afraid.'

They walked back to the village, Richard leading the horse, Biggles. They probably looked like stragglers retreating from a battle lost.

'I'm Michael Sessions,' said the wounded man; 'I'm a literary agent.'

'I'm Richard McAllister.'

'I know who you are. Hiding?'

15

There was a saying Joanna had always loved: 'To see him act is like reading Shakespeare by flashes of lightning.' It was Coleridge speaking about Edmund Kean.

She was on the plane, flying to St John. Actually she was flying to St Thomas, because there is no airport at St John. A fast boat would meet her. Acting was her life. It was a strange expression. If she added up all the hours she had spent acting, actually performing, they wouldn't be a twentieth or a fiftieth of her life. Even long-run soaps and the theatre engagements were a small fragment of her life. It was the flashes of lightning that were her life. Acting is my life, she whispered, as the plane rose above the steel-grey water of La Guardia. She whispered it as an incantation. When she fell in love with Richard, she said to him, to love you is like reading Shakespeare by flashes of lightning.

Below her, Long Island. The plane wheeled sharply for the south. These holiday planes are less formal; they hustle. For an actress to be a success she must have the face of Venus and the hide of a rhinoceros. Who was that? Marguerite Duras, he said. She wasn't sure who Marguerite Duras was. They passed over incidental swamps and then fields. Long Island was guarded by a long spit of sand to the south. The plane banked again and they were in the cloud. The stewardess, who was a tough, raddled broad, was solicitous. Fame was a curious thing: they identified with you, as though you had been batting for them. You were doing it for them, for their inner lives and their humiliations. She was in charge of the First Class section; she had a welcome rum punch or a glass of champagne, or most other beverages. Joanna asked for a rum punch.

When Richard rang as she was packing for London she was happy.

'I'm packing. I'll leave at four for Kennedy. I'm doing Entertainment Tonight first, that's why I'm packing. Actually I'm packing because it makes me think I'm almost home with you.'

'Joanna, I have to ask you something first before you come.'

She felt sick, a churning in her stomach as though some chemical reaction was going on there. A bitter fluid rose to her throat.

'What?'

'There's a report that you were at a party with Case Stipe and someone died of an overdose.'

'I went to dinner with Case, with his hangers-on, and one of them, a model, died much later. I wasn't there. I'm not even sure we met. I told you that.'

'I'm not interrogating you, but apparently you went to Case Stipe's home and spent the night there.'

'I told you that, too.'

'There are photographs.'

'Of what, for Christ's sake?'

She thought that someone must have photographed them having sex.

'You and him arm in arm, going into his house.'

'Richard. Oh Richard. It was nothing, believe me. Believe me. Just actors. Just luvvies.'

'I do believe you. You didn't sleep with him or anything?'

'No. No. Oh please, I love you Richard, why are you asking me?'

He was inviting her, begging her, to deny it.

'I'm so sorry,' he said. 'Did you take drugs?'

'I pretended. I know it sounds foolish, but I sort of went along with it.'

'I'm sorry I'm asking you these things, but I have to know because one of the papers is threatening to run a story, with photographs, of a Minister's lover taking drugs and spending the night with Case Stipe. They're trying to kill the story.'

'Who?'

'Downing Street. For me, the main thing is not whether it causes them embarrassment, or me for that matter, but the fact that it's nonsense, that's the main thing.'

'Richard, I love you so much, it's unbearable. Being separated from you has been like a little death. I think of you all the time. I feel so lonely and lost, as though I'm detained in the wrong place. I try to imagine what you're doing at every moment.'

'I love you, darling. For your sake, I want you to wait until after the funeral on Wednesday. If you came today, all the papers will go for the story. Nobody would be able to kill it. By Thursday or Friday it'll be old news.'

'I can't wait until Friday.'

'I'll come to you as soon as the funeral's over. Let's meet in Nevis or Costa Rica or somewhere. You choose. We'll vanish.'

'All right. I have to get out of here. They'll think I'm nuts. Where are you now?'

'I'm still at Igor's place. I'm going up to London for the funeral on Tuesday night.'

'I thought the hearing was tomorrow.'

'It has been postponed. What a surprise. It's just a magistrate's court where he pleads.'

'Guilty?'

'They say so.'

'Richard, how did we get into all this? This utter fuck-up.'

'God knows. It seems completely unreal. I know that's hack, but that's how it feels.'

'And now these horrible stories. I'm so sorry, I'm making life even more difficult for you.'

'I'll find somewhere for us to vanish.'

'I'll be fine until Thursday or Friday. Do what you have to do.'

'Thank you.'

There was a moment's silence.

'Richard, it's not going to go on for ever is it?'

'I hope not. I've decided not to stand again and as soon as I can, I'm going to leave the Government. I'm not made for this. Funnily enough, that's what Talfryn said this morning.'

'Nobody can take all this, darling. It's too much.'

She went to her interview and they asked her about the new movie and Case Stipe.

'Is it true that you two are an item? You've been seen about town together.'

The question was asked in that breathless, squeaky fashion

by a presenter with hair that could have provided lodging for hummingbirds.

'What sort of fucking question is that? Stop recording. What kind of impertinent rubbish is this?'

She allowed herself to shout and rage: she recognised as she was doing it that she was on a slippery slope. But there was pleasure in frightening the interviewer with the ridiculous hair, and attracting an executive from somewhere in the building, to soothe her. Joanna knew that they would all be sniggering when she left the building. For the moment they were feigning contrition; the interviewer apologised profusely, saying she just read it off the screen. The questions were re-drafted to a level of new imbecility.

Berkovsky's people had booked her into the St Regis, where they were no doubt festooning a suite for her. In the taxi going there she heard again the unmistakable anxiety in Richard's voice: *You didn't sleep with him or anything?*

What could she say? And could she tell him that the day before, Miklos had humiliated her. That he had slapped her. Could she claim loneliness and confusion and cocaine as excuses?

She saw two policemen on horses as they approached the park and she began to cry. The horses were plump and gleaming. Their faces had that dumb beauty. She rang Richard; mercifully he was not there, but she left a message, her voice failing.

'What I told you earlier is not true. I don't love him, or even like him, but I have no excuse. I can only tell you that I love you, I love you, but this torment can't go on. Please forgive me. Please try to forget me. I'll never forget you. I'm so, so sorry.'

Then she rang Case Stipe, and he said, almost as if he couldn't remember the invitation, oh sure, yes, come to St Thomas, US Virgins, and I'll send a boat for you. Stay as long as you like. No problem.

The Russian cab driver took her money with complete indifference. He was faintly lavender round the eyes, and seemed to be too exhausted to look at her, as if he had lost any expectation of human communion in New York. Liveried people rushed out of the hotel to escort her, to assure her of their pleasure in seeing her.

For a while she lay on another huge altar of a bed, richly brocaded. She longed for her farmhouse, with its crooked corridors and creaking floorboards and the view of apple blossom in the orchard. All gone. All gone. Her life had gone. Her father, putting on his sweater with the impressive epaulettes, the gold cross gleaming on the red flashes; she and her mother seeing him off, just down the road. Gone. There are no short-cuts. In a world where nobody believed that there were any consequences, she had discovered the truth of what her father believed in his brisk fashion. She had told Case she wasn't coming for romance or anything, and he said: 'Yeah, yeah, don't take it so seriously, Joanna. You're letting things get to you.' In his world at least, there were no consequences; at a certain level, stars were exempt. He was inviting her to join him up there, a million miles from Ashdown Forest and the apple blossom and the small, mean British politics.

As if to make the invitation more attractive, the water glimpsed below the plane, which had been the colour of salt on a road, was now a lively rich green, with blue highlights, that seemed to be a promise of things to come down there in the lubricious Virgin

Islands. The stewardess, improbably called Chelsea, brought her more rum punch and a meal of expensive fishy ingredients, which presaged island life: *A taste of the islands.*

Joanna was quite sloshed; the rum punch, pre-mixed, was sweet with a metallic aftertaste. She signed the First Class menu for Chelsea. *Chelsea, with thanks, Joanna Jermyn.* And then she slept up here, far from all consequences, it was easy. It was easier than lying on a broad bed in a thousand-dollar-a-night suite. She was miserable, but in that misery there was a small measure of relief which she fostered. It was a fact that you could sleep while consciously nursing a single thought.

When she woke, as the plane began to prepare itself in that clattering, roaring fashion, to land, she saw that the sea was indeed blue, of an unlikely hue that reminded her of Jeremy's mouthwash. Chelsea gave her a warm towel to press to her face. Quickly she touched up her make-up as the plane swooped down past a hillside verdant as a tropical garden (perhaps it was a tropical garden), and low over a bay lined with palms. Richard. Oh Richard. The two of them could be hiding down there in the palm trees if she hadn't been so foolish.

The airport was full of very large people, who spoke amongst themselves in a West Indian patois, but to visitors in American. She was shown to a Jeep by two men, Case's people, and driven through St Thomas and up a steep hill. In the bay below, she could see a cruise liner tied up. It seemed too big for the landscape of green hills and little bungalows. They began to head down the other side of the mountain, and the driver said that was where they would get the boat for St John. She imagined that Richard would have her message by now. How would he take it? Perhaps he would be grateful, even if he didn't fully realise it, to be released. What would he do now? Nobody knew where she was. As a matter of fact, she didn't know precisely herself. In the distance, scattered on the comically blue sea, were fragments of islands. She knew that he would take her confession badly. Unfaithfulness was not something which was easy to explain away. He would be deeply hurt by the thought of her body being entered, her breasts kissed – all the attendant intimacies of sex. Of course, everyone knew that there were degrees of intimacy and detachment. But to the one who is wronged, the surrender of the secret places is intolerable. The dull truth was that she was slightly stoned and Case acted as though sex was the most natural and inevitable thing on earth at that moment. Maybe, as Jeremy was always suggesting, she was just an actress and actresses are congenitally on the make. But Joanna had noticed that the most superficial of men, the most bogus, transparent womanisers, are never short of women to practise their frauds on. It was because they promised absolution from duty and devotion. Richard's father, soon to be buried, was one of these, transmitting a male sonar.

They passed junkyards of old pick-ups, and banana trees and a stone church that looked Scandinavian. Worse than the physical, sensual sense of betrayal, she knew that what would last longer was the awful feeling that everything she had said as they breathed love was a lie. It wasn't a lie. It isn't a lie.

'You okay, lady?'

'I'm fine.' She was crying as the Jeep lurched down the hill past a half-built supermarket. She decided that she would write to Richard, begging for forgiveness, and suggesting that when the time was right, when he was able, he should send for her.

Half in Love

The boat was moored in a marina. It was a drug-smuggler's boat, long and thin with immense engines. The big black man handed her over with her luggage to two big white men, Case's boat people, who were wearing white caps with gold braid like the skipper in *Some Like It Hot*. They fired up the engines and the boat roared through the marina and out into the bay. The noise was awful. Richard said he was leaving politics. He had never felt at ease, because he hated the way every issue had to be over-simplified. It's not easy to do good. That's what I've learned. It's more about claiming to be doing good. And if nobody believes that, you produce figures to show that you are doing better than the last lot.

Why had she told him, when it was the last thing she wanted to do?

A small island flashed by and one of the sea dogs said that W. John Pennebaker lived there. *Oh good. How amazing. Nice guy too. Real nice guy. Always says hi. That's great.*

She had told Richard the unbearable truth because she couldn't lie to him. Not to him. The police sergeant, the maid, some paparazzi, may have told their stories, the papers may have created a scandal. So be it. But if she had lied to Richard she would have been committing an offence against nature. Richard was an innocent. Despite his mother's early death and his urbane old dandy father's carrying on and his early success, Richard was a person who lacked malice. It would be unbearable to lie to him, for their lives to have continued, knowing that she had betrayed him, whatever the circumstances. She couldn't do it, and she took some small comfort in this act of sacrifice.

*   *   *

The boat curved in a huge arc towards a bay which appeared to be completely uninhabited. The jungle fell from a high peak into the water, an avalanche of greenery.

'That's Cinnamon,' the skipper shouted.

He eased the engine down, and Joanna could hear water in its natural state. The boat stopped bounding and settled lower. As they rounded a headland she could see what looked like a Polynesian longhouse on a terrace above the beach. Below it there were other houses, artfully made of wood and bamboo, and there were flashes of water from Buddhist ponds.

A figure, probably Case, was waving and now running down to the jetty. It was Case, in a sarong.

16

It was high tide. The river was part of the North Sea for an hour or so. Even way up here in Chelsea, on a warm spring day, it had that marine glint, a gunmetal sheen of sea water, lightly convulsed, lapping against the holding walls and attended by seagulls.

Joanna's mother came to the funeral. She was, after all, a veteran of bereavement. Perhaps she hadn't heard that her daughter had moved on again. Richard and Tim stood at the head of this congregation of mourners, and she hung back near a pillar. Maybe she had come in an ambassadorial role to represent her absent daughter. A few photographers had waited in vain for her daughter. Richard wondered if she knew where Joanna was.

Chelsea Old Church was filled with the irresistible poetry of the funeral service. The old boy was carried out by six unsteady pallbearers, recruited from his club, and the burial took place across the way in the churchyard. There wasn't much space to be had in Chelsea, but somehow he was admitted. After the burial Richard spoke to Joanna's mother, and thanked her for coming.

'I wanted to come.'

Had she wanted to see what she was denied, the heavy

pebble-infiltrated clay piling in on the coffin? Had she wanted to establish some claim on him — after all, she might believe she was soon to be his mother-in-law?

She was wearing gloves. The touch of them on his hands caused a flick of static. He looked into her eyes to see if he could detect something, a comet trail, left by Joanna.

'Will you come back to my father's flat in Tite Street for a drink?'

'No, no. I have to go. There's nobody to look after the cats. But Richard, I just wanted to tell you how terribly sorry I am.'

'Thank you.' He wasn't sure what she was apologising for. Perhaps she knew that Joanna had left him.

'Do you know where she is?'

'No. Don't you?'

'Not really. She's keeping her head down.'

'Has something gone wrong?'

'There's been a lot of pressure.'

'She loves you.'

She delivered this message so fervently, her handsome Army-wife face so close to his, that he felt a faint dew from her words and he could detect the scent of camomile and rosewater on her English skin.

She loves me, but she sleeps with another man. How can this be?

It was a hot day. The caterers had opened the windows of the flat. They had prepared white tablecloths and small, impeccable sandwiches and some drinks, including tea laid out severely. Tim spoke briefly. He told a story about how his father had sent his school report to his bookmaker and a betting slip to Tim's housemaster. Timmy concluded that his father's life had never quite lived up to its promise, but he was a fundamentally kind and generous man. Igor gave a Tibetan blessing too, which made some uneasy, but which Richard accepted without reservation as part of the ecumenical nature of death. As if to emphasise this fact, Igor was wearing a long embroidered coat, like a vestment.

Being separated from you has been like a little death, she said.

And now he had died too. It was a field of corpses.

Richard had told Igor what Joanna said about Case Stipe. He had tried to explain to Igor the desolation he felt. Igor had said, his face solemn: 'It passes.'

Richard did not want it to pass. Why would you? To let it pass would be a form of self-mutilation.

The conversation was warming up as relatives and old friends were released from their recent solemnity. He knew some of the friends; their pockets were strangely angled, if they were men, and they wore slightly mad hats if they were women. But both sexes were characterised by an unfashionable cheerfulness of expression, as though they knew the lifeboats were leaking, but weren't going to display any fear. They had made it into the new century, but they were on borrowed time. Richard felt guilty now for his selfish misery. He forced himself to do the rounds, thanking them for coming, enquiring after their grandchildren, and reading their desperate, muted appeals for attention. They mostly had anecdotes about his father which they wished to vouchsafe to him: his father's kindnesses and his indiscretions and sense of humour were

221

given to him as parting gifts. They gave the impression that his father knew what he was doing; in some strange way he was party to secrets denied to others. This is what was meant by the triumph of memory over forgetting: these warm human feelings were all that were left. Yet he felt the loss of someone alive far more keenly than the loss of someone dead. He could easily imagine his father's loss passing. The pain travelled through his gut, which seemed to want to give birth to a great foetus of despair.

Igor stood beside him. 'All things pass,' he said, 'dear Ricardo.' *Tout lasse, tout casse, tout passe.*

The little fragile gathering in Tite Street broke up. Gerald Tremayne, a rubicund fellow with yellowing teeth, seized Richard's hand. 'He was a fine man. The finest of us all,' before he lumbered towards the stairs, his back heaving emotionally like a conductor's on the podium. The finest of us all. Richard wondered if this was much of a distinction.

Tim and Richard sat down finally in the heavy, swathed furniture, unmediated at last by the rituals of death.

'There's very little left,' said Tim, 'Hopkinson says.'

'I know.'

'The flat's heavily mortgaged and the shares have gone.'

'What was he living on?'

'God knows. Where's Joanna?'

'I don't know. She's gone her own way too.'

It sounded so pallid, thinned of human meaning.

'Oh, shit, Rich, I'm sorry. What happened?'

'It was just too much for her. I kept having to tell her to stay away.'

'Were they pressuring you?' He pointed down-river towards Whitehall.

'They only see that part of the picture that interests them. They're terrified of chaos or rumour or scandal.'

'I'm sorry, Rich. I'm sorry.'

His younger brother, his hair thinning while his face was thickening like his father's, still looked to him about nine years old, and Richard remembered how terrified and confused he had been when their mother died and their father was crying as he told them.

'What are you going to do?' Tim asked.

'I promised not to resign this side of the election. I'm working on the manifesto. But I won't be standing again. Also I don't want this to appear in your rag, by the way.'

'Don't be crazy.'

But Richard knew that his brother was as susceptible as any other journalist to the belief that spilling the beans was a universal moral imperative. Journalists, although they regarded themselves as hard-bitten and cynical, had a naive faith in the ultimate good of what they were doing. They had to make their offerings to this great furnace of truth, without which the light of the world would go out. As a matter of fact, all professionals believe that they are what makes the world go round.

'I wouldn't do that, Rich,' said Tim sadly.

'You might.'

They were conscious of being alone. Richard wondered if their relationship would change. Brothers are, always, in competition. Their father had at times been as impervious to family affection as a mallard to water, but still he was the conduit to their past as a family. Until he was about fifteen, Tim had always sought Richard's memories of what it had been like before their mother died. His small, thin face – now fattening up – had been chafed by the assurance that they had once had a mother and all the usual trappings of a family. It was as if he needed reassuring that his memories were not too deceptive. In the telling, Richard had to recall certain elements: holidays, Christmas trees, presents. The conventional landscape of childhood was promoted to mythical status.

Now Richard found himself having his own doubts about the veracity of his memory of Joanna. Maybe, blinded by her beauty, he had just imagined their closeness. She had told him only the other day that to be apart from him was intolerable. She had once asked him to beat her, because she wanted something hardly expressible: sex was an imperfect expression of love of this intensity. It was impossible for Richard to accept that this intensity was no more; or worse, that it had never been. Joanna's mother had told him that she loved him too, only a few hours ago. He wanted to speak to Joanna, he wanted to speak to her because he was sure that she wouldn't be able to say, please try to forget me. He couldn't forget her. It was unimaginable.

Tim was going straight back to Berlin this evening.

'What are you going to do, Rich?'

'You asked me that.'

'I mean, now, today, tomorrow.'

'I'm not sure. I'll probably go down to my cottage and hole up there for a while.'

'Until?'

'That's the question, Timmy. Until what? I don't know.

I've started working on a little memoir of our great-uncle the Army vet.'

'And what about Government?'

'I'm still on R & R.'

'Are you any better?'

'I'm fine,' said Richard, fingering his scar dismissively. Look, it's almost gone.

'You've just got to get over the idea that you were to blame in some way.'

'I don't think I was to blame. What happened was that I just began to wonder if I was doing the right job. It made me think.'

'Everybody says you were a huge success. I'm proud of you. I probably got this job because I'm your brother.'

'Don't be ridiculous. You got the job because you're an excellent journalist. The editor himself said so as I was recommending you for the position.'

'Oh fuck off.'

'How's your German girl, the language teacher?'

'She's a maniac in bed.'

'Is that it?'

'That'll do. Until I know the language. I might find she has hidden depths.'

When Tim had gone, Richard looked through his father's papers. There were piles of bank statements unopened. There were letters from women and there were unpaid bills, amounting to twenty or thirty thousand pounds. He felt a great weariness. It was wholly typical of his father to leave this mess. He'd have to sell his own flat to pay the bills and the overdraft. He put aside

the demands for money and the pleas from the bank and looked
at the letters. They were full of demands. He scanned them to
see if he could find out what it was that stirred these women.
They also had the idea that the old boy was hiding something,
denying them some emotional treasure.

'I wish you would tell me what you really think.'

'I can't seem to get through to you.'

'You appear to think there is nothing beneath the surface of
life. Believe me, there is.'

And there was a very poignant note: 'Last summer you said you
wanted to marry me. Now silence. What is it you really want?'

His father had written neatly on the top of the letter: 'Died.'
And the date, a year ago.

His father's life had no harmony. Nothing held it together
in a meaningful whole. It was a succession of small events
and lusts and failures. Perhaps it is because my own life is
in fragments that I think this, or perhaps there is a music I
can't hear.

He decided to walk. If he could smell the river, the way his father
could, he thought maybe that would be a start. But first he walked
up away from the river, towards Royal Hospital Gardens, where
the sound of children playing and the thwack-thump-thwack of
tennis balls attracted him.

The world was going on, of course, except that around
himself he felt a deadness. He sat down under a tree near
the cricket pavilion and made a small pile of the bark of the
plane tree. This bark seemed to fall off in rectangles. Tiny
things were busy in the grass. From the tennis courts he heard

the cheerful apologies: *Sorry. Oh sorry. Ooops, sorry. Sorreee. Oh God, I am sorry.*

He slept for a while, tilted against the plane tree, until his phone rang. He was startled awake. He hoped it was Joanna because only she and Talfryn and his brother had the number. It was the Prime Minister.

'Rich, I'm so sorry about your father. Apologies for not speaking earlier, we both send our love.'

'Where are you?'

'I'm in Vienna. Are you holding up?'

'I am.'

'Good. I want you back as soon as possible. But you must decide. We managed to stamp on the story, by the way.'

'Thank you.'

'And thanks for keeping Joanna out of the way.'

'She's out of it permanently now.'

'Oh no.'

'Yes. I'm afraid so.'

'I'm sorry. I wanted to be best man; I meant it.'

'That's okay.'

'Will you get together again?'

'I don't think so. I hope so.'

'I hope you do. I've got to go, it's more apple strudel for me. Where are you? I can hear tennis.'

'I'm lying under a tree in Chelsea.'

'Lucky boy. Very sorry about your dad, and particularly that we couldn't come to the funeral.'

He was gone. He had told Richard, in the early days, that he sat in meetings with leaders of other countries and asked himself how he had got here. He said he felt like an impostor. No more. He was in the club now, controlling our destinies. His every action, every kindness, every personal message now had a significance and a weight which could not be gauged on the normal scale. Why had he rung? Was it because he genuinely wanted to say how sorry he was? Or was it because Talfryn had suggested it? *Look, Prime Minister, give Richard a call, he's a bit wobbly about Joanna Jermyn. Give him the good news about the Express yourself. Here, I've dialled the number, sir.*

Between rounds of schnapps and glad-handing and treaty-signing, a quick housekeeping phone-call. Where did friendship stand in all this? Who could say? Yet the Prime Minister had told him that he wanted his friendship more than ever now; he knew that people found it difficult to speak frankly to him. The newspaper said that he had aged over the past few years, but Richard found that power had given his old friend a glow, so that he looked like a Renaissance painting, subtly enhanced by a luminous light. His eyes had become almost as blue as Delftware, ecstatic, never dimmed by fatigue or tedium.

Close friendship, however, cannot survive changes like this, because friendship is based on common experience. Whenever they were alone, not often nowadays, the Prime Minister would talk about old times, as if to remind Richard that they still shared something, even if it was past. And that was the trouble, a consciousness had risen up to separate them.

One set of tennis players had a huge jug of cordial, which they were now pouring. Even from here he could see a sheen on them. The two women wore tennis dresses and their thighs were quite stout and pink as they sprawled on the grass. He thought of Joanna's thighs, and the little creases at the top of them and how his tongue had traced that tendon in the very inside, right to the source. These things mean nothing, and yet they mean everything. As he lay propped up against the tree his heart filled his chest to bursting point. The tennis players were gulping their squash; a couple of pensioners walked past, Toby mugs out ambling; a dog yapped, the children were leaving, and his blood was surging uncontrolled round his body.

Less than a mile away his father was experiencing his first of many days down in the deep clay, and he was thinking of Joanna's thighs. His tongue had just reached the first springy hairs. Over there they had finished drinking their cordial and were slicing and chopping the tennis balls in that old-fashioned upper-class English way. All these physical intimacies – he had once thought of them as sacraments – were now lost to him. If he ever made love to her again, which he doubted, he would be too aware that he had lost what he had thought was his to the depths of his being. If they ever made love again, there would be a spectre at the feast; there would be unspoken questions, questions which now he couldn't bear to formulate, because they could turn to bitterness and hatred. A few minutes ago, the Prime Minister had called him. He could picture him, gliding through all those fat suited men who ran Europe: of them, but definitely superior, morally and instinctively. But Richard knew that he was becoming world-weary, like them. European politics had an irresistible allure, a sort of ancient knowingness, which was proof against excessive idealism. Machiavelli believed that politics without cynicism was dangerous. His old friend was being exposed to this five-hundred-year-old seminar. While he was learning about Mitteleuropa, Richard was lying under a tree, painfully remembering his ex-lover's inner thighs. In love, there was a very thin line, a mere tracing, between the noble and the absurd. Tears came, not to his eyes, but to some passage leading there, where they were choked back. He was supposed to be the brains of the Government, the licensed thinker, and what was on his mind was the confluence of Joanna's thighs. It is the day my father is buried. But he couldn't reorder his thoughts, it was impossible. If he hadn't known it before, he knew it now: to be human is to be only partly rational.

He walked down to the river, which was receding. Its marine quality had gone: mud banks were exposed and the water was flowing urgently towards the sea. He tried to smell what his father claimed to be able to detect, but he couldn't get it. Instead he heard the turbine rumble of the great, heedless city, and the screaming of the seagulls. Strange birds: clean, lithe and without scruple.

His phone rang again. A voice he didn't recognise spoke.
'Hello?'
'Hello, is that Mr McAllister?'
'Yes.'
'Yes, I'm Stan Blumberg, Joanna Jermyn's agent. She gave me the number.'
'Yes.'
'This is difficult, Mr McAllister. It's not easy to say. I hope you don't mind?'
'What are you going to say?'

'Joanna asked me to ring you.'

'Yes?'

'She says she wants you to know that she will wait for you to forgive her, and that when you're ready, if you are, she wants you to have her back. That's exactly what she asked me to say.'

'Where is she now?'

'She's at a resort for a few days. The picture starts in Phoenix in a couple of weeks.'

'Is she all right?'

'Richard, forgive me if I call you Richard, she's very unhappy. I have known her for twelve years now, and believe me, she loves you. My wife asked me specially to tell you that. She's spoken to her too. Richard, she's a lovely girl, try and understand.'

'Thank you for ringing me.'

'I believe your father died. I'm very sorry. May he rest in peace.'

'Thank you. The funeral was this morning.'

'Have you got a message for Joanna?'

'Tell her I want to speak to her.'

'I will.'

'Thank you.'

'She said she would call later.'

'Goodbye. Oh, there's one more thing, tell her the story has gone away.'

'Oh, fine, I'm sure she'll be pleased. God bless you.'

'And you.'

Another person had told him that Joanna loved him. Stan. Stan's voice was thick with intensity. The message seemed to be that Joanna's love for him was something very special. It had left the confines of the personal, him and her, and entered another region. Perhaps it had become more public, more symbolic, the way that actresses' lives tended to. Jeremy once said that actors and actresses only live truly at second-hand, through their public selves, the sort of remark Jeremy made, wryly suggesting the price of being married to an actress.

Richard would sit there at that table, wondering why he felt so little guilt about sleeping with Jeremy's wife. Lovers believe they have some moral force behind them, that transcends the lives around them. Now Richard saw that he and Jeremy had been conscripted into the same regiment.

As he walked along the river, he felt the stirrings of bitterness. She loved him. But her love was somehow more important than their love. God help me, I'm becoming petty. The next stage is obsession. Those whom the Gods . . . et cetera.

You should have asked Stan more questions, about who she was with and why she passed her messages through him, but Stan himself seemed to be feeling awkward, as though he had been forced to make the call, by Joanna and by his wife. Joanna had told him that her agent had been in love with her once. 'It's not easy to say.' Perhaps he didn't relish the job of Pander, under the circumstances.

He walked back slowly in the direction of the flat; she wanted to be forgiven and taken back. But a worm had entered the apple. He walked past the front doors, painted with as much meaning as the posts outside Indian lodges, the deep reds and lustrous dark blues and the sober confident blacks; also the ornaments – the 'door furniture' – and the terracotta pots and the flowers in them, and the railings and even the bells told an English story.

He could read it; he was the Schliemann of these artefacts. He was the brains of the Party, he was the Prime Minister's friend. But mostly, he was a cuckold.

A worm had entered the apple.

Instead of turning up Tite Street, as he had intended, he cut back towards the churchyard with the disturbed earth where his father was buried. He half expected, in his turbulent state, to find some fresh flowers and anguished notes, but there was nothing there. No more notes. The old boy was elusive before; now he was for ever beyond their reach.

Richard walked back to the flat. He had a bath in his father's bath. The enamel was stained and the taps released hot water from some central reservoir with dramatic surges and puffs of steam.

Joanna's love was of a high order. He thought that perhaps women wanted to distance themselves in this respect from men. He had read somewhere that lust was, for men, the most wretched form of human struggle, the very essence of slavery. Women didn't want to confuse lust and love.

He didn't know how long he lay in the bath. The pipes were generous with the hot water. The bathroom was fragrant with essences that had belonged to his father. Even these essences spoke an English which was falling into disrepair: Trumpers' Essence of Jamaican Lime, Officers' and Gentlemen's Strong Soap, Almond Shaving Cream, Royal Cologne and Spanish Leather Eau de Toilette.

17

By a strange coincidence, Joanna was taking a bath at the same time. Her room, a pavilion, as Case called it, had a bath outside in a small courtyard. She lay in the water, her back against polished stone. The bath was hollowed out of black rock. It was set into black slate paving stones, and there were two huge Indonesian pots at either side of the bath. In the soap dish, tropical flowers shared the available space with blocks of handmade oatmeal soap. From here Joanna could look directly out to sea, through a narrow opening in the wall of the courtyard, so that the ludicrously blue water formed a kind of David Hockney between the white frames of the walls.

Case was fishing. He had taken up fly-fishing in the sea, for bone fish. When he had done his head in, this was what he longed for, just to get away and do some bone fishing. He invited her to come along, but she was waiting for Stan to call. As always, Stan was punctual.

'Joanna, I spoke to him.'

'And did you give him my message?'

'Yes. Exactly.'

'What did he say?'

'He said he wanted to speak to you.'

'How did he sound?'

'It was hard to tell, as I've never spoken a word to the man before. How did he sound compared to what? He sounded sombre. His father was buried this morning.'

'Did he ask where I was?'

'Yes. I said you were at a resort, until you go to Phoenix.'

'Thank you, Stan. Thank you.'

'The Almeida have been on to me about *Antony and Cleopatra*. You've got to decide.'

'I'll do it. I'm not too young, am I? As long as you tell them that I may not be able to rehearse for a few weeks if the picture goes over.'

'Sure. Sure, they understand.'

When Stan's voice had gone, she felt lonely. Stan had clearly been hurt by having to pass on her message. A few minutes before, Stan had been speaking to Richard. She saw a thin line, a thread stretching from here via Stan, to him. She so wanted to speak to him, but she couldn't trust herself if he asked her why. What could she say she hadn't already said? Last night Case had, of course, proposed to come with her to bed, but she had explained to him that, attractive as he was, she was feeling great remorse for the other night, and that she had told her lover about what had happened.

'So now he knows, let's make the most of it. What's the diff?'

'No, Case, please don't go on. I told you the score on the phone.'

'Okay. Have it your way.'

He didn't seem to be upset. There were other friends in the

pavilions; some were going, some were coming. These expensive bodies were always in flux.

'Joanna, there's something I find irresistible about you: it's this lah-di-dah cold classy bitch, who's really a sex fiend.'

'Case, what a charming recommendation.'

'And it's that voice, "what a simply charming recommendation".'

'I didn't say "simply charming". Anyway, it's all drama school. Totally fake.'

'Was that fake, the other night?'

'Please, Case.'

'Okay. Okay.'

Case had shown her round the property. It had once been the site of a Danish sugar mill. He seemed unclear about the history, but anyway it was way back when. Because the old mill still stood, made of curious blue flint blocks which he said were called 'blue bitch', he had been able to develop the place in this Indonesian/ Colonial style.

'Weren't they Dutch, in Indonesia?'

'Dutch, Danish, same difference.'

All around was forest, and he had two beaches of his own. The pavilions each had a terrace and a small pool. The walkway down to the main building – the longhouse – where meals were taken, was through a jungle of trees and lianas and giant ferns. Butterflies as big as pancakes flapped slowly there, weighed down by the richness of their decoration, like cardinals on a feast day. The blueness of the sea was occasionally broken by expensive white yachts, which arrived suddenly and vanished just as suddenly, although when she'd looked at them for any length of time they appeared to be going very slowly.

Was she a sex fiend? In Case's world, things were quite simple. He made a virtue of a certain shallowness of understanding. His views were eclectic, gathered in the clubs he frequented, on film sets and from television and magazines. Her father had had the military man's sense that the world was increasingly lacking in rigour. Perhaps he was right. And Richard believed that the appearance of things in public life was becoming more important than the substance. Yet how could you argue with Case's uncomplicated enjoyment of the material world? Maybe there was a new type of world which most people already lived in, a world which was there not for duty or sacrifice or – a butterfly marked like a silk chasuble flopped onto the soap dish for a moment – self-sacrifice, but a world simply of gratification. And sex, of course, was the simplest form of gratification for Case. He was extraordinary-looking, with widely spaced brown eyes which suggested some Native American blood; his hair was wheat blond and thick; his skin was a deep brown and his lips were slightly pink. Close up, his skin was minutely pitted. He was lean, so that his body felt sharp and uncomfortable. She had no desire for him. Instead, deep inside her body, she missed Richard. If it was true that she was a sex fiend, it was nothing to do with the mechanics, but with this almost unbearable desire to be close to Richard, to become, as he had said, one person. You couldn't explain this to Case, perhaps not to anyone, except Richard. She would ring him. She had to, even if she was going to be humiliated.

She wrapped herself loosely in a sarong. She lay on the bed, a

Japanese arrangement with a huge bolster, and dialled his number.
She waited for him, her love, her life, to answer.

'Hello?'

'It's me.'

'I'm glad you rang.'

'Where are you?'

'I'm in my father's flat in the bath.'

'Are you speaking to me?'

'I am. Of course I am, but I feel very hurt. I have to tell you
that honestly.'

'Was the funeral terrible for you?'

'No, it wasn't too bad. He's buried near the river in the old
churchyard. Your mother came.'

'My God, why?'

'She came to tell me how sorry she was.'

'How is she?'

'She seems okay, she says she doesn't know where you are.
Where are you?'

'I'm in the Virgin Islands.'

'Is it nice?'

'It is.'

'Are you alone?'

'Richard, whatever happened, however I regret it, however it
has hurt you, please believe me that there's nobody but you. I
love you. My whole body, my soul is aching for you. Please
Richard. Please Richard, I beg you, try to forgive me. It was
nothing, nothing at all. Just a horrible mistake. Please, please
darling, love me. When you're ready, I beg you.'

'I feel almost dead.'

'I can't imagine how I would feel if it happened to me. Just try to believe me when I say I love you.'

From the spaces between his words, she knew he was suffering.

'I can't love you. Not at the moment. I feel awful bitterness.'

'Please Richard. Don't say that. Please my darling. Will you try? I can't bear the thought that you hate me.'

'I don't hate you. Of course I don't. Of course I don't.'

Now she was crying, choking with misery.

'You're crying,' he said.

She couldn't speak.

'Joanna.'

'I can't bear it, Richard. Just say you love me. Lie to me.'

'I can't say it. I want to say it, but I can't.'

'Please, Richard.'

'You've killed something. It's dead. My father's dead. I'm just as dead.'

'Don't blame me. I can't bear it. Forgive me.'

'I can't. It's not a question of forgiveness. All I can think is that I have lost my faith. To the bottom of my heart or my being or whatever, I loved you. I wish it could, but it can't be the same. It's gone.'

'Don't say that, Richard. Don't say that.'

'It's the truth.'

They couldn't speak any more, except for a few words which guttered before the conversation died.

This is worse, this is worse than not speaking to him, she thought. At least before she spoke to him she could nurse the hope that he loved her and would forgive her. She could hope that by abasing herself, he would realise she loved him. But now he was saying that something was dead. That something was love.

She walked down through the forest to the beach, and lay face down on the sand which was white and crunchy with colourful highlights.

It is early in the morning that I saw him coming, she whispered, her warm breath causing a small crab to bury itself in the laundered, minutely faceted grains of sand.

> Going along the road on the back of a horse;
> He did not come to me; he made nothing of me;
> And it is on my way home that I cried my fill.

Richard said that he had lost his faith:

> It was you that put darkness over my life
> You have taken the east from me; you have taken the west
>   from me,
> You have taken what is before me and what is behind me;
> You have taken the moon, you have taken the sun
>   from me,
> And my fear is great that you have taken God from
>   me.

Now she realised that in her anguish, she had not really asked him about his own father. She wanted to call again, to say how thoughtless she had been. But she couldn't bear to hear him tell her again that she had put darkness over his life.

18

Talfryn brought the news all the way down to the cottage himself. Richard wondered how the Prime Minister could spare him for these missions. Perhaps he wanted Talfryn's personal observations about his state of mind. Not that Talfryn's state of mind was too good. Things weren't going well for the Government, and he was discovering every day what Richard had long known, that politics is about as susceptible to control as marsh gas.

Richard had just been riding out in the forest, which was recoiling from the summer sun. The streams were barely trickles and the deep hollows of fern and bracken were lifeless. Most of the year the whole place seeped and wept, but now it was squeezed dry, like the loofahs by his father's bath.

Mimosa was eager as ever. Like barmaids, mares have a professionally flirtatious manner. He had ridden out every day now for the past week, and she approached each outing with eagerness, as though she were expecting a romantic encounter. He drove back from the stables to find Talfryn sitting on his old sofa, reading a book.

'Talfryn. I have a strange thought: if this was a film I'd have to ask you what you're doing here. But as it's you, there's no need.'

'I haven't read a whole book for nearly two years. I used to think I didn't know what I thought until I read it. Now I realise that I don't know what I think until I've said it.'

'Or until the Prime Minister has said it. Can he spare you the time to catch up on literature?'

'Everybody always says what a super bloke you are. I've begun to realise that you can be quite a vicious bastard too.'

'I like the way you say "super bloke". It's like a tug hooting. It's great to see you, whatever you're here for. Have a drink.'

'Just coffee.'

Richard delayed the uninvited conversation by milling some raucous coffee beans to fill the pot from the Algerian Coffee Store and then placing the pot on the stove. He liked the freshly released smell of the ground beans as much as the coffee itself. Talfryn was leafing through the book nervously. He had lost the habit of taking any time. In Downing Street he liked to say, in mock complaint, that he was wired.

Richard was wearing jeans and brown jodhpur boots. He was conscious, as he carried the coffee over, that he must look detached.

'Smells good,' said Talfryn. 'You look happy and relaxed.'

'I'm trying. How about you?'

'Oh, the fucking teachers stabbed us in the back, the fucking nurses are threatening to turn off incubators and the fucking rail operators are arseholes, but otherwise everything's hunky-dory. How's the manifesto? We need help.'

'It's coming on. I got a little bogged down on our commitment to eliminate bullying in schools, but I've found a way round it. We're going to give children of less than average size and weight a can of Mace at the beginning of each term. Why are you here?'

'God, I miss you. So does the Prime Minister. He wants you back.'

'Thank you. Will that be all?'

''Fraid not. There's a few more things.'

'Oh yes?'

'You know the chappie who stabbed you, Carl Panky? It turns out it wasn't so random after all. He was trying to kill you. He's a member of the BNP with quite a long record of violence. He's a football hooligan in his spare time, but it was just chance that you were sitting in front of him.'

'Why did he want to kill me?'

'Because apparently you're a left-wing poofter who likes black people.'

'That's all of us, isn't it?'

'Yes, but you had his cousin locked up.'

'Who is his cousin?'

'He's a man called Denny Tongle.'

'Oh yes. He hit one of my constituents with a tyre-iron.'

'A black constituent.'

'Yes.'

'According to Tongle, it was just a little argument, but you gave evidence against him. Because you are an MP, the police banged him up.'

'He hit a sixty-four-year-old man on the head with a tyre-iron because he hooted at him when he stopped his van suddenly on a double yellow. I was travelling along behind.'

'You may have saved your constituent's life.'

'I doubt it.'

'Anyway, questions of bravery aside, the Tongle–Panky clan have been harbouring a grudge, and when Carl Panky saw you at Wembley, and when you told him to shut the fuck up, the red mist came over him.'

'So?'

'So now there's no question of giving him a lesser charge, he's going to be tried for attempted murder.'

'Which means that I'll be required to go to court and the whole bloody business will start up again.'

'There's not much evidence you can give. But yes, you will have to give it.'

'I don't want to do it.'

'You'll have to.'

'I'll have to if the case is brought.'

'The case will be brought. Obvious reasons.'

'Because he's a racist.'

'Yes. We can't afford to look less than determined. Nor can the police. Not if we're going to have to call the election before the end of the year.'

Richard felt an awful heaviness. His soul dragged. For the past week he'd been trying to live in this darkness in a limited way, like a mole or perhaps some nocturnal creature, and he was beginning to rid himself of the numbness he felt.

Talfryn knew the weight of the news he had brought: 'I'm sorry, Rich, I know you wanted to forget. It's going to be in the papers tomorrow, so I had to come.'

He wasn't forgetting. Instead he had been playing so many moments over and over, and then he had been torturing himself with the thought of Joanna with Case Stipe. He had wondered a hundred times if she had uttered those little cries which to him had sounded like primitive poetry, and worse still, if she had clung tightly to Case Stipe in the night. He had told himself, by force of will, that sooner or later he would grow tired of this dialogue with the unknowable. The human brain is set up to find answers and it would despair of this futile enquiry. Jealousy was utterly unworthy and destructive. He had tried many times to see it from another point of view, as if he were a friend of the parties involved: she, lonely in New York, foolishly taking some drugs, caught up momentarily in Case Stipe's world. It was just a one-night stand. But a one-night stand suggested a kind of heedlessness which gave him more pain.

'Talfryn, I'm not in good shape.'

'Joanna, I suppose.'

'Yes. I've taken it badly. When you first told me the rumours, I didn't believe them.'

'You'll get over it.'

'My friend Igor says everything passes.'

'And your father dying.'

'And that.'

Out in the forest he had a kinship with the leaves and the brackens, and even the streams. It was a vegetable and mineral relationship. He conversed with the horse in warm tones, appreciative of her good-hearted vitality. He had begun to see himself as part of this world, the primitive world of organisms. His father had joined that world too, although of course the spark which made disparate organisms one life had left him. It was strangely cheering to find himself a member of this society: he was operating on a very low level, without pretension. He thought that in this way, riding out, chatting to the horse, allowing the leafy world to whisper to him, he would be re-entering life, by an overgrown path. What Igor had said may not have been absolutely true, but it contained a truth, that life was relentlessly present. Nothing died for ever, although in the dark hours he felt a dreadful numbness of his soul (or his heart). Now they wanted him to go to court to be cross-examined; the court where every human subtlety and ambivalence was derided and he would be lined up against the goose-bumped, home-grown Nazi, Carl Panky, in a show trial. Riding in the forest he saw, too, that much of politics was a kind of ritual into which they were locked as tightly as the cardinals of the Vatican. In politics there was no such thing as rational thought: all was blind ritual and prejudice and antipathy, dressed up in the clapped-out language of public interest.

The public interest – also the up-coming election – demanded that he confront the deluded half-wit who had stuck a knife into his neck.

'We were in Vienna the day of your dad's funeral.'

'I know.'

'The Prime Minister was upset.'

'Do you have difficulty using his name these days?'

'It's a strange thing, but I have gone from his first name to "Prime Minister" gradually, even to friends, and now I can't go back. It's almost superstitious.'

'Maybe it's religious. It's an invocation. Shri Rama Krishna used to say God and his name are identical, and Nicephorus the hermit practised nothing but invocation of the name of God for forty years.'

'Are you okay?'

'Are you here on a psychological mission?'

'Partly.'

'Why?'

'The Prime Minister has asked me to tell you that he wants you as his deputy after the election. John has had enough and the Prime Minister wants you. You have the necessary people skills.'

He had the sense to say 'people skills' with a little extra emphasis for ironic effect.

'I haven't spoken to anyone but my horse for a week. Are you sure I'm the right person?'

'I'm not sure. But he is.'

'Talfryn, you know I don't want to go on.'

'I do, but he wants you to. If you go, he believes it will look as though all the idealism and faith are going.'

'They are.'

'Oh Jesus.'

'Talfryn, Enoch Powell may have been an arsehole, but when he said all political careers end in failure, he was right. You didn't believe it, but I always did. Politics casts a retrospective gloom, like adultery, as someone said.'

'You're so fucking clever, I sometimes wonder how you can be so normal. Apparently normal.'

Richard took Talfryn's arm in his hand.

'If I am so fucking clever, how is it that I can't work out what happened to me? It's not as though I'm the first person to be . . . to be in this situation.'

'We've all been there.'

To Richard it wasn't comprehensible. When Stan Blumberg, Joanna's agent, rang him, he implied that Joanna's feelings were of a special order, exalted above those of ordinary people. Maybe in his own way, he thought his emotions were uniquely important too.

'I know,' he said, 'I'm being boring. Self-obsessed.'

'I'll be going. No answer is expected immediately. Your secretary says that the constituency would like to hear from you sometime.'

'Oh shit. I had almost forgotten them.'

'That's what they're implying. Keep in touch.'

'All right.'

'Don't be alarmed if you see the occasional policeman hiding behind a bush.'

'Witness protection?'

'You could be a heartbeat away from Prime Minister in a few months.'

'Don't be ridiculous.'

'Can we let it be known that you and Joanna have split up?'

'Talfryn, we were getting on so well. Don't fuck it up. Don't try to turn everything into a favourable story. Not my life, anyway. Okay?'

'Okay. Have fun. And when you're communing with the squirrels, give thought to what I said, please. The Prime Minister expects an answer. He loves you.'

Everybody loves me, apparently.

He sat down in an unsettled state with Major Dick's papers.

The Colonel described giving a demonstration of modern horse-breaking to an appreciative audience of Baden-Powell's officers. He told of a conversation in Dixon's hotel after the horse-breaking, which concerned the future treatment of the Boers. Major Dick said that the Boers had been unfairly treated, and found that most of the officers agreed with him, although they thought that the Boer was 'excessively harsh with the darkies'. Baden-Powell believed that the Boer pony, a small tough animal, held the key to the duration of the war. The Colonel wanted to introduce his own irregulars, similarly mounted. He was also forming a group of boys in the town to carry messages. In a footnote, Major Dick added that one of these boy scouts was killed by a shell in December. Major Dick escaped from the besieged town on his best horse during a thunderstorm. It was surprisingly straightforward, until just before he found Plumer's forces on the border, when the horse died of a heart attack. Major Dick walked the last mile or two, carrying his saddle.

'Brave horse. Died for his country. I saluted it.' He had built a small memorial to it later, he wrote.

After his solitude, Richard found that the distinctions between past and present, between the imagined and the real, were becoming less obvious, certainly less important. When he was teaching a course on the political thought of Oliver Cromwell, he found that after a time he could read Cromwell's letters and speeches without having to take into account the vagaries of seventeenth-century language; he was so used to Cromwell, to his letters and his turns of phrase and his biblical metaphors, that he might have been reading a letter from his brother Tim. There were no secrets between him and Cromwell.

When he was out in the forest, these barriers between the human and the animal and the plant worlds seemed to him less clear too. As he thought of Major Dick riding away from Mafeking and as he sat here reading Major Dick's often ridiculous sentiments and commentaries, he saw that all human endeavour, viewed from this fluid perspective, is insubstantial and ephemeral. *Tout passe.* That's what it really means: everything becomes nothing. What he had foolishly believed would last, his love for Joanna, had suffered the same fate.

His mind was disordered. Had Talfryn really offered him the prospect of becoming Deputy Prime Minister? Apparently he had, but they also wanted him to go to court to see Carl Panky. Panky wouldn't be allowed to draw as a defence on the deep wells of myth which had made him. What if Panky's barrister knew that Richard's own forebear used the term 'darkies'? What if his barrister explained that myth and superstition and antipathy had not been eliminated, and never would be, and that Carl Panky represented nothing more sinister than a branch line of English history. And the chief prosecution witness, the man who had been stabbed with a Stanley knife, knew enough about the way things are arranged to feel guilty for having triggered Panky, because he should have known that Panky was powerless to resist when he had told him to fucking well shut up. And, come to that, how did Talfryn know his words?

Would you shut the fuck up?

He thought of his own father, so freshly buried, and Joanna's father, out there in the Falklands. The richness of confusion and conceit and chance – his own stabbing was a case in point – would never end. Likewise, the business of love with its mixture, its ready-mix, of infinite happiness and certain despair, would be engaged in for ever too, the candidates believing, like him, that they were not subject to the rules. Perhaps he could get used to the idea of having Joanna back, bruised and imperfect though their love would be. But then he saw strings of semen, like white roe, on her breasts, and her mouth bruised and avid, and he laid his head down on Major Dick's papers in anguish. From the papers came, he imagined, a faint smell of Mafeking, cinders and wood smoke and horses.

That was it. Jealousy came down to the single, terrible image that his Joanna was smeared with another man's semen. He felt that he could easily kill. He was no different from Carl Panky. His mind was racing. He understood what that cliché meant now: his brain was unable to settle for a moment, before it was off on another chase, like a mad person ransacking a house and flinging open the cupboards in search of something. In this case images of Joanna, garlanded with frog spawn.

But it eased. The skittering brain tired itself. He began to see that Joanna had done nothing very unusual in the broad range of human peculiarity. Perhaps what was unusual was that she felt compelled to tell him. But then maybe that was because, as weary Stan had suggested, her feelings were of a higher order, stamped, like so many of the papers he had to read, PRIORITY. He would have her back. He needed a few more weeks, as his mind settled under this regime of riding and writing Major Dick's story.

He walked into the village to collect the papers from the small

253

store. A woman called Iris worked there, selling stamps, biscuits and drinks. She spent a lot of her time reading and arranging the greeting cards, which featured dogs and horse-shoes and bunches of flowers. She was reaching into the cabinet where the ice creams lived, close to the frozen peas, and Richard saw her hips outlined by the checked housecoat. She had an intensely feminine bottom, like two peach halves, and a short thick waist. Her legs were appropriately stout, solid and practical. She turned to him with her rustic weathered smile: her face was puckered by a chronic but cheerful puzzlement. She had the papers ready. He wondered about female shapes. Joanna was tall, slim, with narrow hips, yet here was this little woman built to last, built for the life of a woman, perhaps better equipped in every way than Joanna. But he could never have loved someone made like Iris, and he felt guilty, as she enquired about his health and speculated about the weather. He felt uneasy about the gulf between him and his fellow countrymen and women. He really had no idea about life in those rows of houses in every town in England, houses he only visited at election time, and which he saw only from the outer limits of their small hallways. You could tell something mysterious was going on in there, the television usually on, the smells of cooking, sometimes a glimpse of sexual disarray, or truculent, blotchy children. These glimpses were like television films of rare and elusive people in the deep jungle. Their inner lives impenetrable to him, the Honourable Member for Smallfield.

'Mr Jeremy was asking after you.'

'Did you tell him where I was?'

'Yes, I did. I couldn't say no, could I? I thought I should tell you.'

'Thank you.'

'How is Miss Jermyn, if you don't mind me asking?'

'She's working on a film in America.'

'Lovely girl. She used to come in here as natural as you like.'

'Thanks for the papers.'

He walked towards the farm, and round towards Jeremy's and Joanna's house. The 'For Sale' sign read 'Sold', but Jeremy's car was outside. He knocked on the door, and Jeremy opened it. Jeremy was wearing a dark polo-neck and his hair was short. It was a theatrical look, which expressed the belief that the theatre, for all its artifice, was close to the street. His skin had a dryness which Richard thought might be the result of some inner contradictions. The skin was a strangely sensitive wrapping for the body in its complicated workings (which in turn was the prison house of the soul, of course). As they shook hands, Richard could see small flakes of skin assembled like lemmings above Jeremy's combative eyes, and feel his parched cold little hands.

'You were asking after me?'

'Yes, I asked Iris if you were about. Your phone is off.'

'Here I am.'

'The house is sold. I wanted to say a couple of things to you.'

'Why?'

'Because you and I were friends.'

Richard wondered if this was true. He had always seen Jeremy in that English way, as an acquaintance who would never become a friend. It was nothing to do with Joanna; it was just that he had never felt any affection for Jeremy at all. There was no

255

human warmth or understanding, as if they were from different orders of life.

'Go ahead.'

'Are you all right?' asked Jeremy.

'Yes. Why?'

'Why? Because I imagine you are suffering. I tried to warn you, actresses are from another planet.'

'What are you getting at?'

'I mean the fact that she is living with Case Stipe.'

'Where?'

'At his house in the Virgin Islands.'

'Jeremy, I can't discuss this with you.'

'I just wanted to say that I don't blame you for what happened. I don't think she can help herself. It's something I've seen with . . .'

'No, Jeremy. I've got to go.'

'Whatever.'

He walked away from the proffered confidences and sympathy and turned his back on Jeremy's invitation to join the brotherhood of cuckolds. He had read in *The Sunday Times* that Jeremy was writing a play about the relationship of the poetic imagination to the new physics. He had told the interviewer that as the big knowledge increased, the creative people must fight their corner. There were different truths. The creative imagination was just as important to scientific knowledge. Jeremy was right; an understanding of natural laws could never equip you to deal with the really big question, which was mortality and its stooge, love. As he walked, more or less aimlessly, he saw again, so clearly, that to lose what you love is to lose your humanity. You didn't die all at once, as most people supposed. And then he thought about Jeremy's play; he couldn't control his mind: a professor of physics, book-lined study in Oxford, beautiful young American graduate student, interested in love poetry, comes to visit. The prof is smitten. He forgets the laws of physics, particularly the one that relates to levers, and we have three comic, but tragic acts where love and indifference, theory and reality, sensibility and rationality are contrasted in that fetching, Stoppardian manner: Jeremy in his new reflective mood, trying hopelessly to emulate Stoppard's lightness.

The Virgin Islands with Case Stipe. Stan had said that she was at the resort, and she had said: 'Just say you love me, Richard,' and of course he loved her but he had said: 'I can't say it,' and all the time she was with Case Stipe. As Stan had suggested, she belonged to another order. These icons, these necessary figures, were probably subject to a kind of gravitational force that draws them together. The real world presents too many problems for them, so they aggregate according to a natural law – a law of physics – into a solar system. After all, they are called stars.

He walked all the way to the stables to see Mimosa, who was bedded down comfortably, her nose in a feed bucket which the stable girl, Jenny, had just given her. Jenny didn't seem surprised to see him. She loved horses herself at some inexpressible level, so it was not odd to her that he should spend half an hour in Mimosa's stall, listening to the crunching of the cubes, the slurping in the plastic bucket and the impatient stamps of the hooves; hearing the occasional low whinny in response to other horses, the snorts and the vegetable exhalations, the equine murmurs; watching the eager but easily bored head burrowing,

257

the restless pricked ears and the thick greasy tail; and stroking her neck, so sleek compared to the pockmarked little Mafeking ponies, descendants no doubt of the Boer ponies Baden-Powell admired, and he could hear now Baden-Powell singing, 'Chin, chin, Chinaman, Muchee muchee sad,' and he could hear Joanna moaning softly in the night with happiness, and he could hear Carl Panky whispering, 'You're a posh cunt, aintcher?'

Jenny came into the stall.

'Orright?'

He was sitting in the bedding. She sat next to him. She was large and awkward, and she contained all the fragrances of straw and horse feed and hay, but her hands were strong and warm with human feeling, as Jeremy's were dry and barren.

He lay in his cottage. Her farm fragrances were still on him. He didn't think of this as levelling the score, or anything as crude as that. Instead he saw himself as accepting the new landscape of his life, having sex with this kind, elemental girl, right there with the horse only mildly interested. It was natural and unexceptionable. She had wiped herself with the back of her hand and said: 'Ooh, that was nice.' Nice. Yes. He felt a calmness which he'd been missing. He also saw that what Joanna had done was not so terrible. The brain, too, is governed by physical laws.

19

Joanna's first scene was to have had her riding a horse as the sun set on the Camelback, a jagged red mountain which rose around the low, spacious houses of Phoenix. It looked as though it might have dropped from space in earlier aeons. Twice she'd been out on the horse, because she thought it was important to look natural and relaxed while riding. The horse was called Big Red and he was handled by the senior wrangler on the picture, Rocky d'Angelo. But the filming was cancelled. Case had changed his mind again: some of his lines had been rewritten at the last minute, and his agent had passed on his client's regrets. His contract had been breached and he would not be showing up for the first day of principal photography until writers appointed by him had reworked the script.

The producers, including Mike Berkovsky, were anxiously checking their insurance policies and consulting their lawyers. Other actors were being approached in secret. Berkovsky said it might be a blessing in disguise: Case's drug problem had made him unprofessional. After just a few days of lighting tests and wardrobe calls and all the other preliminaries, she was free to go while they got the picture back on the rails, as Berkovsky put it. The insurance was allowing them a ten-week break for this purpose.

Joanna rang Stan and arranged to fly back to London: she would start at the Almeida as soon as they were ready. The day before she left, she went for a ride out in the desert on Big Red. A rattlesnake reared up as they passed; the horse shied and she fell off, bruising her arm badly. As she was falling she thought, 'I am going to be bitten by a rattlesnake,' but the snake had hurried off into the spiny undergrowth. Berkovsky was choked with rage at the wrangler. All his anger over Case Stipe's treachery was directed at Rocky d'Angelo. He shouted, he summoned three doctors, he poked d'Angelo's chest with a stubby, white finger; a blood vessel stood out on his head.

'I'm okay, Mike, don't get your knickers in a twist. I asked Rocky to take me in the desert. I'll be fine,' said Joanna.

'You may have asked this schmuck to take you in the desert, but the terms of his employment and your insurance expressly forbid it. If you'd hurt yourself more seriously, we could have kissed goodbye to twenty-seven million and then some, and all because this backwoods cowboy, this fucking hick-town Romeo wanted to go riding with a star. Jesus.'

'Sorry Mr Berkovsky. A snake got up.'

'Fuck the snake, and fuck you. Load your trailer and get your dog-food horses off this lot. Goodbye, you won't be needed when we start again. That's an A-I fucking guarantee.'

Joanna was impressed by the intensity of his vehemence. No doubt back where he started, in the Brooklyn school of hard knocks, it was standard: as the cowboy loped off, light showing between his legs, Berkovsky wiped his brow. He was wearing a Western shirt with one of those bootlace ties and a silver clasp around the neck. But it didn't work for him. His shape was ineradicably urban. Joanna knew that behind his anger was a kind of jealousy. She was given a sling to wear, but advised to use her arm as much as possible. She was driven back to her rented house in Scottsdale.

Case Stipe had left the house in St John after two days. His wanderings were in response to migratory calls, inaudible to Joanna, but which he had to obey. A party in LA, somebody's new yacht in Saint Croix, a gallery opening in New York. The calls reached him in mysterious ways and he was off. She had spent a few more days in luxurious solitude, walking in the clamorous forest and reading on the perfect beach. One morning early she had seen a man removing unsightly debris which had washed up in the night, plastic bottles and nylon rope, but leaving interesting objets trouvés, a piece of driftwood and an old paddle.

Jeremy had found her here. He had just enough clout to talk to important agents and producers. He seemed to be adopting a more sagacious mood, deliberately. The contracts had been exchanged now, he said. He was starting a play, about the new physics, which he had had to read up. It was a learning experience for him. It was a tender love story as well, a Cambridge professor and a PhD student from America, but essentially it was about asymmetry.

'Like us,' she said. 'Jeremy, why have you rung?'

'Just to tell you that the house was finally, finally sold. And to see how you are. You've had a bumpy ride, I hear.'

'Meaning?'

'Meaning that you seem to have been, how can I put this delicately, out and about.'

'I haven't been out and about, whatever that means. It's all nonsense.'

'You are in Case Stipe's house, aren't you?'

'Case isn't here.'

'No, he left yesterday.'

'What are you suggesting?'

'Does Richard know where you are?'

'Richard won't talk to me.'

'Why not? Does he believe the stories?'

'Jeremy, please. It's not easy for you either, but please don't root about in this. Do you promise?'

'All right. I've realised I don't have any life except my work, so I don't want any *Sturm und Drang* either. I just want to move on. The lawyers say it's only going to take a few months.'

'I'm sorry, Jeremy, I am.'

'That's okay. When the dust has settled, and all that?'

'I hope so.'

'Richard's going to give evidence. The little fascist who stabbed him is being tried for attempted murder.'

Jeremy was a connoisseur of injustice and intolerance in society. He said 'fascist' with all the relish of a wine bore saying 'Pauillac'.

'He's being protected,' he added.

She was on her own for three nights although strangers came and went, people who knew Case or knew people Case knew. In her forest pavilion she lay awake. There were tree frogs which whistled, and sometimes she could see the swift movement of bats beyond the screens which covered the windows at night.

The snipe were speaking of you.

She tried to call Richard once more, but his phone numbers were dead. Maybe it was true that he was being protected.

Then she thought of trying his cottage on the off chance. A girl answered, 'I'm afraid he's gone up to London.'

'Who are you?'

'I'm just the stable girl. I'm waiting for the oil man to deliver.'

'Are you going to see Mr McAllister?'

'I'm not sure. He didn't say when he would be back.'

'All right. Just tell him Joanna rang, if you get a chance.'

'Righty-o. I'll tell him.'

Her accent was rural: 'Rye-ee-oh oill tellem.'

Now in her huge unused house in Arizona, which was in the grounds of a country club, she was packing her things one-handed in a troubled state, when Case rang. He tried to explain why it was important to his integrity, as an actor and also as an individual, to stand up for his space. She said it was only a question of five or six lines and they were no worse: 'the bland leading the bland', she said. But he wasn't listening. He was thinking of pulling out altogether, as a statement.

'What are you stating? And what about the rest of us?'

'That would be the one thing which would deter me right now. Hey, I heard you fell off a horse. You okay?'

'Yes, I'm okay, just bruised. A snake frightened the horse. A rattler.'

'A rattler. Cool.'

Perhaps he was thinking of the Viper Lounge. She felt tired. 'I'm packing, Case. Because of your little wobbler I am off for ten weeks. By the way, they're talking to Tom Cruise. Don't say I told you.'

It wasn't true, but she felt he deserved some angst. He had probably forgotten their night in New York already. She hoped he had. The photographs had never been printed, thanks to the action taken by Richard's friends, but she wondered how long it would be before they appeared somewhere.

It was difficult to pack one-handed. She would wait for the maid. She went to swim in her enormous swimming pool, whose depths had those Hockney refractions. She couldn't raise her left arm above the water, but paddling about was pleasant. In ten weeks' time the temperature around here would be unbearable. They must know that. Even now as the sun prepared to set behind Camelback, it was nearly ninety degrees. She had the feeling this picture was doomed. Old actors – particularly the ones who did no film work – talked of theatre as real acting. She was looking forward to her run at the Almeida, face to face with people, real acting.

Jeremy had claimed that he had no life outside his work. She thought that something similar could be said of her, perhaps of all actors, that they are only fully alive in the process of acting.

In the artful garden of rocks and cacti, there were lizards which operated on a similar principle: without the sun their metabolism slowed. A large lizard with a sort of coxscomb of a mussel-shell blueness was even now craning towards the sun from the peak of one of the carefully placed stones. She saw in this a little example of the implacable nature of physics (in which Jeremy was now dabbling): the sun's heat, the chemical reaction in the body of this low life, the inevitable dying of the cells, the doomed, but unconscious struggle. Oh Jesus, my mind is disordered. She wanted Richard's body next to hers so that she could continue the process of exchanging – she could barely articulate the thought – their essences. This would be chemistry, or perhaps bio-chemistry, but in that loose molecular embrace, love was contained. Jeremy probably thought he was making a good shot of reconciling poetry and science, physics and emotions, but the truth was that love, whatever natural laws governed it, was beyond comprehension, a glimpse of eternity.

The lizard, in response to the profound, if intractable, thoughts that were wracking her, lowered its head as the sun dipped and moved off to hoard the energy it had gathered through the sinister umbrella fragment on its head, now furled.

I am floating on this blue blank swimming pool, breathing desert air, watching a lizard, but I wish to be in Richard's damp cottage, where the tulips I gave him a week ago are collapsing gracefully, and the light is filtered through muslin.

I'm a star and I am dying of loneliness. How can this be?

It was less than three weeks since she had last seen him. But a lifetime had passed.

20

Prime ministers and presidents always age in office. Contrary forces are at work – the embalming effects of power, the emollience of celebrity – but the days without respite, the months without sleep, the years without the relaxation of idleness, inevitably leave their mark like the effects of wind and water on the surface of the earth. Nobody could imagine what it was like to have not a second in a day, not a particle or a scintilla of time you could call your own. Richard thought that true relaxation, which he knew riding in the forest or reading at night, consisted of being without purpose, or doing without aim. It was what Nicephorus the hermit sought. Richard had read a book recently in which the last hermit in the Middle East, as he described himself, said that it was a tough life; so even there serenity was hard to come by.

The Prime Minister was about to dismiss him, but he wanted to explain himself to Richard, to rehearse his philosophy, before he came to the task in hand. His face showed the signs of physical strain, but also the coursing energy of his eminence. His skin was tired, but his eyes were fervid. His hair had lost its vitality, but his gestures had quickened, as though he could save time by moving faster through the motor actions, like raising a cup and making notes. Richard had entered Downing Street by the

Cabinet Office. He had been shepherded all the way by Talfryn, perhaps a little too intimately, the way police officers like to have close physical contact with the arrested. But Talfryn was excluded from this final moment.

Carl Panky sat in the dock, wearing a suit which, had he understood judges and barristers and the sort of people who had charge of English law, he would have realised was a mistake. It had small lapels and far too many buttons, and it was too new. When Richard had seen him last, he was wearing a short-sleeved England football shirt, bearing the three heroic lions, and in his ears large solid rings were gleaming. They had gone now. That night he was wearing his native dress; today he seemed to be in costume.

'The point about politics, Rich, is that you have to understand how it works. It's no use having good intentions and some sort of vision unless you can bring it about. You know that. We discussed it a thousand times. This is the great paradox we're up against. We're trying to make a difference, but the press and media in general don't care. They have become completely, insanely, preoccupied with personality. They have come to believe that they, in some way, run the country, although of course they never have to write a manifesto or propose legislation, or balance the books. No. All they're interested in is the day-to-day, who is in and who is out of favour, who is saying things behind our backs, what our real motives are. Almost nothing we say is taken at face value: if we try to bolster the police, it's because we want to win the conservative vote, if we give the nurses more money, it's a PR exercise. But our job is to make sure that we achieve something, and to achieve something you have to have some unity of purpose, and you have to pull the right levers.'

'And I let you down.'

'You are not like other people.'

'I told you I wanted to go after the stabbing. I wasn't up to it.'

'You were up to it. You were, you are, the best minister I have. Everybody liked you. In fact you were almost as popular as me, hard as that is to believe.'

'I thought you weren't interested in popularity.'

Richard was ridiculously happy that even now at the last moment they could joke. It was a return to a state of innocence.

'I'm not interested in popularity for myself, only that a popular Prime Minister is effective; for nearly four years now we have been working ourselves into the ground, not for power or for popularity, but to make a difference. I just can't let it slip.'

Richard wondered if there was any difference between disinterested power and popularity, and the more familiar kind.

'Rich, what I can't understand is why you did it. It looks as though you wanted to make some point.'

'I wasn't making a point.'

'You know how important it is to put away this kind of racist. It's not just him, but the police, the minorities, the whole sense of public unease. There's always been this ambivalence too. You know how I feel, you just can't muck about with these issues. We have to send out the right signals. That's why I'm puzzled, and hurt, if the truth be told.'

'I couldn't do it.'

'It wasn't a question of doing anything. All you had to say was what happened.'

'I no longer know what happened.'

'This is not some Bishop Berkeley tutorial, Rich, this is just a simple identification: "Yes, that's the man."'

'I couldn't reduce it to that.'

'Oh, Richard. Richard.'

The press, the despised press, had been briefed anonymously: the Minister was suffering; he had had a form of breakdown after his stabbing, his father's death, and the end of his romance. It seemed, so close friends said, that he was suffering from a form of phobia: he had been overcome by a panic attack. His betrayal by Joanna Jermyn had left him very hurt. He was deserving of sympathy, rather than condemnation. The Prime Minister was particularly keen to stress his continued affection and support for his old friend.

Now the Prime Minister was showing him draft letters, exchanges of respects and regrets.

'That's fine, I'll sign.'

'Are you sure?'

'Yes.'

Dear Prime Minister,

It has been a pleasure and a privilege to work with you over the last four years. After my recent and widely publicised health and personal difficulties, I think the time is right for me to step down as a Minister and to leave public life. Please be in no doubt that you have my fullest support in the great endeavour on which we embarked.

Half in Love

With deep regret,
Richard.

'Are you absolutely sure about the wording?'
'I couldn't have put it better myself.'
'Oh, please.'
'I mean it.'
Richard could see that the Prime Minister was uneasy. They had embarked on a great endeavour, but Richard had jumped ship. Here in Downing Street, the Prime Minister was feeling the first chill wind of rejection, and perhaps feared increased isolation.
'Please believe me, it's not you. I signed up under a misapprehension. I didn't realise we would ever go to war.'
'What are you talking about?'
'I liked the idea of politics, but I wasn't prepared for the reality.'
'When it came to it, you didn't have the guts for it.'
The Prime Minister was looking at him coldly now. His eyes, Richard thought, had become opaque and implacable and as oily as a seabird's.
'You didn't have the guts for it. And in court you chickened out. You let me down, and you let the country down. And Valerie feels even more let down than I do.'
'I'm sorry.'

While the prosecution was outlining its case against Carl Panky, Richard was being given shelter in a room off the main corridor of the Old Bailey. He wondered why the law and dark panelling and leather-topped desks were always found in company. Who

271

decreed it? Why did lawyers like marble busts and rows of vellum-clad books, and school photographs and framed antique maps? For that matter, why did they favour expensive lace-up shoes and velvet collars on their overcoats? And where in God's law did it say that lawyers should wear pinstripes? Zebras shall wear stripes, sayeth the Lord. Not lawyers.

As he sat in the room, himself a prisoner, he knew that if he continued down this oak-panelled, tongued-and-grooved, ripely-spoken route, he would be kissing goodbye to the remains of his humanity, already tattered.

When he was called, the prosecutor asked him his name. From the press gallery he could hear the flutter of paper and he could imagine the scraping of pens magnified a thousand times. He confirmed that he had been at Wembley on the prescribed date. He confirmed that he had asked a fellow spectator to desist from shouting obscenities. 'And that person was the defendant, Mr Carl Panky?'

'I can't be sure.'

'Mr McAllister, may I repeat the question? Is Mr Carl Panky, the defendant, the person to whom you addressed your remarks?'

'I'm not sure.'

He looked at Panky, sitting with his head bowed, so that his scalp showed nacreous where the very short hair was thinning.

'Mr McAllister, you picked out the defendant to the police from photographs. You gave an affidavit — I have it here — to that effect. I ask you again. Is this the man you identified?'

'I can't be sure.'

* * *

The case collapsed. The press speculated that he might have been threatened by Panky's criminal connections. In this way he let down the Prime Minister, and his wife. The real injury was to friendship, which he regretted. Carl Panky was a nasty racist, and he should have gone down, that was clear enough. But it was impossible for Richard to explain to his old friend that there were other truths. The stabbing had left no permanent damage, apart from the scar which, like a dying battery, had almost ceased its pulsing. And of course he couldn't tell the Prime Minister that it was nothing compared to what the Egyptian writer, Naguib Mahfouz, had suffered, stabbed in the neck by an unknown fanatic and left paralysed. All because of a book he'd written in 1959. The world was irrational. That was a fact. Nor could he tell him that he had lost faith in the great endeavour, because that wouldn't have been strictly true either.

What he had always known about politics is that democracy by its very nature is not a great endeavour: it is a mechanism for tapping off the noxious gases of humanity; it is a marketplace for competing interests; it is a compromise that must be dressed up in the language of idealism in order to make people believe. Above all, it is an attempt to dignify real events and problems. The politician's job is to pretend that all this has a purpose and conforms to some natural laws. So a government's ministers, even the walking wounded, must subscribe to the notion of purpose. The Prime Minister said that good intentions were not enough, but of course the appearance of having the will as well as the good intentions was just another illusion. In the end there were forces which no government could control or predict, and these forces, in a small way, had erupted in the person of Carl Panky.

'I can't be sure.'

Carl Panky looked up; he realised that something was going on. He looked up at the judge with hope. After a brief exchange between the judge and the prosecution, the court rose and Panky was freed. Richard was hurried away past the photographers and television crews who shouted their questions to him, questions which linked him still to Joanna.

In truth he was still linked to her, but in ways they could not imagine. He woke every morning and many times in the night believing that she was there, a hand's-breadth or less away. Each time he found that she was not, he crashed downwards through clouds of gloom. He didn't mean to belittle Jenny. Far from it; he hoped that in time he might adapt himself to her. But leaving the Bailey he saw all too clearly that his interest to the world was only because of Joanna, not because he had engaged in a great enterprise and then chickened out. In politics he used to explain the distinction was clear between the conceptual and the normative. And it was this gap between the ideal and the real that political systems inhabited. In love there was only the ideal. Once love was gone, there was nothing left, nothing to take its place, except perhaps death. Yet he knew that little by little, this being the way human chemistry was organised, he would recover.

When the Prime Minister said to him: 'You have let us down,' he was wrong. He was loyal to a prior commitment, to the sense that there is no truth. What Carl Panky did in stabbing him offered no lessons in morality. Of course, this was an unacceptable way of thinking.

As he walked to the waiting taxi, Talfryn and a few lawyers forming an escort, he looked down at the wet slabs of London beneath his feet, and the reporters called to him: 'Are you going to be seeing Miss Jermyn? Joanna?'

'Where is she now?'

The BBC's legal correspondent, a bald, bearded man, asked him about the implications of the case for the Government.

'I don't believe there are any, Joshua,' he said smoothly.

As he said it, he knew that this would be his last political lie ever, except perhaps for the words of his resignation letter.

And this letter was already on its way to the papers, via the Press Office. Richard knew that the meeting had been planned so that the letters could go out in time for the morning editions and the late television news. The Prime Minister would be balancing the news with his Guildhall speech, and so diluting the effect of the resignation of his good friend. You had to know how these things worked to be effective. You had to pull the right levers. The Prime Minister offered him a curt goodbye.

Talfryn walked with him to the Cabinet Office entrance.

'Do you feel let down too?' Richard asked him.

'I'm very worried about my own state of mind, Rich, very worried indeed. I don't seem to be able to make moral judgements.'

'Have I damaged the cause?'

'The Prime Minister is hurt, but I can't really blame you. I would like to be angry, but I can't do it. Keep in touch, I'm going to miss you.'

A driver was waiting to take Richard away. Talfryn stood for a moment, forlorn, on the top step. Richard embraced him. Only one photographer was there to catch the moment as their shapes separated awkwardly. It would be in one or two papers, but not many. He was fading from view.

The car was only taking him to Victoria Station. Jenny was going to pick him up at the other end. Above the familiar skyline was the Wheel, surreally large, a domestic item inflated out of all scale. They swung past Churchill and Smuts, and the Abbey, where the Westminster schoolboys in their shiny, dowdy grey suits were setting off for home. They looked unhealthy, favouring a lank Dickensian haircut; amongst them were a minority of mysteriously glowing girls.

The train was crowded, and he had to stand at first, swaying in time, a new member of the commuter *corps de ballet*. But he found some comfort in this: just another passenger. In a few months he could have been Deputy Prime Minister; he looked at the others, all swaying, and wondered if they too could have taken different paths and made different decisions. They were tied together, by the train's movement. He felt pain for his old friend trapped there in blind Downing Street, seeing his friends and his ideals, and perhaps his hopes, floating away on tides he could not control.

Jenny would have picked up a ready meal for him. His car, which she used now, was full of bits of bandage and the overspill of horse feed. It had acquired a veterinary smell too. Horse medicines are pungent and old fashioned. At the Guildhall, dressed in a white tie, the Prime Minister would soon be glancing at his speech, as he sat down to six courses, amongst the sleek and plump.

But also Richard had the nagging feeling that what he had done, chickening out, inviting sacking, was not done out of an urge to save his soul, but as a way of reproaching Joanna: look what you've done to me. You've brought me down, you've caused me to live on ready meals amongst horse appurtenances. But he wasn't sure that there was any truth in the charge that he levelled at himself as the train lurched uncertainly and noisily south, as if it had never been this way before. He'd longed to get away from Westminster for many, many months. In those dark irrational hours, he'd asked himself if somehow he'd invited his own stabbing, in order to escape. It was an old idea, that you could court death and put yourself at risk simply by wishing it. He wasn't revelling in his reduced circumstances. No. He simply felt more at ease here, the train playing a fanfare for the common man.

Jenny was waiting. She didn't kiss him in public. She could have been no more than a driver or a groom. She didn't ask how it had gone. The world outside was of little interest to her. She started the car, and headed out of the station compound.

'Joanna rang for you.'

'When?'

'Yesterday.'

They had never discussed Joanna.

'Did she say why she rang?'

'No.'

As they moved out of the little town, down the familiar road that dipped suddenly towards the forest, he looked across at her and he saw how young she was. She was young and chubby and passive, but shrewd too.

'Nothing at all?'

'She rang, because she loves you.'

'And you?'

She didn't answer.

'Do you love me?'

'Do you love me?'

'I can't tell you exactly what you mean to me. You know I'm still half in love with Joanna.'

'Not half in love, Richard.'

She was crying softly now as she drove the aromatic car, and turned off the main road.

'It's true. I love her.'

'I don't mind. I knew. It was obvious. Honest, I don't mind.'

Her face was soft and unformed, with no hard edges or furrows for the tears to roll into, so that – he thought – they moved very smoothly down her face.

'Don't cry.'

'I knew, don't worry,' she said, 'I'm sorry I'm taking it like this. It's not fair on you.'

That night, after the Sainsbury's haddock and mashed potatoes, he drove her back to the farm where she had a room, as she asked.

'I'll look after Mimosa. Don't worry,' she said, as if he were going away.

In his own bed, alone, he missed her, but at the same time he was grateful to her for recognising the truth. She had a kind of honesty which he valued.

Half in Love

'She loves you.'

He lay in bed and read Major Dick's notes on horse management, although he wasn't sure why he felt the need. The toughest horses sent out to the Boer War were the Argentinian. Less than one per cent died en route, although this was also because it was an easier passage. Mules were next toughest: only two point seven per cent died. Major Dick hated the waste and the slaughter of horse, like Robert Graves. When he returned to the front after being wounded, Graves wrote, 'I was shocked by dead horses and mules; human corpses were all very well, but it seemed wrong for animals to be dragged into the war like this.' It was a strange thought for someone who had seen virtually all of his regiment killed.

The cottage in the depths of night was never quiet. Night birds called. The frame of the house itself creaked. The chimney whistled and sighed.

Don't worry, I'll look after Mimosa.

Jenny had vouchsafed to him, in a childish but touching fashion, her loyalty. He saw that this love of animals was a way of expressing feelings about the cruelty and volatility of the world, in a form of code. He saw that his ancestor was a closet pacifist, just as unable to realise it as Baden-Powell was unable to see that he was gay. Jenny had left him with an unmistakable message: whatever she was suffering, she wouldn't visit it on Mimosa. Now, in this creaking, heaving, sighing night, Richard felt resentment against Joanna: she had driven Jenny out; her emotional claims, her concerns were more pressing and more important. Perhaps in that female way, she had understood the situation. He wondered exactly what she had said to Jenny. They were from different orders of womanhood, and here in the deep night he wondered why women had to be locked in a struggle with their natures. In his father's realm, women had only come fully to life in the presence of men. They bloomed like those desert plants which spend the dry years disguised as stones. He remembered these women, in fact he had seen the brave survivors of that regiment at the funeral, and he had read their letters. Since his mother died, and before, he had heard his father trumpeting quietly to them, and he had seen their flanks quiver. But now there was a conflicting call to women to express themselves, to be whole people without reference to men.

In the real world — as Talfryn liked to say — he knew that it wasn't easy to be this kind of woman. There was also another kind of woman, who was elevated out of reality, plucked out of the real world, to represent some inchoate desires and ideals. It was his misfortune, perhaps his stupidity, to have fallen in love with one of these.

But in the night clamour, the country fugue, he remembered when he had met her just up the road. He remembered the first time they'd made love and she said: 'Now you've seen my famous tits,' with a giggle, and he said: 'and you've seen my completely unknown cock.' And they had laughed like children. Like water running down a drain.

He knew that love, like innocence, must pass.

21

The movie collapsed. Berkovsky called her just as she was leaving
New York for London. Her fees were guaranteed, he said, but
the studio had put the movie into turnaround. Turnaround was
the graveyard. When she first heard the word, she imagined
movies being backed up and parked like redundant war planes
in the desert.

'You fell off a horse for six hundred and fifty big ones,'
Berkovsky said, trying to sound wry and worldly. 'How's the
arm by the way?'

'It aches a little, but basically I'm fine.'

'Listen, as you know, I wanted to do this picture with you
more than anything. Please don't just forget us, will you?'

'Who's the "us", Mike?' she asked.

'Me.'

'Oh, you. How could I forget?'

'I mean it. I'll be in London in a couple of weeks, working
with some writers.'

'I'll be rehearsing. We can have lunch.'

'Okay. That would be great. I hear you're treading the
boards.'

'Yes. Shakespeare.'

'Great. The bard. That is so great.'

She knew that he wanted to say more, but also he was aware that his infatuation was ridiculous. He probably hoped that if the movie was a huge success, they'd be joined together in some way. There is always a sexual suggestiveness about film production, in an unspoken but clearly understood compact. Theatre also had its sexual subtexts, further complicated by homosexuality. When she first met Jeremy, he had a string of impressionable admirers. He had just won an award for his play about a powerful newspaper tycoon who was trying to destroy the health service.

Case was already committed to another movie, and Miklos had signed to light it. Miklos had written to her again, saying that he was now a regular attender – he said 'attendee' – at a clinic where he was clearing out his system. A lot of bad things had been flushed away. He was profoundly sorry for what had happened in New York. His handwriting was beautiful, almost Cyrillic, no doubt written with an antique Mont Blanc. As she read, she saw his Orthodox hair damp with sweat.

The dressing room was small, a space made out of a corridor. The chair and the table were mismatched. The light bulbs on the mirror were gap-toothed.

'This is it, I'm afraid,' said the assistant stage manager, an ethereal girl called Emily who wore strings of polished stones around her neck.

'It's fine. It's perfect.'

'We'll do it up next week. It'll be painted and the lights will be fixed.'

'There's no need. There's no need. I like it. I like it.'

'Kevin Spacey said it was echt.'

'It is. Very.'

For her, the scruffy dressing room, the attic clutter, the pots of Ponds Cold Cream, and even the talc in the air, were richly familiar and comforting. When she left drama school she spent nearly two years in places like this, selling tickets, helping out, serving behind the bar, and playing small parts. In an interview she had once said that when she stepped into a theatre she felt at home for the first time in her life. Her mother had been hurt. It wasn't entirely true; nothing said in interview was entirely true, partly because you blurted things out and partly because you wanted to make a good impression. In reality there had been moments of despair and depression. She had met Jeremy too soon. A year or so later, she probably wouldn't have been taken in by his tendency to turn every meeting into a seminar. She remembered him sitting in the stalls at that first read-through with the studiedly patient look on his face, and then he had launched into his own explanation of what the words meant. Apparently they were far richer in meaning than the mere utterance of them by actors suggested. The rhythms and the associations had long tendrils which went back into myth and dialect (or maybe dialectic). He was heavily under the influence of Paul Bourdieu at the time, and spoke to them of their intellectual and artistic capital, and of cultural production. It transpired that they were cultural workers.

The tea was perfect, served from a brown pot in the bar, which smelled of last night's beer and human exhalations. The theatre had a kind of raggedness. The work done here was not like the work done in pristine offices. This was an older world, the world of the voice and illusion. This was a world of emotions and sentiment. It was the closest thing to necromancy left. She was able, just by speaking words, to create intense feelings of sadness and happiness in an audience of strangers. She'd never said it, but she regarded the process, the creation of something from nothing, as sacred. It was a sacrament, a case of trans-substantiation. This was what made us human, she thought; this and love.

The rest of the cast, Emily said, were terribly pleased to be working with her. She would ensure the place was full every night; they would all be swept along by her fame. Actors are always looking ahead anxiously, their fervid eyes cast towards the distant uplands where they would finally be bathed in sunlight.

Stan had found her a flat, and Cynthia had filled it with food and flowers. This was Cynthia's area of special expertise. Jeremy wanted to meet her to talk about their finances but she couldn't face it.

Richard had vanished. She rang his brother, Tim, in Berlin and he said that he had no idea where he was. She told Tim that she was at the Almeida, opening in a few weeks. She asked him to see if Richard could call her, and left her number.

One morning early she drove down to the forest. Richard's cottage was closed up, and her old house was now occupied; there was a BMW in the drive and a children's climbing frame in the orchard. The knot garden, the entwined initials, had been replaced by lavender plants which had not yet joined up.

It is early in the morning that I saw him coming,/Going along the road on the back of a horse.

And thinking of Richard on his horse gave her the idea of going to the stables. She drove into the yard. The horses were feeding, only their strong rumps visible like hillocks above the doors. It was ten in the morning. There were no children about; some usually arrived after school. Richard told her that after his mother died, he spent all his holidays at his local stables. He was the only boy horse groupie.

'Lucky you.'

'It had its problems.'

'Like?'

'They were all after me.'

'And you?'

'I was scared of them. They were always trying to corner me.'

'You're such a liar. I bet you were as happy as a pig in shit.'

'They thought I was gay in the end, because I wouldn't kiss them all. I can still see their eager little milk teeth in my nightmares.'

She walked around the yard. The stables were labelled: Black Saladin, Trigger, Al Barak, Dapple, Marengo. She would have recognised Mimosa anyway. She had her head in a bucket, rummaging about. After a few moments, the horse turned and stuck her head over the door inquisitively. Joanna stroked her muzzle, where the whiskers were as thick as fishing line. The horse began to snort eagerly. Joanna was pleased. She wondered if in some strange equine fashion the animal recognised her, but it turned out the horse was not looking at her.

'Hello.'

'Are you the girl I spoke to on the phone?'

'Yes. Jenny.'

'Hello. I'm Joanna.'

'I know.'

She was a tall strong girl with straight brown hair, and a chubby, pretty but featureless face. It was an English face.

'I look after Mimosa,' she said.

'Where is Mr McAllister?'

'I'm not supposed to tell you, but seeing it is you, he's gone to Africa.'

Joanna watched her go into the box and pour some chopped carrots and horse nuts into a bucket.

'Has he gone for long?'

'He should be back soon.'

'If you see him, will you ask him to ring me?'

'Orright.'

Joanna started to leave, but stopped.

'Are you staying at the cottage?'

'No, I live at the farm.'

She spoke with an upward quizzical inflection as though Joanna might not have known what a farm was. The horse was an intermediary, they were able to talk a little about her welfare: she needed plenty of exercise and had a large appetite.

'I'll just write a quick note,' said Joanna, 'I'm back in London doing a play.'

'That's nice.'

Jenny went into the box and began to brush the horse. Joanna wrote a note and attached her numbers. The note simply said 'Please ring, love Joanna.' She handed it to Jenny over the stable door. Jenny's T-shirt was stained with sweat under the armpits. She put the note into the back pocket of her jeans.

'Goodbye. I just came down to see about my old house.'

'Goodbye.'

'Goodbye.'

Jenny was clucking to the horse as Joanna walked to her car, clucking and shouting in horse language.

'Good girl. There's a good girl. Tchkkk, tchkkk, tchkkk. Move your feet. C'mon. C'mon. Tchkkk, tchkkk, tchkkk.'

Richard had told her that people had been clucking at horses in this way for thousands of years. Xenophon regarded it as commonplace, and that was thousands of years ago. It was an ancient language, as old as Greek or Nabatean or Hebrew. Richard was fascinated by the collaboration of men and horses. The unbroken dependence seemed to him a beautiful thing, a kind of romance written in the margins of history. She wasn't surprised to hear that he had left politics (or been fired). But the way he had gone was disturbing. She had noticed suggestions that he lacked the necessary toughness for the job. One report in the papers said he had had an emotional breakdown. Stan was outraged at his behaviour in court. Stan thought he must have been intimidated by 'the fascist underclass'. But she knew it couldn't be that. It was more likely a certain fastidiousness. He once said, before the stabbing, that he hadn't realised that high office gave them the right to admonish and give moral guidance to the very people who had elected them. This was the closest he had ever come to criticising the Prime Minister.

'He believes in strong families, cherished by a strong community.'

'You don't?'

'Of course I do, but in my heart of hearts I'm concerned about the boundaries of sense.'

287

'What does that mean?'

'It means that a certain kind of idealism, a certain kind of language, can be dangerous. At least it's always been dangerous, as far as we can tell from history.'

'Don't knock yourself out worrying about it.'

'I won't.'

She followed the familiar road home out of the verdant countryside to the dog-eared outskirts of London. The transition was sudden from this rural dereliction, as if the countryside and the city were not related in any way. She picked her way through the squalor until suddenly the majestic river, strung with architectural palaces, opened to view. The river was full and the water had the texture of fish skin, shiny, viscous, alive.

There was a photocall at the Almeida. All the cast and the director assembled on stage, there were at least fifty photographers and journalists. She and the director stood slightly ahead of the cast, as if they were already taking a curtain call. She was asked to say a few words.

'I'm just very happy to be here. I don't want to make any big pronouncements about the theatre versus the cinema, or anything like that. But coming back to the theatre feels right to me, and I'm very grateful to Jonathan and the Almeida for giving me this chance. We have a wonderful cast, wonderful director, and of course, a wonderful play in *Antony and Cleopatra*. So it's up to us. Thank you.'

One of the journalists asked her about Richard. Had she seen him?

'To be honest, I have no idea where he is.'

'Are you hoping to see him?'

'I don't really want to talk about it. I'm sorry. I'm here to talk about our play.'

She couldn't tell them that only a few hours before she had been talking to his horse and to his new lover.

Later her mother asked her about Richard too. She had come to town for the Country Living exhibition. They met at a Tex-Mex restaurant in Islington. It was a poor choice. Her mother was confused by the menu, and the hard, loud room made her uneasy. She looked at the tequila nervously.

'There's salt on the glass.'

'That's how they drink it.'

'Why?'

'It's hot in Mexico. Probably they sweat.'

'Joanna, really.'

'Richard isn't speaking to me. He's in Africa somewhere.'

'What is he doing?'

'I'm not sure.'

'He didn't behave very well, apparently.'

'Apparently not.'

'I quite like this tequila. Once you get used to the salt it's rather nice.'

'Have another.'

'I shouldn't.'

Fine cracks had opened around her mother's eyes. Could they have opened in the few weeks she'd been away? They were like the cracks in a dried river bed. Joanna could see clearly the older woman emerging, competing with the handsome, still girlish features. There was no doubt of the eventual winner of this contest.

'And how's Jeremy?' her mother said.

'I don't know. He rang. He wants to see me to discuss things, but it makes me tired just to think about seeing him.'

'He's writing a new play. I think the title is quite catching: *This is It.* He says it's about science and love. I think he would like you to be in it. Actually, I think he'd like you to get back together.'

'You aren't here as a messenger, I suppose?'

'No, darling, of course not. I do talk to him. He has been my son-in-law for seven years. Don't be unkind.'

'Mum, I love Richard. Whatever you've read in the papers or whatever people have said about him and me, I love him. I'll always love him.'

'Don't cry, darling.'

'I can't help myself.'

'I'll order another of these tequila thingies. Don't cry. People are looking.'

'They expect actresses to be miserable. Don't worry about them, they love it.'

22

When he rang the stables to see how Mimosa had been during his absence, Jenny told him that Joanna had been looking for him.

'How long ago?'

'Last week. She came down here. She left her number and said would you ring her.'

'Thanks.'

'Do you want the number?'

'All right. Let's have it.'

He wrote it on the back of his hand.

'Are you coming down?'

'At the weekend. I've got some things to do in London.'

'All right. I'll get her ready. She's been to the farrier.'

'Thank you. Are you okay?'

'I'm fine. Thank you.'

Her voice, however, had become slightly formal, as though she were having difficulty finding the right tone. He felt a stab of pain.

'Okay, I'll see you on Saturday.'

'I may not be here, but she'll be done.'

To avoid the press he was staying at his father's flat. Tim, too, had told him that Joanna was back. Her film had folded because

Case Stipe had withdrawn and the money had followed. Tim said she was doing *Antony and Cleopatra*. It was going to be played with a post-modern twist, as if it were the making of the Elizabeth Taylor and Richard Burton film, *Cleopatra*; the whole thing was set in a film studio. It was the hottest ticket in town.

'Where have you been?' Tim asked.

'I was in Africa.'

'Doing what?'

'Nothing much. Just keeping out of the way. I took a riding safari.'

'It's probably too early to say, but what are you going to do now?'

'Timmy. A few short months ago you were writing a book and I had a job. Now you've got a job and I'm writing a book. At least I'm trying to. But don't worry, it's only about our ancestor, Major Dick. But I may go to work in Africa on horse safaris for a while.'

Nobody had known who he was. The guide, a South African, asked him after the first week if he would like to come back one day and help out. He had no idea who Richard was either. Richard said he had worked in the Ministry of Transport, but lost his job.

'Ja, well this is transport too, I suppose.'

Richard had spent two weeks in the Kalahari. The possibility of going back appealed to him; in his situation, there was something attractive about the unexpectedness.

'Timmy, how's my press been? Am I a pariah?'

'The papers seem to have bought the theory that you cracked. You were a victim of events. Your friend Talfryn Williams was putting it about eagerly. The Prime Minister feels sympathy for you: stabbing, death of your father, end of . . . Are you going to see her?'

'I don't think so, Tim. I'm trying to keep my head down. I'm going to sort out my cottage and Dad's affairs and so on and then probably go back. I'd like you to come and visit me. There are lions in the area, although I have only heard them, and antelope of all sorts. It's wonderful.'

'It sounds a little short-term, like being a chalet girl or a waiter or something.'

'It probably is. I just don't know.'

It had been cold in the Kalahari at night. A truck went ahead with tents and horse feed, and hot water was poured into canvas buckets hung from trees, so that they could shower after their day's ride by pulling a chain, sending the water cascading down. For twelve nights he had ridden across the plain, along dried watercourses and past the occasional village. The horses were tethered at night in lines behind the truck. A fire was built and a guard was set in case of lions. You could hear the lions roaring hoarsely miles away, but André, the South African, said that they had only ever had one horse killed, and that that was when the horses had broken away from the lines during a thunderstorm.

Richard found himself pouring drinks, fixing tack and giving riding tips. He enjoyed these tasks. The other guests were German and South African, and none of them knew that he had until recently been the lover of a famous actress. He set about with *Roberts Birds of South Africa*, to try to identify the partridge and guinea-fowl and doves. At night he began to be able to locate these new stars and to name them. He wasn't sure why he wanted to know. For nearly two weeks he did not see another vehicle, nor did he see an electric light. At sunset they hung storm lanterns in trees and bathed themselves in firelight. He took to visiting the horse lines two or three times at night, and sat for a while with the watchman by his fire. He was a small, thin man, apparently at least half Bushman, and he wore a huge army greatcoat. André said he had once been an army tracker. He smoked roll-ups and his eyes were yellow. For a few hours each day he slept in the back of the truck. He had an old rifle, which he stood against the nearest rock or tree. Richard wished he was able to speak to him.

On the last day they made camp by a waterhole. It was alive with small doves and sand-grouse, jockeying politely for position, so that the waterhole seemed to be crawling like the sea. That night the lions roared from a few hundred yards away and it was a thrilling sound. Elephants drank there and in the morning there were huge footprints in the mud, although nobody had seen the elephants come or go. André said the desert elephants moved like ghosts.

Richard could see that out here it would be easy to take an interest in rainfall and beetles and bird life, and – perhaps above all – working horses, serving loyally, never questioning where they were headed or why. He remembered a Jewish story: a passer-by watches the driver of an overladen cart beat a horse, which cannot pull the cart uphill. He chides the driver: 'What's the point, it's too heavy.' The driver says, 'To be a horse, that was his choice.' Major Dick had detected a certain tragic poetry, war poetry, in the doomed lives of the horses he had been responsible for.

There were times, usually just after everyone had gone to bed and Richard was sitting alone by the fire drinking coffee infused with wood smoke, when he believed he could lose himself forever out here, free of the constraints that had ruled him until recently, constraints which now seemed absurd. His thoughts were not ordered; perhaps he had suffered a sort of breakdown without realising it. Perhaps it was cowardly to hide himself away. He hadn't done it out of a sense of shame, although the *Telegraph* said that he was a disgrace, on a par with Stonehouse and more guilty than Profumo. He felt no guilt, and he felt no need to explain himself. There were many requests for interviews and articles. He didn't call back.

Sitting by the fire with jackals crying and the horses shifting and stamping in their half sleep, Richard had wondered how long it would be before he no longer missed Joanna. He wondered how the moment would be marked, the moment that he was free. He hoped that he would wake one morning without that sick emptiness. Perhaps it would never go away entirely; but, like the scar on his neck, it would fade, although in the sun the scar had now become more prominent: it was white and tender as the parchment of a lily, so that the hospital stitching stood out and it looked like the fossil imprint of a lost eight-legged insect.

Out in the Kalahari he seemed to be in a state of dreaming. His thoughts, far from logical, were circular like the passage of aortic blood. He could see what Major Dick meant, when, in a blaze of purple, he wrote: 'Camping under the star-washed sky requires a man to confront his own diminutive stature in God's creation, as if in a bold flash of revelation.' Here the night sky rested flat on the earth, so that you had the impression that the stars were not that far away, barely out of reach. Joanna had told him that the most exciting thing she had ever seen as a child was the illusion of flying in *Peter Pan*. He had seen it too, and been consumed by the urge to fly out of the window towards the theatrical stars. The stars here were equally dramatic.

Wrapped up, receiving on the gentle, cold wind the scent of the fire and the watchman's tobacco, he had the impression that the two of them were only lightly moored to the earth's surface. It was no more than a sandy crust, and compared to the extravagant and probably infinite show above and all around, it was nothing much, thinly planted, mere scratching in the dust. You needed no special knowledge to see it for what it was, a chance germination of life in this vast, unimpressionable universe. The belief that he had taken on something of Joanna's substance, and that it was lodged within him, at the cellular level, didn't seem to him unlikely in this vastness. And maybe, he was able to hope, something of him lived in Joanna. You were said to get over love, to see that in some way you had been deceived, and to return to the real world. But the truth is that love gives the illusion – if it is an illusion – that there is a more real world. That was surely why love corresponded so exactly to human longings.

He relished these thoughts – harmless thoughts – and they began to lessen the turmoil he felt when he woke two or three times in the night, sometimes sitting bolt upright. Where his great-uncle had seen God in these extravagant thoughts, brought on by the hallucinogenic properties of the landscape and the night sky, Richard saw that there was also pleasure to be taken in the inscrutability of it all, the mineral indifference. As for his memoir of Major Dick, he had begun to expand it in his mind, so that it became an account of how the limitations and virtues of the horse have influenced language and ideas. For instance, when Shakespeare wrote that Caesar and Antony could not be 'stalled together', he was thinking of stallions. Richard wondered how long horse imagery would survive or be understood. Take the evocative word 'horsepower'. What size of horse was used for the measurement?

Richard had made a small expedition before he came home. Major Dick wrote that he had erected a monument after the siege to his horse where it had died on the banks of the Lobatse River. Baden-Powell, now a General and a national hero, came to the unveiling. Major Dick had penned these words:

> Here lie the bones of my horse, Percy. He was a faithful friend to the last. This monument is dedicated to Percy and all the horses that died in loyal service of the Empire during the siege of Mafeking.

Listening to the South African's translation, the guide seemed to know exactly the spot his great-uncle had described, under a huge tree on the curve of the dry river. The tree went many years ago, he said, but the place was familiar. Baden-Powell had made a sketch, which amused the guide. André drove straight to the spot in less than an hour, and indeed there was a scattered pile of brown stones on the river bank, although the plaque had gone.

Major Dick, Baden-Powell and his aides, a few watching Africans. Horses held by uniformed grooms. Sumptuous picnic. Perhaps a bugler or two. B-P speaks. Richard cannot hear what he says: instead he hears him singing in his light tenor 'Chin, chin, Chinaman, Muchee muchee sad . . .' and he sees his great-uncle overcome with the moment ('Privately I shed a few unmanly tears') and he sees something that had been stirring in his mind for the past few years: that we are all blundering about in the dark and that we are all consoling ourselves with lies and myths. But it is the nature of the human enterprise — B-P, Major Dick, the Prime Minister, not excluded — to live as though none of this was obvious.

And worse, the dark is no less impenetrable than it has ever been. Nothing has changed since B-P and his great-uncle stood here in their shiny boots, remembering a horse.

It was clear that to pay his father's debts he would have to sell his cottage and move into the flat, which had a few years to run on the lease. His own flat, near the House of Commons, was rented. He didn't discuss paying the debts with his brother: he believed that this was his task. He estimated that once he had sold there would be a small amount of money left, enough to keep him until he had finished the book. The lawyer said that he had no obligation in law to pay the debts. In fact he recommended not admitting any obligation. But there was an obligation. He wasn't sure exactly what it was, but perhaps it was a simple matter of blood. The fact that his father had managed to spend a large amount of money on his indulgences and vanities made the obligation the stronger. Also there were some tottering old friends owed money, including two of the women whose letters he had read. He didn't care that drawing a line under his father's heedless life would impoverish him. But he was sorry that he would no longer be able to keep a horse. He decided to give Mimosa to Jenny, if she wanted her.

He visited the grave by the river and placed some late tulips in a vase. The tulips were yellow, a washed-out sulphurous yellow, the colour of his father's Royal Cologne from Trumpers. Tulips don't have much scent, but still, he thought, they might convey a reminder of Jermyn Street to whatever presence lingered down below in the London clay.

23

Joanna read that when Antony returned to Rome to marry Octavia, Cleopatra was pregnant with twins. She didn't tell Jonathan or any of the others. To her, it made some of her lines unbearably poignant, although nothing in the play suggested that Shakespeare knew of Cleopatra's pregnancy. On the first night she was thinking of these lines as she took the asp from the wicker basket.

Peace, peace. Dost thou not see my baby at my breast that sucks the nurse asleep?

The asps were real snakes — small, sleepy, black slow-worms, that were kept cold until the last moment. Tears welled in her eyes; she opened her robe on her breasts, which she had never done in rehearsal. It was a small theatre, and the audience, so close, froze. She took a second asp and applied it to the other breast (although Shakespeare specified: 'applying it to her arm'). When she sank onto the bed, a Hollywood chariot of a bed in pharaonic reds and gold, the audience too were in tears. There was horror, as the small snakes moved slowly on her punctured breasts for a moment, before they found refuge out of the light.

The critics thought that she surpassed the National's Cleopatra, and the production's evocation of Elizabeth Taylor's and Richard

Burton's drunken and chaotic love story was moving and appropriate in an age of celebrity, of which Joanna, of course, was a victim too. All fears that she was too young to be a convincing Cleopatra were forgotten. Most of the critics referred to the moment when her breasts were exposed – a *coup de théâtre*, said *The Guardian*. Jonathan offered to change the line about there being another bite on Cleopatra's arm, in the hope that she would expose herself again. He said that if she did, she would need more make-up, as Shakespeare described Cleopatra as having 'a tawny front'. One critic applauded the sly reference to the obsession with breasts in Fifties and Sixties Hollywood, where breasts had become cult objects divorced from their original purpose. Nobody knew that she was imagining carrying Richard's child as she was applying the little snakes. And there was nobody to tell.

Already there was talk of taking the production to Broadway, and of a film version. She was pleased but still she was lonely, desolate during the long day which was nothing but a blank interlude before the performance.

She rang Richard's brother, who said that Richard was back, and assured her that he had passed on the message. He promised to speak to Richard.

'I know I'm making a fool of myself,' she said, 'but I love him.'

'You're not making a fool of yourself. Believe me.'

He spoke gently, and she heard Richard's warmth in his voice.

'Please tell him.'

'I will. Congratulations on your play, by the way.'

'It's not me. I'm just the keeper of the famous tits.'

He laughed, and again she was reminded of Richard.

'Joanna, he loves you, I promise.'

'Thank you.'

Jeremy called to say he was coming to see the play. He asked her to meet him for a drink after the performance, but she refused. She knew that he would quickly find her wounds and poke his fingers in them. He said that he had almost finished his new play, *This is It*, and would welcome her opinion. She said she would read it, although she knew that he was hoping she would agree to do it. Things had changed. A few years ago, he had belittled her acting, not directly, but by his habit of suggesting a better interpretation, as if acting were done through the intelligence, which of course was his domain. The night Jeremy was in the audience she was unable to bare her breasts. But she spoke the words 'happy horse, to bear the weight of Antony' directly towards where he was sitting. The lines were amongst Shakespeare's most sexually charged, said Jonathan.

Since the news of Joanna's semi-nudity got around, the price of tickets had doubled on the black market. Richard bought two.

Now he was walking along Upper Street from the Underground with Igor. Igor was wearing a prayer shawl of hand-carded yak's wool, wound around his nose. The air in London was foul. Actually, Richard thought, the air was pleasantly savoury with the scents of pizza, mesquite wood, oregano, garlic and Thai curry. They passed a pub which was breathing hops onto the street in gusts.

Tim had said that she was in a bad way. Richard had

promised Tim that he would go to the theatre and maybe say hello afterwards.

'You must.'

'Don't play Pander, Timmy. I'm just getting over it; there's no point.'

'Are you sure you're getting over it?'

'I think so.'

It wasn't true. Deep inside him — (how banal the images of love are) — there was a longing which never went away; a sense that he had lost the use of some vital organ. But he had no wish to make the pain worse. Igor, too, believed that Richard should go and see her.

'Ricardo, old fellow, you have to do it. What have you got to lose?'

Plenty, thought Richard. Igor explained the importance of propitious moments, which was something he had studied in depth. His voice was muffled, but the gist of it was that this evening, which had turned out warm and scented, was one such occasion.

Outside the theatre there was a long and gleaming limousine and a group of photographers; they were in an animated state. Richard and Igor slipped by, through the archway which led to the theatre, and presented their tickets.

When the lights went down they were looking at a film set, with two carpenters in shiny brown overalls finishing a piece of scenery and putting it into place. When it was positioned, the picture became clear: it was a room in an Egyptian palace. They had filled in the last snake-and-ibis-embossed piece to complete the puzzle. The two carpenters were working men with

a world-weary, self-serving, building-site knowingness about the
ways of women:

> His captain's heart,
> Which in the scuffles of great fights hath burst
> The buckles on his breast, reneges all temper,
> And is become the bellows and the fan
> To cool a gypsy's lust.

'It's just a play,' whispered Igor. He had removed the yak
purdah.

Strident MGM trumpets sounded and Cleopatra entered with
Antony. Joanna was wearing a black, absolutely straight wig. And
on her head was the cobra crown.

Joanna said, 'If it be love, indeed, tell me how much.'

Her voice was urgent, yet sensual, offering from the first line
a sexual challenge.

'Shit or bust,' whispered Igor, enthralled.

'Jesus, Igor.'

His own heart was threatening to burst out.

Case had insisted on taking over the whole bar. His people
turned the playgoers away, while the theatre staff made piping
apologies.

Joanna was removing her make-up when he came in. It
was a time-honoured scene: the actress sitting in front of
the mirror, the male admirer standing in the doorway. The
dressing room was full of yellow roses mixed with bright
orange blooms.

'Joanna, you were better than good. You were amazing. Outstanding. Awesome.'

'Thanks for the flowers. They're gorgeous.'

'That's what you theatre actors do, I believe,' he said with a poor English accent. 'Jesus, this is real. You couldn't swing a fucking gopher in here.'

'It's the theatre, darling. We suffer for our art.'

'I've bought the rights in the production. Am I too young to play Antony?' He kissed her. 'There's just one thing, you're part of the deal.'

Richard and Igor were at the stage door, which was guarded by a large bald man in sunglasses.

'Could I see Miss Jermyn, I'm a friend?'

'No, mate, it's a private function.'

'I just want to say hello.'

'Not tonight, mate.'

'Okay. Can you give her a message?'

'No, mate. I can't. It's not me job. I'm nuffink to do wif the theatre. I'm on Mr Stipe's team.'

'Let's go, Igor.'

When Joanna emerged from the dressing room with Case, the photographers lit up the small courtyard with the flashes. Case and Joanna posed for a few moments as arranged, arm in arm.

Emily, the assistant stage manager, put her hand on Joanna's wrist. Her touch was bird-like, a robin pecking at a window, but insistent.

'Joanna, can I have a moment, it's important.'

306

And indeed she was trembling with what she was about to say: 'Mr McAllister was here a few moments ago, asking for you, but these security goons turned him away.'

'Where is he now?'

'He was walking towards Upper Street, with a friend who was wearing a sort of scarf over his face. Over the lower part.'

'Igor. Case, Case,' said Joanna, 'you've got to help me.'

Richard and Igor were just about to go into a Tex-Mex restaurant when a limousine pulled up next to them. Two large men jumped out.

'Mr McAllister?'

'Yes.'

'There's been a mistake, sir. Mr Stipe wants you to come to the party. My fault, sir. All my fault.'

Case was in the depths of the car: 'Hey Richard. I'm Case Stipe. You must be Ivan?'

'Igor.'

'Igor. Welcome. We didn't know you were there. Quick, get in, get in.'

They paused. The big men had them hemmed in.

'I don't really think this is the right ...'

'Don't be a prick, Richard, don't be so fucking British. Let's go. She loves you, man, believe me. Welcome to the movies, Ivan.'

He was laughing wildly.

24

Richard and Joanna lay so close, you couldn't have fitted a piece of paper between them, as the saying goes.

Igor was in the next room, but he was a reassuring presence, from which goodwill emanated, even while asleep on the sofa.

'Oh happy horse,' she whispered, 'to bear the weight of Antony.'

Before the words were out, she was asleep, as though a tombstone had closed on her for ever.

Some time earlier – perhaps an hour ago – when Igor was crashing about in the bathroom, when their bodies were trembling, when the city outside was groaning – she said: Give me a baby, Richard.

He understood it for what it was, the promise of love, which is a filament in the dark.